Beth closed her eyes as if to block out the reality of what was happening. Jared kissed her eyelids, her cheeks, then her mouth, his tongue parting her lips as he pulled her closer. Her robe, already loosely tied, fell open, and Beth, her own passion rising, went to close it, but Jared's hand was there first, cool against her warm stomach. He touched her breast lightly; then, abruptly, drew away from her and stood up. Beth quickly pulled the robe tightly about her and sat up straight.

"I have to go," Jared said huskily, then caught a lock of auburn hair between two fingers. "But I'll be back for you, Elizabeth Harte, I promise you that."

She swallowed hard, and her violet eyes met his. "Will I have to wait seven years this time?"

"I have no intention of waiting seven years to complete what we just started," he said and, with a grin, kissed her on the forehead. "Two days at the most, Beth."

Outrageous Desire

Carla A. Neggers

Weston, Florida
32038 - 701

This novel is a work of historical fiction. Names, characters, places and incidents relating to non-historical figures are either the product of the author's imagination or are used fictitiously, and any resemblance of such non-historical figures, places or incidents to actual persons, living or dead, events or locales is entirely coincidental.

EXCLUSIVE DISTRIBUTION BY
PARADISE PRESS, INC.

ISBN #1-57657-407-5

Printed in the U.S.A.

PROLOGUE

"Beth," Ginny whispered nervously as she ran across the crowded ballroom floor after her friend. "Beth, what are you going to do?"

Beth stopped abruptly. She was as dark as Ginny was blond, but both were seventeen, dressed in elaborate hoop skirts, Beth's of deep violet taffeta, Ginny's of light rose silk.

"Ginny, don't follow me!" Beth said, her voice low and intense. "You'll only get yourself into trouble."

The color drained from Ginny's rosy cheeks. "Oh, Beth,

5

don't do anything crazy. Please! I thought you were having a good time, for once. You've danced with nearly every man here—''

''Precisely,'' Beth said, sighing at the delay Ginny was causing. ''And each of those men ridiculed me for advocating women's suffrage. They all asked me what I intended to do now that Congress has refused to give women the vote and I won't be able to devote myself to becoming President after all.''

''But, Beth—''

''Now I'm seeking my revenge,'' Beth said dramatically, but her eyes suddenly lit up, the deep violet irises sparkling. ''A small revenge, to be sure. The real revenge will come when women receive the vote!''

Beth resumed her course through the ballroom, where over a hundred people had gathered for a summer's evening dance, but Ginny pressed on behind her. ''Beth, I don't believe they all were that nasty and insensitive,'' she challenged.

''Oh, but they were. Every one of them gloated. I'm sure they all think I'm going to give up my plans to go to Vassar College and take up looking for a husband.''

''Even William?''

''Most especially William.'' Beth blinked back an unwelcome tear of anger and humiliation. She had had a crush on Ginny's older brother for years, but she had never suspected his entrenched opposition to her favorite cause. William Prentiss, Jr., had been the worst offender of all. She drew herself up to her full five-feet-eight inches. ''I shall teach them all a lesson.''

''Then I'll go with you,'' Ginny said courageously.

Beth flashed a grin, and Ginny smiled, reassured. This was the daredevil, outrageous Beth Harte she knew. They had been constant friends throughout their years at a private academy for girls in New York City. Ginny had always tagged along when Beth was carrying out one of her rebellious plots. Once they had nearly been expelled for standing outside the headmaster's house in the middle of the night to read Milton and Shakespeare aloud. He had told his students that long hours of study would damage a woman's delicate physique, and Beth had been determined to prove him wrong. Only the intervention of Judge Robert Lowell Harte, Beth's father, saved them from such an ignominious end to their education.

"No, Ginny, this is my fight," Beth said. "But, of course, if they decide to put me in front of a firing squad, you can always rescue me."

Ginny laughed, then winked conspiratorily. "Well, good luck. You won't tell me what you're going to do?"

"You'll hear about it, I'm sure," Beth said.

She gave her friend a quick hug as the orchestra tuned up for yet another Strauss waltz. Beth glanced one last time at the glittering ballroom. Everyone who was anyone in Saratoga Springs must be here tonight, she thought, wishing she weren't. She should never, never, never have accepted Ginny's invitation to spend part of the summer at the opulent Prentiss "cottage" on Lake Saratoga. The Prentiss men were dead set against women receiving the vote, and she should have known the refusal of the Congress of 1867 to extend voting privileges to women would have to come up in conversation. Her father and all the old veterans of the suffrage movement—her namesake Elizabeth Cady Stanton included—had taken the defeat in stride, but not Beth. Youthful optimism does indeed die hard, she told herself as she pushed through the ornately carved double doors into a quiet, cool hall.

She lifted up her skirts, cursed the awkward hoop and, her heart pounding, hurried down the hall to yet another set of ornately carved doors. She swallowed, catching her breath, and smoothed her flowing skirts. Then, from her tiny taffeta purse she withdrew a long, thin cigar and a match. Her nervousness vanished. She struck the match on the heel of her shoe and lit the cigar, taking a few puffs. It tasted vile, she thought. Then she grinned to herself, and, without knocking, pushed open the heavy doors.

William Prentiss, Sr., overweight and an inch shorter than Beth, stood with his back to the door as he gave a lecture on what the transcontinental railroad would mean to industry—if the Union Pacific and the Central Pacific ever got the thing finished. In their hurry to lay the rails across the great West, Beth knew, the railroad men were encouraging shoddy work, playing games with the lives of their workers and future passengers, and becoming more and more corrupt. But that wasn't bothering William Prentiss, Sr. He wanted the railroad finished, and quickly. That was a different fight, Beth thought, and glanced at the smoke-filled, hushed room.

She stuck the cigar in her mouth, drew in as much smoke as she could tolerate, and blew it out at her host's back. "Hello," she said cheerily, and smiled as William Prentiss, Sr., turned around. "I understand this is where one can smoke and discuss politics without offending the ladies."

Ginny's father sputtered in fury. "What in the name of heaven do you think you're doing, girl! Judge Harte—"

He whirled around and looked expectantly at the judge, who was sitting in a corner quietly nursing a glass of whiskey. He was a tall, lean man with his daughter's chestnut hair, just beginning to turn gray, and her sparkling eyes, only his were the darkest of blues. The judge responded with a shrug and a smirk of amusement. Beth knew he understood that her actions were but a protest—a gesture—that the men in the room had earned and richly deserved.

All but two eyes were on her. Jared Inman had but

glanced indifferently at the girl in the door and resumed his game of pool. Beth had decided much earlier in the evening that he wasn't the kind of man she would want to notice her—for any reason. He had appeared on the ballroom floor once, briefly, and danced with no one, but whispered rumors followed in his wake. Jared Inman of San Francisco was a friend of outlaws, said one, an outlaw himself, in the opinion of another. At the very least, he was deeply involved in the corruption in the race to lay railroad tracks across the continent. He had hired thugs to supervise the work crews and had left no holds barred in their treatment of the workers. He had worked as a supervisor himself and beaten men mercilessly. He had killed a man in San Francisco.

The rumors had one common thread: Jared Inman was not the kind of man decent people needed to know. And always there was one understood and unspoken question: What was he doing at the Prentiss ball in Saratoga Springs, New York? Even now, glancing at him out of the corner of her eye, Beth could see he was different from any of the men in this elegant but most masculine of rooms. He had the stamp of the untamed West about him: tall, broad-shouldered, strikingly handsome, casually dressed in brown sack coat and trousers. No formal black tail coat, trousers, and waistcoat for this crude man from San Francisco. Beth was just as glad he would rather play billiards than watch her smoking a cigar in the doorway.

When no help was forthcoming from Judge Harte, William Prentiss, Jr., strode past his father. He was just an inch taller than Beth, trim but not muscular, as blond as his sister, and elegantly dressed. Not long ago, Beth had thought him the handsomest man in the world.

"Elizabeth," he said, his clean-shaven face red with anger, "have you no respect for your hosts?"

Beth held her head high and flicked her cigar ashes onto

the deep red Oriental rug. "Why should I when you have no respect for your guests?" she asked, but she didn't wait for an answer. "I have never asked you to agree with me, only to respect me for what I believe is right and just."

"You're completely impossible, Elizabeth!"

She flashed a devilish, beautiful smile. "Thank you, William."

William sucked in a breath, controlling his anger, but Beth, continuing to smile, lifted one of his soft white hands and dropped her cigar into it. Then she folded his fingers around it and patted them. "I'll be going now, William," she said coolly.

"Elizabeth," he said sharply, his tone commanding her to listen, but she turned her back and started out the door. "Elizabeth!"

She was through the door, and as she closed it, she could hear the billiard balls crack and the loud, hearty laugh of Jared Inman. She *knew* it was Inman. Her face reddened. He was laughing at her! Better to draw jeers and anger than laughter!

A wave of nausea overcame her, and Beth fled down the hall, away from the ballroom, past the center front staircase and outside. The cool night air revived her, but the nausea wouldn't subside. She lifted her hoop skirts even higher and ran through the gardens and down the sloping lawns toward Lake Saratoga. Above her to her right, she could see the lights of the ballroom, the silhouettes of people dancing on the terrace, and she could hear the bright chords of the "Vienna Waltz."

The moonlight glistened on the large, still lake. Lake Saratoga, Beth thought. It was nine miles long, packed with fish, quiet, beautiful. On warm summer afternoons, hundreds of guests from the sprawling village hotels, just four miles away, would join the carriage parade to the lake, where they would enjoy boating, bathing, strolls along the shore, and perhaps dinner at Cary Moon's Lake House, renowned for its wafer-thin fried potatoes, "Saratoga chips." But Beth cared nothing for such elegant routines.

She stumbled into a stand of birches along the shore of the lake, then fought her way into the brush, leaving the trim Prentiss grounds. She vomited until her stomach was empty, and then again. Her skirt caught on a bramble and she yanked it free. .tearing the taffeta. Unmindful of the damage to her dress, she pushed her way further into the brush, until at last she came to a small inlet, where the water lapped onto granite boulders and only the full, round moon provided a warm glow of light. The Prentiss mansion seemed far away.

Without another thought, Beth quickly dropped her dress: the tight bodice with its puffed sleeves, the yards and yards of taffeta skirts, the black buckle shoes, and, above all, the hoop skirt of whalebone and muslin. She even pulled off her underclothing and dopped it atop the pile. Then she lowered her tall, slender body into the water, welcoming its soothing coolness. She had never swum naked before. She pulled the pins and bows and ribbons from her thick chestnut hair, running her fingers through it as it tumbled down her back. This was freedom, she thought, and dove deep.

She luxuriated in the cool water swirling around her body, and soon she began to relax. She floated on her back, kicked up her feet, and plunged deep, swam agilely on her stomach, losing track of the time and even where she was.

Then, as she surfaced from a dive, she gasped at the figure of a man on the boulder beside her doffed clothes. William? But then she heard the deep, hearty laugh of Jared Inman. Her heart beat wildly, but she boldy swam closer to shore. His figure took shape in the moonlight. He was sitting on a rock jutting out of the water while she splashed about naked in Lake Saratoga, but Beth couldn't take her eyes off this man whom rumor had declared unsavory and even beastly. Common sense told her to swim away at once and take her chances naked on the opposite bank rather than stay here under his scrutiny. His dark hair was longish and tousled, and even in the dim light Beth could see the rugged, tanned features of his face: keen, dark eyes, straight, arrogant nose, firm mouth, square jaw. And so tall and so broad.

How long, she wondered, had he been spying on her?

"I didn't think proper young ladies swam naked," he said.

"Proper young ladies don't swim at all," Beth countered, careful to keep just her head above water.

His grin broadened, and Beth's uneasiness grew. "And how," he went on, ever so casually, "do you propose to get back to your room while dripping wet?"

Beth pursed her lips, her uneasiness quickly yielding to outrage. How dare he! "My predicament is none of your concern. If you were a gentleman, you would turn your head, and leave."

"Ah, but I'm no gentleman."

"How long have you been watching me?" she demanded, her tone haughtier than she felt.

"Long enough, Miss Harte, long enough."

"You're crude."

He laughed. "And you're in a mess. Half a dozen men are combing the grounds for you right now. They think you might have made yourself sick on that cigar or gone off and drowned yourself. Women who want the vote are unstable creatures, you know."

Beth scowled in disgust.

"Yes, well, apparently only your father isn't worried about you. He's practicing his game of billiards and smoking his pipe. He thought you might be off swimming, so he asked me if I might take you a few towels since he didn't expect you'd thought of how you were going to get yourself dry again. I'll leave them with your assorted underclothes."

He rose, and Beth bit her lip as she took in his size. He had none of William's fine features, but instead conveyed power with his broad shoulders, muscular arms, and long, thick legs. Beth was all too aware of her nakedness beneath his gaze. How much could he see? He grinned down at her. "Can you get out by yourself, or would you like a hand?"

"I can manage quite well by myself, thank you," she said tartly.

He turned away and jumped lightly off the boulder. "Mr. Inman," Beth called. He glanced around at her. "Thank you for the towels."

He shrugged, grinning. "My pleasure."

Beth was glad he was already pushing his way through the brush so he couldn't see her reddening face. She waited until all she could hear was the lapping of the water on the rocks, the crickets chirping in the brush, and, across the lake, the distant hoot of an owl. The orchestra, she realized, had stopped. She quickly crawled out of the water, dried off, and donned her clothes. She dried her hair as best she could, but with the pins and bows and ribbons at the bottom of Lake Saratoga, she had to leave it hanging.

She hurried back to the house and, without meeting anyone, snuck through the kitchen and up the back stairs to her room. On her bed was a scrap of paper: "I had to leave suddenly, but, outrageous Beth, I'll be back for you one day. Jared.''

Beth scowled. "The arrogant swine," she muttered, but carefully folded the note and slipped it into her journal.

CHAPTER 1

Seven years, Beth thought, smiling to herself as she looked up at the elegant stone mansion. Seven years since she had last come to Saratoga Springs. Where had the time gone? She had been a girl then, naive, optimistic, free-spirited. No longer. She had learned that optimism and free spirits would do nothing to secure the vote for women or end the corruption that was tearing at the very fabric of American society. That required work, and so Beth had tried to rein in her free spirits and had allowed her optimism to languish and die a natural death. Now she was twenty-four, an educated, mature young woman.

She laughed aloud. And what, she wondered, would her father the judge have to say about that summation of her young adult life? She laughed again, knowing the answer, and tried in vain to shake the wrinkles from her brown linen traveling dress. He would say—and had said many times—that pessimism and propriety did not mix with Harte blood, and try as she would, Beth would never be able to rein in her free spirits for too long a stretch at a time. And never had. "We have too much life in us, Beth, to waste it obeying all those silly damned rules of so-called maturity!" Those would be Judge Robert Lowell Harte's very words.

He had urged her to come to Saratoga. When she had received Ginny's letter and cry for help, Beth had been reluctant to alter her busy summer schedule to go to her friend. But her father had interfered this one time. "You need a vacation," he had said.

She had denied it.

"You've been behaving yourself for far too long," he had gone on lightly, but his tone had suddenly turned serious. "You've worked hard, Beth. You deserve to have some fun."

"Ginny's letter doesn't make Saratoga sound the least bit fun," she had pointed out.

Her father had waved a hand. "Ginny Prentiss always exaggerates. Elizabeth, I'm worried about you. You're becoming too serious, and that's not like you. You're losing your perspective on your work. Go to Saratoga and let yourself be entertained and pampered."

Beth had sighed, still unconvinced. Over the years there had been no time for vacations, no time for frolicking in the foothills of the Adirondacks, no time even for thinking about love and marriage. But long ago Beth had given up on finding a man who suited her temperament and beliefs the way her parents had suited each other. Marriage, she

had decided, was not part of her destiny. There was always William Prentiss, Jr., but Beth knew he would never understand that she simply wasn't going to outgrow her zest for reform. They had argued that point so very many times.

But then her father, not getting any response from his daughter, had smiled and continued, "You could also do a little job for me while you're in Saratoga."

Beth had looked up sharply, a smile at the corners of her mouth. What was her father up to?

"The railroads are in a mess, you know that, don't you?" he asked. "Last year's panic has brought most of the construction to a standstill, and everyone—even Cornelius Vanderbilt himself—is worried about what the country's financial instability, labor unrest in the railroad industry, and rate wars will do to the railroads. Some people are even suggesting the day of railroad expansion is over."

Beth had listened in silence. None of what her father had said was news to her. The country was still reeling from the financial panic of 1873.

"So it strikes me as very interesting that so many of the top railroad men in the country are talking about being in Saratoga Springs this summer," the judge had added mildly. He looked pointedly at his daughter. "I would like to know if they are planning something they have neglected to tell the public. If you are in Saratoga as the Prentisses' guest, Beth, I would think you might hear some interesting things."

She had smiled broadly. "And could report back to you?"

And so Beth's defenses were battered down, and she agreed to join her friend Ginny in the country's favorite watering spot. She had tried to persuade her father to join her, but Judge Harte claimed to have had enough of Saratoga Springs during his trip north seven years ago.

So, Beth thought as she deftly pinned up a stray lock of her thick chestnut hair, had she, except for the one thing she had never told her father about—her swim in Lake Saratoga and Jared Inman's "rescue." Even now the memory brought a flush to her cheeks, but Beth held her head high and, hoping she at least looked twenty-four, educated, and mature, she marched up the walkway of tiny cobblestones toward the Prentiss mansion.

The carriage she had rented in the crush of people at the train station had let her off beneath the canopy at the main entrance of the Prentiss summer cottage, and the driver had dumped her large trunk, a Saratoga trunk with its rounded top, onto the walkway, leaving Beth to wonder how many such trunks he handled in one day. If anything, Saratoga Springs had grown even more popular since her first visit in 1867.

It was midafternoon, and Beth knew she was expected to arrive on the evening train. She had considered spending the extra hours wandering around the village, but she was sure to meet some member of the Prentiss household and create even more confusion. Beth smiled to herself once again as she reached for the heavy brass doorknocker. Educated, mature young women, she thought, weren't supposed to parade about a town alone, particularly a town known as much for its gambling and discreet forms of prostitution as for its mineral springs and healthful mud baths.

Just as her hand touched the knocker, one half of the massive double door opened and Virginia Prentiss slipped out. Her golden hair was piled up in a thick braid with ringlets hanging down her back, and she wore a dress of cotton lawn. Its tunic overskirt was a sage green, tied up and behind her to reveal a deep forest-green underskirt, both pulled tight over her slim hips. Her bustle protruded in an assortment of flounces and just a yard or two of train. Just a simple, daytime dress, Beth thought dryly.

"Oh, Beth, you did come!" Ginny cried, and threw her arms about her friend.

"Of course I came," Beth said, as though the decision to leave New York had been easily made. "Didn't you get my wire? I—"

Ginny was already sadly shaking her head. "Father and William are censoring all my messages. I thought they had forbidden you to come. Last night at dinner, Father said it would be best if I didn't have any guests for a few weeks. I assumed he had wired you not to come."

Beth frowned. Perhaps Ginny's dilemma hadn't been overstated. "Well, if he did, I missed it. My message said I wouldn't arrive until after dinner tonight, but an acquaintance of Father's was coming on the morning train, and I decided to join him. So here I am, early and unwelcome." She flashed a smile at Ginny's tired face. "Nothing so unusual about that!"

"You mean you'll stay?" Ginny grabbed Beth's arm as though she were an illusion and might suddenly vanish. She smiled, tears glistening in her wide blue eyes. "Oh, Beth, I can't tell you how glad I am you're here."

Beth draped an arm over Ginny's thin shoulders. They were the same age, but Beth had always felt older. She laughed to herself: older and more mature. "I'll stay," she said. "Unless, of course, your father and William pick me up and throw me out bodily."

Ginny gave her friend a sideways, very serious glance. "They might, you know."

"That I would like to see!" Beth said, laughing. "Are they here, or do we have a few minutes before we test the will of the Prentiss males?"

"They're down at the stables. William has a horse that has a good chance to win the Travers. Jacques—" she smiled and blushed prettily, "Jacques says he's the quickest horse he's ever trained. Anyway, they shouldn't be back until tea time, if then. But Mother's inside and doesn't know you're coming, I'm sure, and Father has spies among the servants. Oh, Beth, are you certain you want to go through with this?"

Beth patted her hand and spoke confidently. "Ginny, I have an entire trunk full of clean clothes. I took an interminable train ride with the most boring man and his most mindless niece to get here. I canceled all my speaking engagements for the summer. Do you think the mere threat of the wrath of William Prentiss, Sr., and Jr. is going to force me out?" She flashed her violet eyes. Perhaps her father was right and this was exactly the sort of vacation she needed! "You should know me better than that, Virginia Prentiss."

"Always ready for a good fight," Ginny said, and tried to smile. "I wish I were as brave."

Ginny darted from Beth's embrace and led the way into the mansion. Beth suddenly realized how difficult it must be for Ginny to stand up to her father and brother. She had lost weight since Beth had seen her last, just before her family's annual pilgrimage to the spa, and her round, pink cheeks had become wan and hollow. With a pang, Beth remembered a few words from Ginny's letter: "I am a prisoner here." Beth had discounted them as emotional and exaggerated, but now she wasn't so sure.

The foyer with its wide, carpeted center staircase was even more elaborate than Beth remembered. The hardwood floor gleamed underfoot, sun streamed through the leaded glass windows, and the walls were so white they glistened. An Italian Renaissance painting of a Madonna and child hung on one wall, directly opposite a huge full-length mirror. A potted palm stood in a corner next to a bench, ornately carved and covered with a red velvet

cushion, and a set of windows overlooking the trim front lawn.

Beth was still eyeing the painting when Ginny took her hand and started to drag her up the stairs. "Wait, Ginny!" Beth said, stopping. "My trunk! If I'm going to sneak about, I shouldn't leave my trunk on the front walk."

"Oh, heavens, yes!" Ginny turned and ran back down the stairs and out the door. Beth followed. "We can carry it upstairs to your room ourselves, and then you can change and relax and—and make your grand entrance at dinner," Ginny said, speaking quickly, thinking as she went along. "We're having guests tonight, so I'm sure Father and William won't make too big a scene. Oh, Beth, it's the only way! It'll work, I know it will. If I could hide you here all summer, I would, but . . ."

She trailed off with a little shrug of the shoulders. "That's an excellent plan," Beth said, not sure it was. She would rather have the two William Prentisses toss her out the front door without an audience. "Here, you lift one side, and I'll lift the other. It's quite heavy."

Beth managed her side of the trunk with no difficulty, but Ginny, smaller and not used to lifting anything heavier than a whalebone bustle, groaned and turned red with the effort. They got the trunk to the bottom of the staircase before Ginny dropped her end.

She smiled weakly at Beth. "Can we switch sides? My arm—"

Already, Beth thought. "Sure," she said. "Look, Ginny, if you want, we can hide the trunk in a closet down here and wait—"

"That's too risky," Ginny protested. "No, Beth, I can do it."

They switched places and clearing her throat and lifting the yards of green cotton and lace of her dress with her free hand, Ginny picked up her new end of the trunk. Beth glanced at the long flight of stairs, then at Ginny, and knew they would never make it. Perhaps she could carry the trunk herself. But Ginny was determined to try, and so Beth lifted her end and mounted the carpeted stairs with her friend. Beth was glad for her practical dress. She had refused to wear a bustle or corset while traveling, and although her skimpy underclothing had drawn a scowl of disapproval from her companions on the train, she was at least comfortable. Her dark brown linen dress had buttons from neck to hem, with just a hint of white ruching at the collar and along the long belled sleeves, and only a cameo brooch for jewelry. It was shorter than was fashionable, but that enabled her to carry a Saratoga trunk up a flight of stairs without tripping over a multitude of cloth.

"I don't suppose you two would like a hand?" asked a deep male voice behind them.

Ginny flew around, dropping her end of the trunk and collapsing against the railing, but Beth held steadfastly to her handle. She tried to balance the trunk herself and keep it from bouncing down the stairs, but the man leaped from the bottom step and took charge of Ginny's end before it even reached the carpet.

"Sorry to startle you, Ginny," he said, more matter-of-fact than apologetic.

"It's all right, Jared." Ginny said, catching her breath. She straightened her skirts and squeezed past him to the step above. "Would you help us, please?"

"Sure."

Beth stood motionless, one hand clinging to the trunk, the other to the railing. She stared at the man on the opposite end of the trunk. He was still as tall, still as thick and muscular, still as dark-haired and informal. If anything, he was more ruggedly handsome, more square-jawed and arrogantly masculine. Beth swallowed hard, and the memories of seven years ago rushed at her.

Jared Inman.

What was *he* doing here? Did he recognize her? Did he wonder if this mature-looking young woman was the wild-eyed girl who had flaunted the rules of the Prentiss household? The seventeen-year-old suffragette he had caught skinny-dipping in Lake Saratoga?

Did he remember the note he had left on her pillow?

The note still folded, untouched, in her journal.

He grinned at her stare, and Beth blushed, catching herself. "Ready?" she asked.

He laughed the same deep, hearty laugh that echoed in her memory. "Here, let go. I can carry this thing better alone."

"There's no need for you to break your back—"

"If you want my help, you'll take it as it comes," he said, not entertaining any arguments, and yanked the trunk from Beth's grasp. He hoisted it on his shoulders and grinned down at her. "Much quicker this way, and I gather you want to be quick about this."

"Oh, yes, please!" Ginny said above them, and led the way.

Beth trailed behind, watching Jared Inman as he carried the trunk. She noticed his leather boots were worn and unpolished, his trousers a sturdy twill as brown as her dress. He wore no jacket over his plain muslin shirt. Since she had arrived in Saratoga, at the train station and then during her carriage ride through the resort town, she had seen only elegance, spit-polished boots, fine lightweight suits, fancy day hats, neatly combed hair. She had seen nothing at all that even resembled Jared Inman, but, then, she thought, had she ever?

Ginny hurried down the hall, made a ninety-degree turn down a shorter hall, and, finally, pushed open a door to a large, sunny bedroom. It was simply furnished with a brass bed, a marble-topped bureau and nightstand, and a small secretary.

"I know it's small, Beth, but will it be all right for now?" Ginny asked.

Beth smiled, trying not the think about the man in the room with them. "It will be fine for as long as I stay."

Jared plopped the trunk down on the floor at the foot of the bed. His eyes narrowed sharply at Beth, but she turned away quickly and gazed out the double window at the view of the back lawns, the lake, and the mountains beyond.

"By the way, Ginny," Jared said, "your mother was looking for you. You might want to catch up with her before she finds her way up here. She was in the rose garden a few minutes ago."

"Oh, I'd better run then. Beth, will you be all right? I'll be back as soon as I can. You have your own bath and . . ." Her voice trailed off, and she seemed slightly awkward. "I'm so glad you're here. Make yourself at home. I'll sneak up some food if I get the chance. And, Jared, thank you."

Ginny raced out, and Beth returned her gaze to the view. She could still feel Jared Inman's presence in the room. She swallowed hard and opened one of the windows.

He walked up beside her and leaned against the windowsill, folding his arms across his chest, studying her face. Beth tried not to look at him. She recalled everything anyone had said about him that night seven years ago.

"I didn't recognize you with your clothes on and no cigar."

She flew around at him, but restrained herself. This man, she remembered, had been said to have taken part in the brutality that went into building the transcontinental railroad. "I am not seventeen anymore, Mr. Inman," she said, very coolly.

He grinned. "That you aren't, Miss Harte."

She nearly choked. He even remembered her name. But again she covered her shock and turned away from the window. She had to get rid of him! "If you'll excuse me, Mr. Inman, I would like to get some of the road dust off me." She brushed a post of the brass bed with one hand and smiled politely. "Thank you for carrying my trunk."

She thought he would accept her thanks and leave, but he didn't. "Why are you here?" he asked.

She had no intention of telling him about her father's spying assignment. "That's up to Ginny to answer—or not." She sat down on the bed, sinking into the white down coverlet, and looked up at Jared. He had abandoned the windowsill for the spot directly in front of her. "But I hope you will keep her confidence and not tell anyone I am here."

"And I hope," he said slowly, "you're here to talk her out of running off with that stinking horse trainer."

So he was in accord with William Prentiss, Jr., and Sr., she thought. It was only to be expected. "I am here to be Ginny's friend," she said firmly. "That's all."

She saw Jared Inman's eyes narrow and his fists clench. "If you're her friend, you'll keep her away from Jacques LeBreque."

Beth swallowed hard as she heard the contempt—the hatred—in Jared's tone. "Why?"

"He's a little weasel, a scoundrel, the worst sort of man I can think of—"

"Worse than you?" she asked quietly, sarcastically.

He took two steps toward her, his face a dark mask. "The man is no good," he said, biting off each word. "That's all I can say."

And what, she wondered, did Jared Inman of San Francisco propose to do about one little horse trainer by the name of Jacques LeBreque? "Ginny's a big girl now, Mr.

Inman," she said coolly. "I don't intend to encourage or discourage her."

"Jared."

"I beg your pardon?"

He put his index finger under her chin and lifted it, tilting her face up so that her eyes met his. "I've traveled three thousand miles to see you, Beth Harte, and whether it was worth it or not, I won't have you calling me Mr. Inman like some mealy-mouthed damsel. It's Jared."

Beth held her breath. "Certainly," she said coldly, not daring to think.

He stood up straight and gave her one long, appraising look, which she met directly and frostily. Then he stalked to the door, but stopped abruptly and turned to her with his hand on the brass knob. "And, Beth," he said, not grinning, "I may like your flat behind, but if I were you, I'd be decked out in full corset and bustle when I came down to meet the Prentisses."

"My behind," she said icily, steadily, not flinching, "is not yours to like or dislike," she paused so he would know she was intentionally thwarting him and, bowing slightly, added, "Mr. Inman."

He shut the door hard when he left.

CHAPTER 2

Jared Inman of San Francisco had traveled across the continent to track down a violet-eyed girl he had caught swimming naked in Lake Saratoga seven years ago.

What nonsense! Beth sat on the very edge of the soft bed and stared at the floor. It *was* nonsense. Only the Prentiss family had known she would be traveling north, and from her brief words with Ginny, Beth had gathered they weren't anxious to have the young suffragette as their guest and wouldn't just mention it casually to someone like Jared Inman. So he couldn't possibly have known

Elizabeth Stanton Harte would be in Saratoga Springs. He had said that merely to upset her.

Of course, the Prentiss summer cottage was where he had last seen her, and perhaps he had decided that was where he could best pick up her trail—

Beth sprang up from the bed. "Ridiculous!"

He knew Judge Harte was her father. All he had to do was look up the judge in New York. No, her presence and Jared's presence at the Prentiss cottage on the same summer afternoon was an unfortunate coincidence.

Beth unpacked enough to get her through the evening. She fully expected that she wouldn't be staying with the Prentisses past dinner, but she wasn't too disturbed. Her hosts couldn't very well throw her out of Saratoga. She would stay if she pleased, and as long as she pleased.

Her thoughts drifted insidiously back to Jared Inman. Was *he* staying with the Prentisses? And in the seven years since she had seen him, what had he done with his life? Beth had never once spoken his name or heard it spoken in her circle of friends in New York City. She supposed, with her Harte connections, she could have found out anything she wanted to about the tall, broad-shouldered man from San Francisco, but she never had. Instead, she had locked away everything about that evening in her memory and left it untouched.

Jared Inman of San Francisco, she had been certain, would never walk back into her life as easily and maddeningly as he had walked into it that warm summer night so long ago.

She groaned aloud. "How could I have been so wrong!"

Ginny burst into Beth's room at three and said she couldn't get away from her family without causing suspicion. "Mother wants me to go riding with her," she said, her face flushed. "I'm on my way to change now—and Father and William insist I have tea with them. Oh, Beth, I have so much to tell you, and I'm so sorry to abandon you this way! I don't know what else to do."

Beth assured her she would be fine, and indeed appreciated the time alone. "I have to plan my entrance," she said with a sly smile. "Now go on and don't worry about me."

Relieved and reassured, Ginny slipped back into the hall. Beth sighed and wished she had had time to ask her friend about the man who had helped with the trunk. Would he be at dinner that evening?

Only for Ginny's sake did Beth wear corset and bustle when she dressed for dinner, but she searched her trunk for her simplest dress. Bows, ribbons, beads, lace, and skirts fitting tight over the hips with yards of flounces and trains behind them were fashionable, but Beth didn't overly concern herself with fashion. She hated being weighted down with so much cloth. She chose a gown with a short, gray tunic of silk faille that had a plain, square neck, no belts or trim, and a bustle but no train. It fit rather loosely over her hips, and had a carob-red underskirt, which hung to her instep. She wore the same high-top black satin boots she had worn on the train, but she dusted them off first. Her hair she wound in a thick braid and pinned high on her head. She clipped on simple pearl earrings, glanced with satisfaction in the full-length mirror, and was ready.

The knock came. Beth sighed irritably at her trembling hands. She hadn't trembled in years, not even when she faced hostile audiences on the subject of the vote for women. She strode boldly across the room to open the door. Jared Inman or no Jared Inman, appearing uninvited for dinner was nothing.

"Nothing at all," she whispered stoutly, and pulled open the door.

Jared grinned at her, and Beth tried to shut the door hard

in his face, but he stopped it with his boot. A shiny leather boot, Beth noticed, and glared up at him.

"A bit dowdy," he said, "but proper."

"Please leave," she told him firmly.

He took her elbow and turned her around, checking her bustle. "It'll do, I suppose."

Beth yanked her arm free and felt her face flush red. How dare he! "I don't care whether it will or it won't. I would like you to leave, Mr. Inman."

"Pleasant little thing, aren't you?" he said, undeterred. "I've come to take you down to dinner."

"I prefer to go alone."

He sighed and crossed his arms over his chest, leaning against the doorjamb. He narrowed his black eyes at Beth, and she met his gaze with her chin held high. He was dressed comfortably—a little too comfortably for a formal dinner, Beth thought—in a brown twill sack coat, loose-fitting with high, short lapels, a broadcloth shirt with a low collar, and a narrow black string tie beneath a double-breasted vest. His brown twill trousers were just a bit dressier than the ones he had worn earlier. Beth noticed that her throat had gone dry. She reminded herself that this man was an outlaw or at the very least a friend of outlaws, and most certainly part of the railroad corruption and brutality she and her father stood so firmly against. Jared Inman, Beth reasoned, was not the kind of man with whom she should involve herself.

She *had* to make him understand that she was Elizabeth Stanton Harte, suffragette and reformer, a mature, educated, responsible young woman—

Who happened to be hiding out in the Prentiss cottage as an unwanted guest!

"You're no fashion model yourself," she said quickly, recovering. "Thank you for your offer, Mr. Inman, but Ginny and I—"

"Ginny asked me to make it."

Beth couldn't hide her shock. "What?"

"She said if I were willing, I could help convince her father to let you stay." He grinned at Beth and brushed her cheek lightly with the back of his callused hand. "And I do want you to stay, Beth."

She drew back instinctively, refusing to acknowledge the tingle his hand had caused in the small of her back. He held out his arm, and seeing she had no other choice, Beth took it. Ginny's health and peace of mind, she told herself, were more important than the pride of Elizabeth Harte. She would deal with Jared Inman once she was accepted as a guest at the Prentiss cottage.

But would a man like Jared be a help in getting her accepted? She glanced at his casual dress and dark features and recalled every rumor about him and wondered.

"Are you nervous?" Jared asked as he escorted her down the wide stairs.

Beth glanced up at him and smiled, her violet eyes suddenly twinkling. "Not at all."

Jared laughed, throwing his head back and pulling Beth closer to him.

"It's true," she said, acutely aware of his strong body against hers. She couldn't allow herself to be distracted! She had to concentrate on Ginny and what her father had asked her to do—and she didn't dare to trust this man. "I'm not nervous."

"I know," he said, loosening his hold as they reached the bottom of the stairs and turned down the hall. He patted Beth's hand, which was politely holding his elbow. "But you probably should be. Well, at least he won't gun you down with me beside you."

"That's absurd. William Prentiss would never shoot me—or anyone."

Jared gave her a skeptical sideways glance. "And I

thought you were a woman of the world. Beth; the Prentisses have become a rich, powerful family. William Prentiss doesn't want his only daughter to marry a horse trainer like Jacques LeBreque, and I don't blame him. He won't stand for anyone, including you, encouraging Ginny.''

Beth groaned. She had no intention of encouraging Ginny, only of being her friend and letting her make up her own mind about her horse trainer. But Jared Inman was no doubt incapable of such a subtle distinction. ''I will do as I please,'' she said haughtily. ''It's a free country—for men at least.''

They had come to the open dining room doors. ''My point exactly,'' Jared said, and escorted her into the room.

They were late. The women, all formally and brightly dressed, were already seated at the long mahogany table, sparkling with silver and expensive china. The men were just about to sit down. Beth recognized none of the dozen guests, but she quickly noticed the four Prentisses: Ginny, seated at the far end of the table studiously not looking at Beth, her mother, Sophia, a tiny, fair woman seated next to her daughter, and the two Williams, the senior standing at the nearer end of the table, the junior at the far end. The shock on the Prentiss men's faces was palpable when they looked up and saw Beth.

She smiled her prettiest smile and, before Jared could say anything, left his protective arm and strode over to her host. The look of controlled anger on his ruddy face had silenced everyone in the room. ''Mr. Prentiss,'' she said, extending her hand, ''it's wonderful to see you again. I know you didn't expect me this early, but—''

''Elizabeth Harte,'' he said and grunted unpleasantly. He was even more overweight than Beth remembered when she had last seen him over the winter, but he was dressed elegantly in black. No finery could hide his often crude, volatile temper, which he was visibly controlling now. "I didn't expect you at all."

"Is that right?" Beth said, feigning surprise. "Well, perhaps I should leave at once. I'm sure I can find a room in town somewhere. I've been meaning to come to Saratoga for a long time, and Ginny's very nice invitation was just what I needed to get myself going. I'm not very organized, I'm afraid, and—oh, please don't tell me I forgot to wire you I was coming!"

William glanced quickly at his guests. Beth wondered how many knew of Ginny's desperate letter and the Prentisses' telegram telling Beth not to come—indeed, the entire mess about Jacques LeBreque. She was hoping William wouldn't want to start a public scandal, which would surely result if he threw the daughter of Judge Robert Lowell Harte out of his house. People would want to know why he had reacted so rudely and ungallantly to her unexpected appearance for dinner, and if he didn't explain, she would.

Suddenly, he smiled and put out a plump, ringed hand. "Come, sit down," he said. "You can tell me later about all your adventures in getting here."

There was an audible sigh of relief, and conversation started up again as the men sat down. William Prentiss, Sr., pulled out a chair at the corner of the table next to him and invited Beth to take it. She obeyed, as demurely as she could, but caught her breath when Jared Inman came up between her and her host. He bent down and spoke in a low voice to the older man, who looked at Jared, then at Beth, and then spoke quietly to Jared. Jared nodded and, with a slight smile at Beth, walked past her to the middle of the table. He was the last to sit down.

As white-coated waiters brought out the food, William leaned back in his chair and gave Beth a searching look. She had long guessed he was against his son's maintaining any sort of romantic interest in her, but unlike Ginny, William listened to his father. "I understand you arrived this afternoon," the older Prentiss said. "I'm sorry I couldn't have been there to meet you."

"I didn't expect to get here so soon," Beth said, speaking to William Prentiss, Sr., as an equal. "Mr. Albert Shaw was leaving on the nine A.M. train and was kind enough to invite me to join him."

William plucked a delicate, steaming roll off a platter and raised an eyebrow at Beth. "Alone?"

"Oh, no," Beth said, snatching herself a roll. The smell of food had made her aware of her hunger. "His niece Rachel Shaughnessy came along."

"Rachel Shaughnessy?" William shook his head as he added oysters to his plate. "Miss Harte, for a young woman who advocates so loudly for her sex to be granted the right to vote, it amazes me how little you actually know of the world. Rachel Shaughnessy is not Albert Shaw's niece."

Beth forced herself not to look shocked. Saratoga Springs was notorious for its "love cottages" and discreet style of prostitution. No one was supposed to ask questions about supposed nieces and secretaries traveling with supposed gentlemen, but everyone was supposed to know who was a niece, who was a secretary, and who was a prostitute. Beth sighed.

"I didn't know," she admitted, then smiled devilishly. "They behaved in a most uncle-to-niece manner. I only know of the world what I see, Mr. Prentiss, and don't judge what I can't see."

"*I* see the years haven't made you less bold, Miss Harte," the senior Prentiss said dryly.

"No," Beth replied matter-of-factly, "but I've given up smoking cigars."

Her host looked at her, appalled, but then, seeing the twinkle in her eyes, broke into a loud laugh. "I had forgotten how much fun you Hartes are. I don't see you often enough, to be sure! How is your father these days?"

"Quite well, thank you."

"Taking on railroad 'corruption,' I hear," Prentiss said, shaking his head. "Still clamoring for better wages for working people as well?"

"And an eight-hour day and an end to child labor," Beth added lightly, as though such reforms could and should be won easily. She spooned fresh broccoli smothered with a thick cheese sauce onto her English bone-china plate. "We Hartes have based our entire philosophy on just one maxim. We believe there is enough wealth to go around so that workers can feed their families and have decent housing, children can go to school, and employers can still grow fat and rich and spend their summers in Saratoga."

"Bah! And no one listens to you, because neither of you knows what you're talking about." Prentiss stuffed an oyster in his mouth, swallowed it without chewing, and barely batted an eye when a huge platter of lobster was held out to him. He forked a pile of the expensive delicacy onto his plate as though it were common fish. "Robert Harte was probably the only judge in New York state who couldn't be bought. It's just as well he's retired."

"To devote himself to reforms," Beth amended.

The older man waved a hand. "He doesn't know a damned thing about industry and what it takes to make those filthy, lazy people work. And when's the last time you've taken a tour of the tenements, Miss Elizabeth Harte?"

Beth narrowed her eyes at him, thinking. Then she held out an index finger as the platter of lobster moved around to her. She shook her head at it, then sighed at William. "A week ago Friday."

"You're making that up."

"I'm not."

And she wasn't. It had been a shocking, painful experience, but William Prentiss would no doubt call her an overly sensitive, silly fool if she tried to describe the horror she had seen. Besides, she thought, he knew only too well what the conditions were. But he blamed the workers and only the workers, never himself. Beth and her father knew better than to try to change men like William Prentiss. They hoped instead to change the laws to protect workers and guarantee them better working conditions and to get men—and perhaps, one day, women—in public office who respected the law. And they hoped change would come without a rise in violence.

Now Prentiss was laughing at the idea of a genteel young woman, a judge's daughter, venturing into the slums of New York City. "Well," he said, swallowing his last oyster and starting on the lobster, "I hope you didn't go alone. Isn't safe for a woman there alone."

Beth shrugged, unconcerned. She hadn't gone alone, but with three other women, which would be just as bad in her host's estimation. "I don't believe it's safe there for anyone, including the people who live there."

William scowled and dismissed the subject. "You'll be fun to have around here for a while, Miss Harte, but don't think you'll bring any tears to my eyes." He raised his fork at her and leaned toward her as he said, quietly, seriously, "You may stay as a guest in my house as long as you like, but I warn you: Don't provoke me. I can be very mean if provoked, even to a woman."

Beth thought he looked very much like an angry bulldog and had to smile, but she knew he meant what he said. "I would do nothing intentionally to provoke you, Mr.

Prentiss," she said sweetly, not for a moment thinking he could detect her sarcasm.

He grunted approval and began eating in earnest. The platters of roast beef and ham were still to come, not to mention more vegetables, potatoes, wine, cheese, and, finally, fruits and scores of tiny pastries.

"Well, Mr. Dobbs," Prentiss said as he cut into a huge slice of roast turkey, "how are you enjoying our beautiful resort so far?"

Elijah Dobbs. He was on the list of men Judge Harte had told his daughter bore watching, although most of his money was in steamboats, not railroads. Beth observed and listened without seeming to. Dobbs was a balding, ruddy-faced man sitting diagonally across from her. What hair he had was iron gray and curly, but Beth guessed he was only in his mid-forties, perhaps a few inches taller than she, but barrel-chested and muscular. He didn't look comfortable in his black swallowtail evening coat.

"Just wonderful," he said, gesturing expansively. He laughed. "Though I've never seen two women take so much time dressing as my wife and daughter have since they arrived here!"

The young woman sitting beside Beth tittered. "Oh, Daddy," she said, blushing.

The daughter was no more than twenty. Her hair, a wheat-colored blond, was piled high onto her head and held there with a deep pink velvet ribbons but for the strand of perfectly shaped ringlets that hung down to her shoulders. Her dress was an elaborate array of flounces, drapery, bows, lace, and train, and Beth was reminded of a peacock carrying his tail feathers behind him. It was always a challenge to sit in such a gown, but the young woman didn't seem to mind. Her tight bodice and low, fringed neckline revealed the white curve of her breasts and didn't at all give the impression of dowdiness.

"Now, Melissa, you know it's true," her father said, chuckling, obviously proud of his beautiful daughter, who, Beth thought, had so little to do beyond pleasing him.

His wife, sitting beside him, smiled. She had the look of a woman who had once been thin and beautiful, but who had put on too much weight and begun to feel the years. Her hair, the color of her daughter's, was streaked with gray and braided on her head without bows or ringlets, and her face seemed very pale and plain above the bright blue fabric of her silk dress. "We're just trying to keep you happy, dear," she said to her husband in a sweet voice.

"Well, that you are, that you are," Dobbs said pleasantly and, leaning back, cleared his throat. "I haven't seen too many other steamboat men around this town. Maybe I'm the only one."

He seemed pleased with the idea, but his host laughed and said, "You might be the only one left in the whole country before too long."

Beth saw it was meant to be a joke and left at that, but Dobbs grew red in the face. He set his fork down. "Don't count on it, Mr. Prentiss," he said, picking up his knife. "We steamboat men are going to protect our north-south trade route, railroads or no. I don't mind them going east to west so much—the Mississippi River doesn't run that way—" he laughed at his witticism—"but they'd better not fool with my route from St. Louis to New Orleans. I won't have it."

Beth wondered what he proposed to do about it, but she decided that for now she should just listen. She could ask questions another time.

Down the long table, Jared Inman laughed. "And what do you think you're going to do to keep the railroads from going exactly where they please, eh, Elijah?" he asked easily.

Prentiss, who never liked to discuss business at dinner,

particularly in front of women, tried to laugh off Dobb's mild outburst and keep him from answering Jared. Beth was wondering why Jared had been so tactless when Prentiss waved his fork at her. "You look like you're setting all this down and storing it in that incredible memory of yours, Miss Harte," he said good-naturedly. "For your information, this is Elijah Dobbs of St. Louis."

Beth didn't tell him she had guessed as much.

"He probably owns more steamboats than anyone I know and is one of the richest men in the Middle West, but he hates the railroads. This over here is his wife, Beatrice Dobbs, and you're sitting next to his daughter, Melissa Dobbs."

"I'm delighted to meet you all," Beth said formally, suddenly awkward and embarrassed by her host's crude introduction. "I hope to see you again while I'm here. Where are you staying?"

"At the Grand Union Hotel," Elijah Dobbs replied, his normal ruddy color reappearing. "We have a suite—the first family to stay there since the renovations were finished."

"How nice," Beth said, and glanced at Melissa. Further down she thought she saw Jared Inman hiding a smile. "Perhaps we can take a walk together to one of the mineral springs sometime," she offered absently.

Melissa beamed. "Oh, that would be lovely! I've only been to the Congress Springs so far. There's just so much I want to see and do while we're here!"

"Yes," Beth said, warmed by the younger woman's enthusiasm. "I know what you mean."

Beth looked around and saw that William Prentiss, Sr., had taken in the conversation and seemed pleased that his unwanted guest was willing to stay among the ladies. But, of course, she wasn't. Beth had her mission for her father to consider, not to mention Virginia Prentiss's dilemma

over her unpopular choice of lover—or Jared Inman. Beth
didn't for a moment expect that she would be able to find
out all she intended to about the disturbing man from San
Francisco by waltzing off to the mineral springs with
Melissa Dobbs.

Finally, the meal ended. Beth had eaten until her corset
felt unbearably tight, and she thought of her father sitting
over his simple meal of steamed fish, plain vegetables, and
boiled potatoes. She wished she had been able to persuade
him to join her. She felt so alone. Sighing, she took a tiny
French pastry and hopped out of her chair unaided as the
men helped the other women to their feet. Prentiss announced that the drawing room and terrace were open to
all and the billiard room to the gentlemen. He sought out
Beth's eyes, but she quickly averted them. She didn't need
to be reminded again of that night seven years ago. Jared
Inman had taken care of that quite handily already.

"Nicely done," Jared said behind her as the guests were
filing into the drawing room. "He played right into your
hands, didn't he?"

"This time," Beth said, observing that William Prentiss, Jr., seemed to be avoiding her. "If you'll excuse
me—"

Jared pulled her by the elbow as she started toward the
drawing room. "Don't you and Ginny sneak off together
yet. I'm betting Prentiss is having you both watched."

Beth looked coldly at the strong hand on her arm, but
Jared didn't remove it so she looked coldly at his face.
"You make him sound like some sort of dangerous
criminal."

"If that's what you want to call a man who spies on a
daughter he adores to keep her from doing something
idiotic."

"You have no respect for women, do you?"

"Jacques LeBreque is a dangerous man, Beth," Jared

said seriously. "Ginny should stay away from him—and so should you."

"I shall do as I please," she retorted haughtily.

His grip tightened on her arm, then loosened suddenly. "Come walk with me on the terrace," he said mildly. "I told Prentiss I was partly responsible for your being here."

Beth didn't argue as Jared walked her through the french doors at the far corner of the dining room and onto the side terrace, but she silently told herself she was crazy. She must get rid of this man! He was like all the rest in that he wanted to control and direct her, and despite the way his laugh made her pulse quicken and his strong frame made her knees grow weak, she knew he would not approve, never mind encourage, her devotion to women's suffrage and reform. She couldn't possibly have him watching her, in any case, while she observed for her father. She required her freedom and independence, and Jared Inman hardly seemed ready to respect either.

The evening air was cool and pleasant, a welcome change after the heavy meal. Beth told herself she was trying to keep Jared from making the scene he would no doubt create in order to get his way. She breathed in the night air and asked, "What did you tell Mr. Prentiss?"

"I lied," he said, and grinned. "I said I had rescued you from Albert Shaw at the train station and took you here myself. I also mentioned that you had come expressly to discourage Virginia from her infatuation with LeBreque."

Beth whirled around. "How dare you!"

"Ah, Beth," he said, stepping from the terrace to the grass of the rose garden. "You'll discover I'll dare to do just about anything."

They were almost eye-to-eye, and Jared put his huge hands about Beth's slender waist and lifted her onto the grass behind him. His hands remained around her waist, and he drew her close. Before she realized what he intended, he covered her mouth with his in a hard kiss. Beth didn't respond, but he pulled her tightly against him, giving her arms no other place to go but about him. His lips softened, then parted as his tongue found hers. Beth kept telling herself to pull away, that he had no right to behave so rudely, but she could not. The strength of his arms, the taste of his lips, his passion, all were so new to her, so different from anything she had experienced at suffragette luncheons and reform meetings or with men like William, that she couldn't pull away. Instead, she found her hands clinging to his muscular back and her lips responding to his.

And then he released her and asked indifferently, "Will you be going to the casino this evening?"

He wasn't even breathing hard. Beth caught her breath and stifled a flush. She was aware of amusement in his eyes, and her own embarrassment. "Will you be going?"

He grinned, missing the reason for her question. "Yes."

"Then I won't."

"Ha! Coward. You won't go simply because of a silly little kiss. I thought you had more backbone than that."

Beth felt her spine stiffen. "The kiss was nothing. I'm not going because I'm tired."

"Liar."

"Mr. Prentiss wouldn't approve."

"What do you care whether Prentiss approves? Besides, he takes his own wife and daughter with him. Admit it, Beth, you won't go because of me."

She stuck out her jaw. "I admit nothing of the sort."

"Then go."

Beth flew around and stomped onto the terrace, then turned her head toward him. "All right, I will."

"With me," he said, his voice quiet, challenging.

She smiled coolly, raising her chin so she had to look down her nose at him. "Is that a dare, Mr. Inman?" His silent grin was his only answer. "Then I accept," she said, and snapped her head around and walked as elegantly as she could back into the dining room.

Behind her, Jared Inman was laughing.

CHAPTER 3

The Prentiss carriage led the parade along the wide, shaded boulevard to the village of Saratoga Springs. Beth wasn't in it. She had accepted Jared's challenge, and with no invitation to ride with his family forthcoming from William Prentiss, Sr., she had been forced to ride alongside Jared Inman. Beth was beginning to suspect that Jared was one of Prentiss's spies and meant to keep her away from Ginny.

Beth sat with her hands folded primly on her lap next to Jared on the elevated driver's seat of the four-horse carriage.

Behind and below them were two transverse seats, facing each other, occupied by the Dobbs family. Beth ignored Jared and tried to listen for any mention of steamboats and railroads from the trio behind them, but all she heard were coos about the beautiful evening. Beth had to admit the ride from the lake was pleasant, the road, an extension of Union Avenue, flanked with elms, a row of graceful trees down the middle so carriages could go to the lake on one side and return on the other. But she was too impatient to find out Ginny's view of her relationship with Jacques LeBreque and too nonplussed by Jared Inman's reentry into her life to pay much attention to scenery.

"Nice night, isn't it?" Jared said after a mile of silence from his companion.

"Yes."

"So you're going to be a sore loser, eh?"

Beth blinked at him in controlled surprise. "I wasn't aware I had lost. I accepted a challenge. I never promised you would find me interesting, Mr. Inman."

He laughed heartily, and Beth, without looking around, wondered if the Dobbses were listening in. "You never had to promise me anything of the sort, Beth my love," he said.

"Don't call me that!" she whispered fiercely.

"Better get used to it, darling dear," he said, and patted her on the knee. "A day hasn't gone by these past seven years that I haven't thought about that outrageous, beautiful girl I found swimming bare-assed in Lake Saratoga."

Beth pulled in her upper lip and carefully avoided clenching her hands into tight fists. "I am not that same girl anymore, Mr. Inman." She looked at him very loftily. "I am twenty-four. I have studied law and philosophy and literature since you saw me last. I am committed to securing the vote for women. And I wear dowdy gray dresses at the country's most fashionable spa. So you see, I am no longer beautiful or outrageous.''

Jared gave her a quick look that told her he knew better. ''We'll see about that.''

''No. You will,'' she said pointedly. Irritated with herself for showing her frustration, she returned her gaze to the gracefully arched elms. She couldn't resist adding quietly, ''I already know who I am.''

Beth rode the rest of the way to the Club House without looking at her escort, but her self-control was only on the surface. Her stomach was knotted with tension, and, as the horses clattered along, she had to fight her thoughts. She told herself very firmly that Jared Inman was insolent, boorish, corrupt, and no friend to women in general or herself in particular. He was merely playing a game with her: Show the smart suffragette she's just as susceptible to my overpowering masculinity as any mindless little snip. Then drop her and laugh. Yes, that was his game. Jared Inman didn't for a moment think he was in love with a Yankee judge's daughter. Impossible! She grimaced. But what if he were? What would she do then?

She was hardly aware when Union Avenue narrowed into Congress Street and they arrived at the elegant red brick building that was John Morrissey's infamous Club House. Jared, already out of the carriage, came around and put his arms on her waist to lift her out.

''I'm not an invalid,'' Beth said sharply, but he was already plopping her onto the ground. ''People will talk.''

''Now ask me if I care,'' he said and laughed, and Beth remembered people had said far worse about him than that he was seen with a bold young suffragette. ''Tell me your lucky number, Beth. I'll bet it all night and win us a fortune.''

Beth smirked, disgusted. "I suppose all that matters to you is money."

He gave her a broad, lecherous grin and ran the back of his hand lightly along her jawline. "No, not all."

Beth pulled away and started briskly up the walkway to the casino's front entrance, but Jared, laughing, caught up with her and took her arm in his. Just behind them were the Dobbses; just in front, the Prentisses. Ginny glanced over her shoulder and gave Beth an apologetic smile. Beth smiled back, hoping she revealed more self-confidence than she felt. She didn't want Ginny to worry about whether she could handle Jared Inman, or to feel guilty about deserting her.

Nevertheless, Beth did feel alone and deserted, and she wished her father were with her. But he was determined to stay in New York and try to figure out what the railroad moguls were up to while his daughter fulfilled her errand in Saratoga and had herself a little vacation at the same time. He had blown out a mouthful of pipe smoke and said, "It's a damned gaudy place, if you ask me."

Beth smiled as she recalled her father's opinion. Saratoga Springs was certainly boldly and unashamedly gaudy, but it also rang truly American. It was democratic and egalitarian to a fault. Anyone who could pay his gambling and hotel bills came to the spa, and thousands did every summer. Some of the newer resort villages—Newport, Cape May, Long Beach—were much more elitist in their tone, but not Saratoga.

Not, Beth thought, with John "Old Smoke" Morrissey in town. His Club House—casino was too vulgar a name and too obvious—stood on thirty impeccably landscaped acres adjoining the Congress Spring estate of Dr. John Clarke, and in the five years since it had opened, Morrissey had done everything he could to give his gambling establishment an aura of respectability—and keep the reformers quiet.

"This should be amusing," Jared said as he led Beth, who wasn't sure what he meant, inside.

The Club House was just as elegant, even tasteful, on the inside as it was on the outside, and Jared and Beth quickly caught up with the Prentisses in the softly carpeted, chandeliered dining salon. This, Beth knew, was the only part of the casino open to women. Handsomely dressed bouncers stood guard at the entrance to the public gaming rooms downstairs and the private rooms upstairs. No women were allowed to pass. They could spend the evening gossiping and looking lovely in their exotic, fashionable dresses, being entertained with sweets and ices and every other kind of refreshment, but no cards or roulette wheels.

Beth eyed the brightly colored dresses, elaborate hairstyles, and plethora of sparkling jewels. She leaned closer to Jared and whispered, "I feel like a pilgrim."

He laughed and squeezed her hand. "I told you this would be fun."

"You have a strange sense of humor."

"You should talk," he said quietly as William Prentiss, Sr., turned to him. "You'll be joining us upstairs, Mr. Prentiss?"

"Certainly, just as soon as I get these ladies settled. Miss Harte, is there anything you would be desiring?"

Beth smiled, and several answers popped into her mind, none appropriate. "No, thank you."

He nodded, asked his wife and daughter the same question, got the same answer, and left with Jared. His son lingered behind and came up to Beth as she watched the men disappear behind the guarded doors of the public gaming room. The high-stakes poker games were in the private rooms upstairs, and Beth had a strong feeling that was where her escort would end up.

"Elizabeth," William said, "I want to talk to you."

She smiled. "Yes, William, of course. I thought you were avoiding me."

"Avoiding you? And when, Elizabeth, have I ever been able to avoid you?" he asked, almost bitterly.

She smiled again and hoped he wouldn't go into all *that* now. William had pursued her after a fashion for years, but he had always mixed his declarations of love with the uncompromising demand that she divorce herself from the suffrage movement and her various other reforms. Beth hadn't seen him for several months and rather suspected he had given up on her ever swearing off her causes to become his idea of a proper wife and mother.

"I can't stay very long, Elizabeth," he went on more briskly, "but I did want to warn you about Jared Inman."

Beth frowned, but she saw nothing patronizing in William's pale blue eyes and fair face. He had grown heavier over the months, and his hair had thinned, but he was still a good-looking man. "What do you mean?" she asked.

"Just because he is a guest in our house doesn't mean he's a man you should trust, Elizabeth," William said quietly. "I don't think you'll find a man in Saratoga that would trust Jared Inman, much less a woman."

"Why?"

"Elizabeth, please trust *me*. I wouldn't interfere without good cause. Jared's from San Francisco. That's a wild town with different ideas about right and wrong, and I daresay it wouldn't produce your type of gentleman."

What, Beth wondered, was her type of gentleman? "But, William—"

He touched her arm briefly. "I thought I should warn you, that's all. If you'll excuse me."

She mumbled a polite thank you as he hurried away to join his father at the poker tables. Beth shook her head in confusion. So Jared *was* a guest at the Prentiss cottage, which meant he wouldn't easily be avoided. But why was he staying there if William didn't trust him? Was he doing business with the senior Prentiss? And if so, what? Well, it wasn't her concern. Or she hoped it wouldn't be. Virginia Prentiss, Beth reminded herself, was her reason for putting up with all this.

Not to mention Judge Robert Lowell Harte.

"Oh, Beth," Ginny said, coming up beside her, "I'm so sorry to have abandoned you, but there was no other way. Please forgive me—"

"Don't be silly. Everything's working out beautifully," Beth said, wishing her words would reassure herself as well as Ginny. "I just wish we could have a chance to talk. Do you suppose we could sneak outside for a walk around the terrace—"

But Ginny was already shaking her head. "I have to stay within sight of Mother, and Father said he or William would be checking on me regularly. They're afraid I'll go off to Jacques." Tears sprang to her eyes, but she smiled through them. "Let's at least try to have a good time while we're here. Would you care for something to drink?"

"Sure," Beth said, glad for any kind of diversion. They ordered a glass of mineral water, and Beth shook her head as she glanced at Ginny's canary-yellow dress with its huge, lace-trimmed bustle and train. "I guess I'm out of step with spa fashion," she added with a laugh, glancing at her own prim gray dress.

"Oh, no, Beth!" Ginny protested. "You look lovely. The gray sets off your eyes—"

But Beth was laughing before her friend finished her compliment, and Ginny joined her. They both knew that Beth was the most simply dressed woman in the room, and they both knew she could afford diamonds and lacy dresses if she chose to wear them. The waiter brought their water—a light carbonate from Pavilian Spring, he said—and the two women began walking among the crowd. The mineral springs had been the original attraction of the Saratoga area, and many people—Beth's father included—regarded those earlier decades as far more civilized than the present. When John Morrissey had arrived in the foothills of the Adirondacks thirteen years ago, everything changed. He opened a casino on Matilda Street, and, in August 1863, with the horror of the Battle of Gettysburg still weighing on the nation, he opened the racetrack. After the war, he built his Club House, which opened in 1869.

Now Saratoga was known as much for its casinos and racetracks as its health-inducing mineral springs and mud baths. A symbol, according to Judge Robert Lowell Harte, of the decay of postwar America.

"Is this Jacques very handsome?" Beth asked idly.

Ginny blushed and lowered her eyes innocently. "Oh, yes! He's very French. New Orleans French. He's not tall, but he has the most magnificent face, and he's ever so charming."

"Pity your father doesn't think so."

"Oh, but he does! That's the problem. He thinks I've been swept off my feet by a lying, stinking little Frenchman. His words precisely."

And Jared Inman's, Beth thought dryly.

"I can't tell you how much he disapproves," Ginny went on. "Everyone does. I haven't a friend in the world, Beth, except for you. I just know you'll adore Jacques!"

"I hope so, Ginny," Beth said. "But what I or anyone else thinks really doesn't matter. You're the one in love with him."

"Yes," Ginny said simply, and let it go at that.

Beth started to ask her friend what she knew about Jared Inman and his reasons for staying at the Prentiss cottage, despite William, Jr.'s opinion of him, but Melissa Dobbs appeared beside them, clapping her hands.

"Isn't this wonderful!" she exclaimed. "I can't think of anywhere I would rather be than right here." She lowered her voice, but not her excitement. "Did you know President Grant is in town? He arrived yesterday afternoon—"

"I know," Ginny interrupted, sounding bored. "My father said he was supposed to be here tonight."

Melissa clapped her hands together again. "No, really? I do wish we could get into the gaming rooms, don't you? Daddy came with just the biggest pocket of money! I think he's getting into a poker game with your Jared, Miss Harte."

Beth had been perfectly content to sip her mineral water and listen to the exchange between Ginny and Melissa, but now she nearly choked. She covered herself with a smile. "Beth," she said. "And I assure you he is not my Jared."

A brightly colored Japanese fan appeared in Melissa's hand, and she fluttered it in front of her pretty face. "No?"

Beth remembered that Saratoga Springs was a town remarkable for its rumor-mongering and that Melissa Dobbs had little better to do than gossip, so she kept her tone firm but her smile in place when she said, "No."

"It was terribly nice of him to escort you," Melissa added, unwilling to drop the subject. "Mr. Morrissey doesn't allow unescorted women in, did you know?"

"Jared was just being kind," Ginny said irritably, and Beth wondered what her friend thought of the pretty young woman from St. Louis. "And even if he hadn't offered to escort Beth, my brother or father would have."

"It seems," Beth said, steering the subject of the conversation away from herself, "that Mr. Morrissey doesn't have a very high opinion of women."

''On the contrary!'' Melissa countered. ''He worships women.''

''Precisely,'' Beth said dryly.

Ginny, used to Beth's suffragette opinions, giggled.''He's called Old Smoke because he 'worshiped' a woman.''

''I don't think we need to repeat that story,'' Melissa said primly, pursing her pink lips.

''Kate Ridgely was a prostitute,'' Ginny said, turning to Beth and ignoring Melissa's protest. ''Morrissey got into a fight over her and was pushed into an overturned stove, but he still managed to beat the other man insensible and win his woman.''

''You would think she was a horse,'' Beth muttered.

''The story goes,'' Ginny went on, eyeing a disapproving Melissa out of the corner of her eye, ''that Kate supported him with her earnings of the flesh, so to speak. In any case, now everyone calls him Old Smoke.''

Melissa flushed red. ''Yes, but that's all behind him now. He married Susie Smith—''

''The high-class daughter of a riverboat captain,'' Ginny informed Beth wryly.

''And I understand he's terribly faithful to her, and he's quite the gentleman.'' Melissa insisted. ''My father would not have brought me here if he weren't!''

Beth quickly took a gulp of water so she wouldn't laugh. John Morrissey, in her estimation, was no better nor much worse than most men who were too deeply involved in politics and gambling. Judge Harte had nearly sent him to jail on a number of occasions, when Old Smoke was a thug for Boss Tweed in New York City, not to mention an elected official people didn't dare to trust.

Ginny's attitude toward Melissa seemed to soften somewhat, and she said more amiably, ''Will you be at the regatta tomorrow, Melissa?''

Melissa smiled, showing she wasn't offended by her

disagreement with the older, richer Virginia Prentiss. "I wouldn't miss it for the world."

Beth hated to be stupid, but she had to ask, "What regatta?"

"Why, Beth, where have you been?" Melissa asked, shocked.

"In New York," Ginny replied stiffly. "Beth only arrived today, remember?"

"I only arrived two days ago—and from St. Louis—and I know all about the regatta!" She took Beth's arm, rather like a sophisticated older sister. "Tomorrow Saratoga is hosting its very first Intercollegiate Regatta. The town is just crawling with students and alumni of all the most prestigious schools, hadn't you noticed? And you should see the oarsmen! There must be seventy here at least. Yale, Cornell, Dartmouth, Columbia, Harvard—they'll all be in the race."

"And Princeton," Ginny added. "This will be their first regatta. Anyway, Beth, that's why Saratoga's so crowded this week. This is supposed to be its biggest summer yet."

"Oooh, it's just so exciting!" squealed Melissa. "You'll be at the Prentiss party tomorrow, won't you, Beth?"

"Father's having guests over tomorrow to watch the race from the grounds," Ginny explained. "Of course you're invited."

Beth wondered if Jacques LeBreque would be around— and if his sweetheart remembered he was the ostensible reason for Beth's presence in Saratoga Springs. She also wondered if Ginny was more infatuated with thwarting her father and brother than she was with her horse trainer.

Beatrice Dobbs dragged her daughter off to meet Susie Morrissey. Beth watched the two women scurry off in their elegant dresses, and noticed the dark-haired, magnificently dressed woman they greeted. The wife of the whoring, streetfighting, ex-heavyweight champion and consummate politician John "Old Smoke" Morrissey. Beth smiled to herself and wondered what it would be like to be married to a man like that.

"That girl!" Ginny muttered. "If she ever gave a second's thought to what she's about to say, I just might be able to tolerate her. Oh, look who's coming to pay the ladies a visit. Old Smoke himself. Come on, I'll introduce you—"

"No, don't worry," Beth said quickly. "I'm sure I'll meet him in due time."

Due time turned out to be immediately. Morrissey strode directly over to Virginia Prentiss and Beth Harte. He was over six feet tall, a heavy man, broad-shouldered and deep-chested, still powerful but no longer in prizefighting condition. He had a big black beard and neatly combed black hair, and he wore a black silk broadcloth suit.

"Well, well, well," he boomed. "Judge Harte's daughter."

Beth held her head high and extended her hand, which he took briefly in his own huge, callused hand. A fighter's hand. "I'm pleased to meet you, Mr. Morrissey," she said clearly. "I'm Elizabeth Harte."

"I thought I'd never see a Harte in my Club House," he muttered, but he seemed pleased that she was there. "Welcome to Saratoga Springs."

"Thank you."

"And how is your father?"

Her father, Beth thought, had suggested that John Morrissey bore watching. He had been involved in more than one railroad scheme over the years, although politics was more his game. "Very well, thank you," she replied, bowing slightly.

"I'm sure the old man would like to see me on Blackwell Island, too!" he said loudly. "Now wouldn't he?"

"In the old days, perhaps," Beth admitted, "but no longer."

Judge Harte had been involved with Samuel Tilden and the Committee of Seventy's maneuverings to get William Marcy "Boss" Tweed indicted in 1871 and convicted in 1873. Tweed was presently sitting in prison on Blackwell Island. Morrissey had led the gang of meats, as the judge called them, that had helped elect Fernando Wood to two unbelievably corrupt terms as mayor of New York. Old Smoke had been a part—and an occasional victim—of the corruption that had looted the city's citizens of millions of dollars before Tammany Hall leader Boss Tweed, then a state senator, was finally arrested.

Morrissey laughed, and Beth could see remnants of the brawler belied by his sleek clothes and the huge diamond stud on his white linen shirt. Try as he would, Beth thought, Old Smoke would never be wholly and completely respectable. "One of my better days was when your father retired from the bench," he said. "So long as he doesn't devote himself to closing down gambling casinos!"

"He believes you aren't robbing unsuspecting people, Mr. Morrissey—"

"I'm not robbing anyone! I run a fair house—"

"And take money only from those who come here willing to lose it," Beth finished for him, and she noticed Ginny had retreated. "Only those men, though, right? You wouldn't take even a penny from a woman who chose to gamble, now would you?"

"I don't allow women or year-round residents of Saratoga Springs into my gaming rooms," he said coolly. "Those are my rules, and this is my club. If you don't want to respect my rules—"

"I have no interest in gambling, Mr. Morrissey."

He frowned down at her, not convinced. "You're a suffragette."

Beth smiled.

"I don't hold with that, you know. Don't believe in it. Women don't need to vote."

"I have often wondered," Beth began calmly, "if the Tammany Hall gang would have come to power if women had been among the voters."

He turned red in the face, and Beth thought he was going to motion for his bouncers to rid his drawing room of one troublesome judge's daughter, but he didn't. He calmed himself and said politely, "I hope you enjoy your stay at the Springs, Miss Harte."

"I'm sure I will, Mr. Morrissey."

He bowed and left, but Beth suspected he didn't trust her entirely. She grinned to herself. Rightly so! Her father had said that if a railroad meeting was going to take place in Saratoga, John Morrissey would know about it.

"So you're Judge Harte's daughter," a woman's voice said behind her. Beth turned and faced a plump woman in her forties with graying black hair, decorated with innumerable ribbons, and wearing a shimmering black satin gown. "And Jared Inman's lady for the evening."

Beth nodded. "How do you do?"

"I'm Betty Bowman." She smiled, revealing pearl-white teeth and a curiosity about Elizabeth Stanton Harte. "Tell me," she went on, "what's a prim-and-proper girl like you doing with a man like Jared?"

Beth took a step away, attempting to ignore this coarse woman.

"Little wild, isn't he?"

Beth spun around sharply and saw the sardonic smile on Betty Bowman's face.

"Don't look so shocked, honey," she went on. "If

you've been hanging around with Jared, you know what I'm talking about.''

"No, I'm afraid I don't," Beth said.

Betty Bowman gave a loud, ribald laugh. "I wouldn't have thought you'd be Jared's type, but you never know what a man likes.''

"Miss Bowman—"

"Mrs. Bowman, honey." Her eyes narrowed suddenly, and the grin vanished. "If you want to know how I became a widow, ask Jared. He knows.''

Beth felt her face go pale. "What do you mean? Mrs. Bowman, I hardly know Jared.''

"You will, honey. Believe me, you will. But if you want to get the lowdown on him before you get to 'know' him too well, you just come by and see me. My place of business is on Caroline Street.''

Place of business? Beth swallowed, and suddenly Jared Inman was between them, his black eyes glaring at Betty Bowman. She smiled graciously, but the hatred was there. "Jared," she said, and bowed.

"What are you doing here?" he asked quietly, bu tone was menacing. Beth took a step back to m₁ retreat, but his hand shot out and caught her on the ₍

"What have you been telling her?" he asked Betty, not even looking at Beth.

Betty inhaled deeply and threw her head back. "Nothing she couldn't find out in any stinking barroom in the West.''

Jared clenched his teeth. "Stay away from her.''

Beth didn't know what to do or say, but she could feel Jared's grip hard on her arm. He escorted her through the crowd, away from the woman in black satin. "You're not my lucky charm tonight after all," he said.

"Where are you going? Mr. Inman—"

He tightened his grip. "It's Jared, dammit, and you're coming with me.''

"I am not!"

"I'm your escort, remember?" he said, tossing her an angry look.

Beth stiffened, but she didn't want to create a scene in Morrissey's Club House on her very first night in town. So she pulled her arm free and stalked out ahead of Jared Inman.

CHAPTER 4

They rode down the wide boulevard toward the Prentiss cottage, Jared a sulking shadow next to Beth, Beth silently holding back her anger and fear. They didn't speak until the lights of Saratoga were well behind them.

"Who is Betty Bowman?" Beth asked.

"A madam."

She had, during the quiet ride, begun to suspect as much. "You know her."

"I know many people, Beth."

"I'm sure you do."

She heard him sigh, but he didn't speak at once. The four horses clattered along the street. "Beth, why did you just stand there and listen to her?"

"I was interested in what she had to tell me," Beth replied, "especially since you have told me so little about yourself."

"You looked as if you were ready to faint when I saw you," Jared pointed out. "Why?"

She decided she would rather ask Betty Bowman about her dead husband than the man who had supposedly killed him, especially since they were alone on a deserted road. "She was rather—insulting."

"Why did you stand there and take it?"

Beth sighed and looked straight ahead at the dark road. "And what would you have had me do? Oh, I see. The Beth Harte you met ever so briefly seven years ago might not have shown such poise in a similar situation. I have already told you I am not that same girl."

Out of the corner of her eye, Beth saw the rawhide reins tighten around Jared's big hands, but he said nothing. Suddenly, she noticed her heart was beating rapidly and her body was rigid with tension. She had to find out what kind of man Jared Inman was!

As they approached the lake, Beth wished he would say something—explain about Betty Bowman's husband, or his three-thousand-mile journey supposedly to see a prim-looking judge's daughter, or anything at all about himself—but instead he said nothing. And she was too stubborn herself to open a new conversation. She sat with her spine very straight and her head held high, until Jared guided the horses and carriage down to the Prentiss stables.

She quickly gathered up her skirts and climbed out, even as Jared was jumping out himself and calling for someone to take the horses.

He caught up with her as she was hurrying across the

lawn. "Don't be in such a rush," he said, taking her by the arm. "It's too beautiful an evening to go inside yet. Let's take a walk."

"You forget I have had a long train ride today," she said politely. "I'm tired."

His hand slipped down her arm into hers. "Beth."

Across the lawn, she could see the moon glistening on the water, irresistible. "It is beautiful," she said, and smiled up at Jared. "William warned me about you."

"Did he?" Jared said, and laughed. "I can always count on William."

They started down toward the lake. The night air was cool, and Beth felt herself relaxing. "Jared, are you a criminal?"

"I suppose it depends on your definition."

"I've heard rumors about you."

He smiled, unwilling to be serious. "And I've heard rumors about you."

"Why are you here?"

"To see you."

Not *that* line again. What, she wondered, would her father say when she told him Jared Inman was in Saratoga? Perhaps Judge Harte could tell her something about this man from San Francisco. "Are you still with the railroads?"

"Still?" he asked, then grinned. "Always so full of questions, Beth."

She pursed her lips and reminded herself she was in Saratoga to be a friend to Ginny and ferret out information for her father. She was not supposed to be taking evening walks with unsavory men. "Cornelius Vanderbilt is in town, isn't he?" she asked, refusing to be deterred by his teasing.

"I suppose you think he's a criminal."

"Not a criminal as such," Beth said, not wanting to elaborate on her definition of criminal. "But he is crooked."

"Perhaps," Jared said, indulging her. "But he isn't as bad as some others—Jay Gould and Jim Fisk, for instance."

"September 24, 1869."

Jared grinned. "So you do read more than *Godey's Ladies Book*."

"From my inelegant dress, you should be able to tell that I don't read fashion magazines at all," Beth said, laughing. "September twenty-fourth was our first Black Friday, and it was all thanks to Fisk and Gould. They tried to corner the gold market, but an informant told the government, and so disaster was circumvented. My father and I believe we need controls so this sort of thing can't happen. Two scheming, crooked men brought this country to the brink of financial collapse."

Jared sat in the grass above the lake and watched Beth speaking so animatedly about corruption and reform. He smiled. "Where were you then, Beth?"

"In 1869? At Vassar." She sat beside him, a yard away, but she didn't want to talk about herself. "Fisk was murdered two years ago," she said.

Jared edged closer to her. "I know."

"I thought you might not have heard in San Francisco." She felt him near her. "Fisk and Gould were in cahoots with Daniel Drew when Vanderbilt tried to gain control of the Erie Railroad in 1867," she added quickly.

"I know that story, too, Beth."

As treasurer of the Erie, Daniel Drew had more control of stocks and bonds than its board of directors wished. He would change bonds into stock at will and flood the market beyond its buying power, and when the price went down, he was there to buy up all the bad stock. Then the price would go up, and he would profit. But the directors could do little to stop him. He held the railroad mortgages, and he could ruin the Erie whenever he wanted to. When Vanderbilt got on the board, he started buying up every share in the Erie at any price offered. Finally, he demanded delivery of what he knew were imaginary shares. Drew had not simply watered his stock. He had cranked up the printing presses and printed shares for Vanderbilt to buy! They each bought judges and politicians, and finally Drew came out on top when the legislature passed a law legalizing the stock issue and forbidding the consolidation of Vanderbilt's New York Central Railroad and the Erie. Everyone knew justice had nothing to do with the final outcome, only who paid whom how much how fast.

"Why do you suppose Vanderbilt is in Saratoga?" Beth asked idly.

"Because he always comes to Saratoga during the summer," Jared replied. "He's an old man, Beth."

"A rich old man." The richest, it was said, in the country.

Jared grinned. "And you don't think his days of manipulating and outmaneuvering are over. You're always so willing to be suspicious of anyone, Beth."

She looked at him and saw that he was very close to her now. She would have to ask her father about Jared to be sure and find out what role he played in the railroad corruption. "You never answered my question," she said. "Are you a criminal?"

He touched her shoulder and looked at her seriously. "Beth, I don't know any man as good and honest as your father. I don't know whom you've been asking about me—"

"No one!" she said sharply, aware of how close he was to her, and how alone they were. She drew back. "I just listen to the gossip."

"Beth—"

She rose quickly. "I'm tired. I think I'll go inside. If you'll excuse me—"

But he sprang up beside her and wrapped her in his

arms, not harshly. "Who are you, Elizabeth Stanton Harte?" he whispered. Before she could answer, he covered her mouth with his. He kissed her passionately, and she didn't, couldn't, didn't want to resist, her own passion equaling his. When he began kissing her neck, she threw her arms around him and pulled herself even closer. What was she doing! His lips found hers again, briefly, before he pulled away.

He smiled and wound a stray lock of her reddish-brown hair around his finger. "Was traveling three thousand miles to come for you a mistake, Beth?"

She drew away and turned her back to him. "You couldn't possibly have known I would be here," she said, and suddenly flew around at him, her silk skirts rustling in the still night air. "Never lie to me, Jared Inman. Laugh at me, kiss me, talk railroads with me, make fun of my most sacred beliefs, but never lie to me. I cannot tolerate lies."

And with that, she lifted her skirts to her knees and stalked up to the house. She half-expected him to follow, but all he did was stand on the shore of Lake Saratoga and laugh. "You haven't changed, Elizabeth Harte," he called to her back. "Not one damned bit!"

But she didn't linger to argue. She raced back inside and couldn't find her way to her room quickly enough. She must have been out of her mind to let him kiss her! But she smiled in her mirror and bit her lower lip. It had been, she thought, a wonderfully tantalizing kiss.

Then she remembered Betty Bowman and William Prentiss's warning about Jared and, with a heavy sigh, prepared for bed.

Beth nearly screamed when she heard someone in her room the next morning. In her panic, she thought it must be Jared, but as she rolled over, she saw it was Ginny.

"Beth," she whispered. "Beth, I'm sorry to wake you,

but I—Jacques is here on the grounds, down at the stables. Father doesn't think I know, but—''

Beth threw aside her covers and scrambled out of bed. "It'll only take me a minute to get dressed," she said, already pulling off her nightgown. "I gather your father and William aren't at the stables with him."

"No, they're still in bed. They won't be up for hours, I'm sure," Ginny volunteered, still keeping her voice low. "I haven't seen Jacques in days. He probably thinks I want to be rid of him—"

"Now don't start that," Beth cautioned, rummaging in her closet for her riding outfit, olive-bronze breeches with a short jacket. She smiled at Ginny. "This way I can take the blame for our being out there."

Ginny was dressed in a simple day dress of pink-and-white striped cotton, unsuitable for riding but eminently suitable for a tryst. Beth washed and dressed as fast as she could, leaving her hair in a thick braid down her back. When she was ready, she noticed Ginny's cheeks were flushed and her hands trembling.

"Come on," Beth said cheerily. "I've been dying to meet this horse trainer of yours."

Ginny smiled, flushed even more deeply, and, warning Beth to be very quiet, led the way down the hall to the back stairs, then out the kitchen and through the rose garden. In a moment, they were slipping into the stables. Beth noticed a small, wiry man leaning against a post beside a sleek black horse, but before she could make out his features, Ginny was in his arms.

Beth stood aside politely and concentrated on the horse. It was as magnificent a thoroughbred as any she had ever seen, its black coat glistening, its young body firm and muscular. This, she thought, must be William's prize horse, Louisiana, which she had been hearing about for the past year. William had boasted all winter that Louisiana would win both the Travers Stakes and Saratoga Cup, and looking at the horse now, Beth could see why.

"Jacques," Ginny was saying, "I'd like you to meet my friend Beth. Beth—" she paused and blushed happily, "this is Jacques LeBreque."

Beth smiled and extended her hand, which Jacques took in both his. "Ah, Beth, I have heard so much about you," he said, revealing only the slightest trace of an accent. "You have come to help convince Mr. Prentiss that he cannot keep two lovers apart, am I right?"

No, Beth wanted to say, you are not. She pursed her lips and studied the Prentiss horse trainer. He wasn't as tall as she, but his short-sleeved shirt revealed tanned arms with well-defined muscles, and his sturdy pants hung low on his tight, flat waist. He wasn't particularly handsome. He had an aquiline nose, a small mouth, and a long face with prominent high cheekbones, but Beth could see that he radiated charm. Still, something about his manner struck her in the wrong place. His confident smile irritated her, but she told herself Jared Inman's opinion of Jacques LeBreque was coloring her own. She was determined to be fair.

"It's a pleasure to meet you at last, Mr. LeBreque," she said formally. "Tell me, is this the famous Louisiana?"

"Oh, yes, yes, of course," he said quickly, sensing, Beth thought, her hesitancy. "He's the best horse I have ever trained." He turned to Ginny and held both her hands. "It has been so long, Virginia! We cannot go on like this. You must speak to your father. We can win his approval. Maybe your friend here—"

"Jacques, no," Ginny said. "I can't ask Beth to risk confronting Father. I only wanted her to be here as my friend. Besides, what can she do?" Ginny sobbed, her voice pained and pleading. Jacques turned away angrily. "Oh, Jacques—"

"No!" He spun around, and Beth found herself drawing back at his fury. "You are toying with me, Virginia. I wait here for you, and you don't come and you don't come and what am I to think? I am the rich lady's plaything. No. It is time we make a decision. We go to your father together. If he won't give us permission to be married, then we get married without it. That is how it must be, Virginia."

His voice had softened with his last words, and now he opened out his arms for Ginny. She obliged by falling against his chest. He stroked her fair hair and said loving things to her in French. Beth stroked the rump of the horse. Jacques LeBreque, she couldn't help thinking, had put on a fine performance. She had hoped she would find the Prentiss men—and Jared Inman—poor judges of Ginny's lover, but Beth suspected they were right and the horse trainer had deliberately charmed his way into the heart of a millionaire's daughter. To her, Jacques's chicanery was obvious, but Virginia Prentiss had always been reluctant to see others' faults.

No one, she reminded herself, was asking her for her opinion.

At that moment, William Prentiss, Jr., ran into the stable and jerked his horse trainer out of his sister's arms. Ginny screamed, but quieted herself quickly and covered her mouth, tears streaming down her face. "I thought I told you to stay away from this snake-charmer!"

Ginny sobbed and fled from the stable, lifting her skirts high and running. Beth noticed that Jacques was not moving to her defense, but, she reasoned, William still had him by the shirt and was a somewhat bigger man. "Stay away from my sister," he snarled, and shoved LeBreque back against the stall.

Beth, wondering if William had noticed her at all, quietly

slipped out of the stables. Ginny was almost back to the house.

"Elizabeth!"

Beth sighed and glanced at William as he came up beside her. "If you just left Ginny alone, she might make up her own mind about Jacques," she pointed out levelly.

"My sister's a fool," he spat. "And so are you, Elizabeth. Did you drag her down here?"

"I wanted to meet him," she said simply, skirting the truth. "And Ginny is not a fool, William. She hasn't run off with that man yet, has she? Give her some time to make up her own mind."

He stared at her, trying to appraise what she was saying, and whose side she was on. "Father said you came here to discourage Ginny from this ridiculous affair."

"I came," Beth repeated, "to be Ginny's friend."

"But you don't like LeBreque."

Beth shook her head. "Not what I saw this morning, at any rate."

William smiled suddenly. "Maybe you are getting some sense, Elizabeth, after all these years."

She wondered what he would have said if he had seen her in Jared Inman's arms last night. She smiled and excused herself to take a walk along the lake. Ginny would no doubt want a little while alone to recover from her humiliation. Beth, too, wanted some time alone, to think of what to say when her friend asked her what she thought of the horse trainer.

"The truth," she finally decided as she sat on a rock above the lake. Before she headed back to the house, she wondered if she would ever get the truth from Jared Inman.

CHAPTER 5

Thirty thousand people gathered on the shores of Lake Saratoga that afternoon for the long-awaited Intercollegiate Regatta. Several hundred were on the Prentiss lawns. Publisher and sculling enthusiast Frank Leslie had opened up his estate, Interlaken, for the event, and a huge grandstand had bēen built next to his Swiss chalet.

Beth stood on a rock above the lake, away from the crowd, and looked out at the glistening, rough waves. The gale that had already delayed the four o'clock starting time blew the skirts of her pale blue dotted-swiss dress, a simple affair with a gathered bustle but no flounces or train or any other drapery, and no hat or parasol to match. The skirt was fashionably tight around her hips, but the bodice extended to her neck, with a light ruching serving as a collar. That way she didn't have to drag along a shawl, but was still respectably clad.

She could see the crews from the nine colleges all along the shore and the multitudes waving their college colors, but the gale that had made the lake water dangerously rough didn't seem to be letting up. Beth suspected the race wouldn't be run today. She liked rowing, and the regatta would have been a pleasant diversion from her thoughts of Jacques LeBreque and Ginny and William and railroads and, of course, Jared Inman. She hadn't seen him all day.

"Trying to get a better view of all those lean young bodies?" Jared's voice said behind her.

Startled, Beth flew around and nearly slipped off her rock. Jared steadied her by the elbow. She scowled and pulled her arm away. "What do you want?"

He grinned broadly. Blushing, Beth turned back to the lake. "I don't think they'll have the race today."

"Oh, you don't? You think the rowing association is going to disappoint thirty thousand people?"

"I'd rather disappoint them than risk the lives of seventy young men," Beth countered. "Look at that water. They'll never be able to have a proper regatta in those waves."

"You surprise me, Beth," Jared said, but his tone was perfectly matter-of-fact. "I didn't take you for a sports fan."

Beth shrugged and stepped down off the rock, avoiding Jared's helping hand. She had thought of him more than once today, of his kisses, his strong arms around her. His reputation. His presence now only reminded her of how physically attractive she found him, and this more than anything disturbed her. Any kind of romance with Jared Inman, she had told herself, would be a disaster.

"If you'll excuse me, Mr. Inman," she said formally, "I think I'll go find Ginny and—"

"Ah, yes, I heard about your little adventure this morning," he said lightly, but his face darkened. "And what did you think of Monsieur Jacques?"

"I didn't like him, but I saw him only for a moment," she replied frankly but coolly. "And my opinion isn't what counts. Ginny is the one who's in love with him."

"You call that rebellious infatuation love?" His voice lowered as they walked toward the lawns. "Or don't you know what love is, Beth?"

She narrowed her violet eyes at him and noticed his casual dress, his dark, arrogant eyes, his strong body. If nothing else, her hours away from him had convinced her to remain on her guard. She straightened up and decided to ignore his last question. "No, I don't think Ginny is truly in love with Jacques, but I think she'll find that out soon enough—and on her own terms."

Jared's fists clenched at his sides. "I think you should stay away from LeBreque, Beth," he said, obviously trying to keep his opinion just this side of a command.

"Why?"

"I don't trust him."

"And why not?"

She stopped and looked up at him, waiting for an answer. His eyes seemed distant, but the wind caught his dark hair and he met her gaze. "It's none of your affair, Beth," he said curtly. "Just stay away from him."

"You sound like William," Beth replied calmly, sarcastically.

His hand shot out and grabbed her wrist, spinning her around as she started off. "What's that supposed to mean?"

Beth's heart was racing, but she glared up at him unafraid.

"I am not yours or anyone's to command, Mr. Inman," she said coldly.

"Jared," he whispered fiercely, and dropped her wrist.

Beth stood still in the grass and watched him stalk off. The wind rustled her skirts while she caught her breath, and her throat was tight. She had the horrible, terrified feeling she was going to cry. She had never cried over a man in her entire life, she told herself firmly, and she wasn't about to start now.

She smoothed her skirts and raised her chin. Her confidence rekindled, she walked toward the main crowds of the lawn party.

"Ginny's in the rose garden with a friend of mine," William said, coming up beside Beth. "Richard Hoskins. Maybe he'll divert her attention from LeBreque."

Beth tried to smile. "Is that the plan?"

"Mine, not Richard's. I'm not so bad as that, Elizabeth."

"If you dislike Jacques LeBreque so much, why don't you fire him?"

William smiled indulgently. "Because racing season is almost here, and he's the best trainer I can get for Louisiana."

"Your horse is more important than your sister," Beth scoffed.

She thought William would explode, but instead he smiled wryly and said, "You're as impossible as ever, Elizabeth."

She had to grin. "I know," she replied and shook off her lingering anger and frustration. "Would you introduce me to some of your friends? I'm afraid I don't recognize too many people here."

"I'd be delighted," he said, smiling, pleased.

But Beth was thinking she had better start finding out a few interesting facts for her father, and there was no better place to start than with a group of men. William took Beth gently by the upper arm just as she spotted Jared Inman standing beneath a giant maple talking intently to Melissa Dobbs. She turned away sharply and allowed William to introduce her to a group of men his age, every one of them a Columbia alumnus like William, and at least four involved with railroads. Two were sons of board members, one worked for the crippled Erie, and one was a board member himself.

They did not, however, want to talk railroads with Elizabeth Stanton Harte. They recognized her name, and knew her father the judge and their mutual commitment to women's suffrage. The race had been canceled for the day, and so the young men had no better way to amuse themselves than by teasing the bold young suffragette.

"Where's the Vassar team?" asked one.

Beth sighed. She had been in similar situations countless times, and by now she knew that the men considered themselves having a little "harmless fun" at her expense and that only if she went on the offensive would they get angry. Sometimes she preferred jeers to laughing taunts.

"I thought I saw a Vassar banner round about," the board member said. "Someone with a sense of humor. If women want to vote, Miss Harte, don't you think they ought to be able to row a regatta as well?"

"No."

"No? Well, *I* think they should! If they want the same rights as men—"

"They ought to be men?" Beth finished with a cool smile. It was one of her standard phrases. She yawned. "Rowing is very good exercise for both men and women. I used to row on the Hudson River when I was at Vassar."

They all thought she was joking and laughed heartily, William the most loudly. But Beth wasn't joking. She was telling the simple truth.

She ignored their laughter. "I understand there are a

number of railroad executives in Saratoga Springs this summer—''

But they didn't want to discuss business on a windy, sunny afternoon, and most certainly not with her. Beth despaired of ever finding out anything noteworthy at all for her father and excused herself. No one followed her. She glanced at the maple, but Jared and Melissa were gone. With a snort of irritation, she marched down to the shore, away from the crowds, where the wind was still blowing hard.

A small fishing boat was tied to the dock just below her. She noticed it and grinned.

She quickly walked down the beaten dirt path onto the dock and, gathering up her skirts, held onto a post with one hand and stepped into the center of the boat.

"Oh, good heavens, what is that girl doing!"

Beth smiled as she heard the shouts above her.

"Miss Harte!"

"Someone should stop her!"

"Elizabeth!"

She slipped the rope from the post and pushed off with one oar. Her face was to the crowd. A half-dozen men were racing toward the dock, and she could see the women standing in their beautiful summer gowns looking horrified. William Prentiss, Sr., was frozen a third of the way up. Beth wondered if her actions constituted provoking him.

William reached the dock first. "Elizabeth, don't do this! That lake is dangerous. You'll kill yourself, you fool!"

She ignored him and rowed out of the protected inlet into the rough, open lake. She had no intention of killing herself. The lake was choppy to be sure, but the fishing boat was built to handle the waves and she intended to stay close to shore. As she rowed away from the crowd gathering by the dock, she found she didn't care who was amused and who was shocked.

The bright, cool air, the exercise, and the solitude all felt wonderful to her. She grinned and laughed aloud. Then, when she rounded a point and the Prentisses and their guests were lost from view, she rowed confidently along the shoreline. Her strokes were careful, methodical, not very fast. She breathed deeply and felt herself growing stronger. It was a gorgeous if windy day, not a day for sculling, but a perfect day for a challenging row along the edge of picturesque Lake Saratoga.

Beth was glad that the founders of Vassar College had instituted a strict program of physical education for its women students, whose health, the theory went, might be damaged if their weaker physiques were submitted to intensive study. Beth had thought that was nonsense, but the balance between physical and mental exercise was carefully maintained, and it meant, now, that Beth was not afraid to row alone—and perhaps make a point or two.

But another rowboat rounded the point, and Beth grimaced. William was rowing furiously toward her. She sighed and, before he reached her, turned the boat around and started back to the Prentiss estate. She smiled as she passed him. "Nice afternoon for rowing," she called at his livid red face.

"You haven't changed, Elizabeth!" he yelled hoarsely. "You're no lady! You never will be. Now get back—"

She laughed, and the wind carried away his last words.

Jared Inman was waiting on the dock. He took the rope from her and tied it around the post himself. Then he hoisted her out of the boat by her elbow. "Have a nice ride, Beth?" he asked sarcastically.

She smiled. "Exhilarating."

He tightened his grip on her elbow. "Why?"

"I felt like it."

"If I were Prentiss, I'd kick you out," he said, but a smile escaped past his angry words. He dropped her arm and laughed. "You're so educated and mature, Beth."

She tossed him a haughty look and started away from the dock, but she stopped when she saw William Prentiss, Sr.'s stocky figure marching toward her. Behind her, Jared said, "I can't help you, Beth."

"I don't need your help," she muttered, and smiled broadly when Prentiss stood in front of her. "A wonderful party, Mr. Prentiss, but there's no need to thank me for livening things up after the regatta was postponed. I was glad to."

Prentiss's face became less red, but his words were still choked. "You could have gotten yourself killed!"

"Oh, nonsense," Beth said cheerily. "I stayed close to shore. I'm a very good swimmer, Mr. Prentiss, and I've been rowing since I was a child." Beth kept smiling, and her violet eyes sparkled. She was neither afraid nor embarrassed, but rather found she was quite amused. Perhaps her trip to Saratoga would do her good after all. She hadn't had so much fun in years! "I don't think my father would have worried about me," she added.

"Your father doesn't worry about you half as often as he should, Elizabeth Harte," Prentiss retorted, his tone still furious but his face its normal ruddy color. "You're a silly, rebellious girl."

She shrugged, unoffended. She had been called worse. "Perhaps, but at least your guests won't go away bored."

"You weren't doing me a favor, Miss Harte."

"No? Ah, but I will, Mr. Prentiss." She gave him a knowing look, suddenly serious, and said quietly, "Ginny has to make up her own mind—I can't change it for her—but I won't encourage her, and I'll tell her frankly what I think. If you throw me out now, against her will, I think she might be more convinced that she's in love with Jacques LeBreque, just to thwart you."

Prentiss looked straight ahead, past Beth. "Do nothing to embarrass me, Miss Harte."

"Yes, sir," Beth said, and walked away smiling to herself.

She was laughing by the time she reached the refreshment tables, and she grabbed a glass of mineral water and a light pastry filled with crabmeat. She was gobbling it down when Melissa Dobbs joined her. Melissa's hair was in ringlets, and she wore a dress of red-and-white candy stripes with a matching parasol and a white mohair shawl. "I should think all that exertion would make you quite hungry," Melissa said sweetly. "But I would be afraid of gaining too much weight."

"Not me," Beth replied, and grabbed another pastry as the waiters started clearing off the tables. "I've been slender all my life and probably always will be. My mother was built just like me, and my father's skinny as a rail. You should try rowing, Melissa."

Melissa paled at the thought, but rallied, pulling her shawl tightly around her when a breeze rose. "My father probably will be furious if he sees me talking to you."

Beth almost choked on her crabmeat when she laughed. "I'm harmless, I assure you."

"But you're—you and—" She bit one corner of her mouth and blushed a pretty pink. "I hope you won't think I'm impertinent, but the rumors about Jared Inman don't make *him* seem harmless, and he escorted you to the Club House last night and you left with him alone."

Beth raised her eyebrows, impressed. So Melissa Dobbs wasn't as mindless as she took pains to appear. "I don't think you're impertinent at all," Beth said vaguely, unwilling to explain her relationship with Jared. "I don't particularly trust Jared myself, but I don't know that much about him."

"I only met him on the train," Melissa said.

"The train?"

"From St. Louis. Actually, we didn't meet until Chicago. I think he and Father plan to do some business together."

"Oh?" Beth asked, trying to sound interested but not as rivetingly interested as she was.

"Of course, *I* wouldn't know all the details, but they spent quite a lot of time together," Melissa said, smiling coyly.

"Then Jared is looking into steamboats? Do you think he wants to invest in your father's business? They didn't seem to agree at dinner last night—"

"Oh, that's just Daddy! He's *so* worried about the railroads taking over his route. *I* think he and Jared get along very well." She pursed her lips, the coyness gone. "I don't mind saying that worries me, Beth. Jared Inman scares me."

"What have you heard about him?" Beth asked quietly, deadpan.

"Nothing you haven't heard already, I'm sure," Melissa said, unwilling to repeat the rumors, Beth thought, at the risk of seeming stupid.

"I saw him talking to you this afternoon," Beth commented idly.

Melissa lowered her eyes. "He was the perfect gentleman. He just wanted to know how I was liking Saratoga and our rooms. And he asked about Daddy. He came with Mother and myself, but he wasn't around all afternoon. I think he had business with some of the men here." She laughed and waved her hand. "He always has business everywhere."

Beth was prevented from getting further details about Jared Inman and Elijah Dobbs by the appearance of Ginny. "Elizabeth Harte, I don't believe you!" she said, laughing. "I just heard about your latest escapade. I swear, that's even better than the cigars! And you looking so prim and proper."

Beth smiled, her eyes twinkling, and as she drank down some mineral water, she noticed the man standing beside Ginny. Richard Hoskins, she supposed. He was a few inches taller than Beth, lean and erect, and dressed conservatively in black coat and checked trousers. He had short-cropped, sandy-colored hair, clipped sideburns, and a long but attractive face with hazel eyes, a straight nose, and a pleasant mouth. He smiled at Beth.

"Richard Hoskins, right?" she said, extending her hand.

He took it briefly, still smiling. "And you're Judge Harte's daughter."

Ginny covered her mouth, embarrassed. "Oh, I'm sorry! Beth, Richard is a lawyer from Baltimore, but he's rooting for Harvard, if that makes any sense."

"I'm a Harvard alumnus," he added with a sideways smile at Ginny.

"And Beth is one of our guests and absolutely the only person here who would venture out all alone on these waters," Ginny said, and pretended suddenly to notice Melissa standing beside her. "Oh, and Richard, this is Melissa Dobbs."

Melissa smiled prettily. "I'm terribly pleased to meet you, Mr. Hoskins."

Before Richard could reply, Beth put a hand on Ginny's arm and said, "I'm going to sneak off if I possibly can. I want to bathe and change before dinner and—"

"Well, go before Williiam catches up with you!" Ginny urged. "I know what he's like when he's furious. Go on, I'll cover for you. I owe you."

Beth saw Ginny's blush and guessed her friend was reluctant to mention Jacques LeBreque in front of Richard Hoskins. Perhaps, she thought, William's hopes weren't unfounded. She gave Ginny a quick, grateful smile and, nodding at Richard and Melissa, hurried toward the house.

Upstairs was cool and quiet. Beth found a servant and

ordered hot water for her bath. Then, inside her room, she suddenly drooped with exhaustion. She undressed slowly, her body relaxing as the corset and bustle fell away, and she put on a simple white silk robe. The servant, a young woman from the village, slipped in with the hot bath water and slipped back out again, returning Beth's smile as she closed the door behind her.

The bathtub was of Vermont marble with silver fixtures, and was the focal point of the small, elegant room with its white tile floor, marble washbasin, and, in a separate wood-paneled cubby, toilet. Beth dropped her robe and eased herself into the steaming water. Her muscles began to loosen up at once, and in a moment she was resting her head against the marble with her eyes closed. She thought she would recline thus until the water grew uncomfortably cold or her thoughts grew uncomfortably confusing.

She wasn't worried about William or his father, or Ginny and Jacques, or Ginny and Richard Hoskins. She had dismissed them all with a sigh and a shake of her head. It was only Jared Inman who confused and worried her. Jared and his reasons for being in Saratoga and what he knew about Jacques LeBreque and planned with Elijah Dobbs and—

Beth opened her eyes and splashed the water. With a sigh and a shake of her head, she tried to dismiss her musings about Jared Inman, but failed. If only she could ask her father about him! If the judge had known Jared would be in Saratoga, would he have put him on her list of men that bore watching, below, perhaps, Elijah Dobbs or one of a dozen other names?

But it wasn't only her suspicions about Jared that Beth tried to shake off. It was also his image, his laugh, the very idea of him. He had imbedded himself into her mind, and she couldn't rid herself of him. She told herself he was nothing but a handsome, lying, crass sneak toying with the feelings of the seemingly hardhearted and implaccable suffragette from New York City. He hadn't traveled a single mile to see her. He didn't care about her. He was insensitive and arrogant and she didn't want to think about him while she was trying to relax in a nice hot bath.

So what were he and Dobbs up to? Why did he want her to stay away from Jacques LeBreque?

Beth groaned and sank lower in the tub. "Who cares!"

With that, she was able to dismiss him for a few moments, but when she remembered his daring kisses the evening before, she promptly stepped out of the tub, dried off, and pulled on her robe. Facing William was better than facing her own thoughts, she decided, and went back into her bedroom.

And there was Jared Inman, stretched out on her bed with his boots on and his legs crossed, grinning at Beth as she slammed the bathroom door behind her.

"Get out of here," she said, her teeth clenched, her body rigid.

"Relax, will you? At least I waited out here. I could have barged in on your bath." He laughed when Beth paled. "There, you see, I'm not such a cretin after all. Now come over here. I want to talk to you."

Beth remained in front of the bathroom door. "I would like you to leave, Mr. Inman. We can talk this evening at dinner. I would like to rest."

"That's what I have to talk to you about," he said, sitting up and dropping his feet to the floor. "I won't be here for dinner. I have to go away for a day or two. Ah-ha, you're disappointed."

"Surprised, Mr. Inman," Beth corrected, careful to keep her tone steady. "Not disappointed."

He walked over to her and, not smiling, not speaking, unpinned her hair and ran his fingers through the chestnut tresses as they tumbled down her shoulders, then held her head in both his hands and tilted her face up to his. Beth swallowed hard.

"Tell me you don't want me to kiss you," he said, and before she could answer, his mouth covered hers, briefly, gently. He looked at her and smiled. "Well?"

Beth put a hand on his wrist. "Jared, please," she whispered. "I'm afraid—"

"Of me?"

"Of myself. I—"

But one arm slid down her back, and in one smooth motion, he raised her up by her waist, caught her beneath the knees with the other arm, and easily carried her over to the bed. He laid her gently on the white spread and, still leaning over her, slowly pulled his hands from beneath her and let them explore her body through the silk robe, up her thigh, along the curve of her hip, then pausing at her waist as she slipped one arm over her head.

Beth closed her eyes as if to block out the reality of what was happening. Jared kissed her eyelids, her cheeks, then her mouth, his tongue parting her lips as he pulled her closer. Her robe, already loosely tied, fell open, and Beth, her own passion rising, went to close it, but Jared's hand was there first, cool against her warm stomach. He touched her breast lightly; then, abruptly, drew away from her and stood up. Beth quickly pulled the robe tightly about her and sat up straight.

"I have to go," Jared said huskily, then caught a lock of auburn hair between two fingers. "But I'll be back for you, Elizabeth Harte, I promise you that."

She swallowed hard, and her violet eyes met his. "Will I have to wait seven years this time?"

"I have no intention of waiting seven years to complete what we just started," he said and, with a grin, kissed her on the forehead. "Two days at the most, Beth."

He turned to leave. "Where are you going?" she asked.

"New York," he replied, not turning around.

"Why?"

"I haven't got time to explain, Beth. I suppose I should have taken the time, but look what we both would have missed." He had turned to give her a wide grin. "I'll be back."

Beth reached down off her bed for a shoe and flung it at him, but he was already gone and it hit the door. She watched it fall to the floor.

"Well," she said aloud to herself, clearing her throat as she smoothed her robe. "That was an interesting experience."

She looked at the closed door and sighed heavily. She didn't for a moment doubt that Jared Inman would be back.

CHAPTER 6

The Intercollegiate Regatta was postponed again on Friday when the calm waters of early morning gave way to white-capped waves by midafternoon. For the second day in a row, thirty thousand onlookers and seventy college oarsmen returned home disappointed. Now the race was to be held on Saturday morning at ten, instead of four, when the lake was more likely to be calm.

All this was discussed in minute detail at the Prentiss lawn party. Dressed in simple white cotton and determined to blend into the crowd, Beth found herself less and less interested in the regatta. Yale had won last year, someone would win next year, and it didn't make any difference who won this year. She felt abandoned. Ginny stayed close to the lawyer from Baltimore, leaving Beth to wonder more than ever how much the wiry horse trainer meant to her, and many of the other guests were wary of the violet-eyed suffragette. But Beth had no intention of venturing out on the lake again today. She had pushed the Prentiss men far enough. Any further and she expected she would find herself on a train back to New York.

Not that that would be so bad, she told herself. She could ask her father about Jared Inman and perhaps track down the man from San Francisco herself.

Nevertheless, she behaved herself on Friday afternoon.

And on Saturday she awoke to a warm, bright, beautiful morning with hardly a breeze in the air. She dressed in yellow, and when the throngs again arrived from the village, she sensed the relief that today nothing could stop Saratoga Springs's first regatta. She couldn't have been more relieved herself, and stationed herself in the shade.

"You look bored, Elizabeth," William said, coming up beside her. "I suppose a ladylike existence can only interest you for so long." He leaned against the thick trunk of the tree. "Or is it Jared Inman's absence that has suddenly made your life dull?"

"What do you have against Mr. Inman, William?" Beth asked, not angrily.

"Let's just say I put him in the same category as Jacques LeBreque, who, I might add, seems to have lost the affections of my sister."

Beth was relieved to have the conversation directed away from herself and Jared. "This isn't a plot on your part, is it? You haven't put Richard Hoskins up to charming Ginny—"

"Elizabeth, Elizabeth, I've already told you I would

never do such a thing to my own sister," William said, more pained than angry.

"I hope not," Beth said quietly.

William caught her arm, and looking at him, Beth thought he seemed tired, even confused. "You're restless," he said softly, pausing, then adding, "and beautiful. I don't know if I've ever told you how beautiful you are, Elizabeth."

"No, you haven't," she said, aware that just a few months ago William's words would have encouraged her to believe that he might change and accept her as she was, but now, after she had been in Jared's arms . . . She smiled lightly. "How beautiful am I, William?"

He half-closed his eyes, looking at her, and at last he said thickly, almost inaudibly, "Very."

"Then you're not angry with me any longer?"

He shook his head. "No, Elizabeth. I never can stay angry with you for long."

The starting gun of the regatta saved Beth from having to respond. William joined his friends, who had staked out a spot right along shore, and Beth once again found herself standing alone. The lake was glistening blue, and the scullers in their college colors were picturesque as they rowed furiously, smoothly, in the flat boats with their sliding seats. Beth became absorbed by the rhythm of the oars dipping into the water, and she hardly noticed the roar of the crowd all along the lake.

Or the approach of Melissa Dobbs. "Why, hello, Elizabeth," she said sweetly. "Do you have a preference for any particular crew?"

Beth shook her head, glancing at the pink-clad woman beside her.

"Neither do I, really. Will you be going to the ball tonight?"

"I don't know," Beth said truthfully. The College Grand

Ball had been twice postponed, as had the regatta, but it was to be held that evening at Saratoga's three largest hotels. The general opinion was that it would be the spa's biggest, grandest ball ever. "I hadn't really thought about it."

Melissa looked shocked. "Beth, this isn't something you decide to do at the last minute! I've been planning what to wear all week! And I've already promised dances to someone from every crew. You know, if you want some help picking something out—" She stopped herself suddenly and put her right index finger to her pretty mouth. "You're not waiting for Jared to return, are you?"

Color rose in Beth's cheeks, and she turned away sharply, as though she were trying to get a better view of the race. "No, of course not," she said dully.

"Oh, Beth, there you are!" Ginny called cheerfully as she joined the two women in the shade. "Did you see Harvard break Yale's rudder? Yale's out of it now. Richard is down defending his alma mater against cries of foul. He says the starboard stroke 'accidentally' broke the rudder when Yale tried to pass Harvard too closely. And so the Harvard-Yale rivalry continues is what I say."

"Isn't it exciting!" cooed Melissa.

Ginny ignored her. "Beth, would you mind taking a quick walk with me? I need to talk to you. Would you excuse us, Melissa?"

"Of course. You two go on. I think that's Columbia crossing the finish line. Maybe I'll just go on down and watch William gloat!" She giggled. "We'll talk again, Beth."

Beth nodded and followed Ginny around to the side lawn.

"I try to be nice to her," Ginny muttered, "but she's such a nitwit! Beth, I'm sorry I've deserted you. I don't know what's gotten into me! You're going to think I'm fickle, but—Beth, I think I've been a fool about Jacques. He's not the man for me. Oh, he's charming and wonderful, but—well, he'll always be a horse trainer, and I'll always be William Prentiss's daughter.'' She stopped at the edge of elms lining the cobblestone driveway in front of the cottage. ''And I never thought I'd meet someone like Richard,'' she added humbly.

''I see,'' Beth said. ''You've only known him two days, Ginny.''

''Oh, but he's so kind and intelligent—and charming, too!'' She spun around at Beth and fought the tears in her wide blue eyes. ''I've never felt about Jacques the way I feel about Richard. Oh, Beth, what am I going to do?''

''Does Richard know about Jacques?'' Beth asked carefully.

''No! I didn't tell him, and I'm sure my father and William would *never* tell him!''

''What about Jacques?''

The tears welled and began dripping down Ginny's cheeks. ''I hate to hurt him,'' she mumbled.

''Jacques doesn't strike me as the kind of man you can put off, Ginny,'' Beth said kindly. ''You have to tell him. You remember how angry he was when he couldn't see you for a few days. Imagine what he'll think if you continue to meet Richard and don't tell Jacques where he stands.''

''I know, but—'' She bit back the tears. ''Beth, I just can't do it alone! Please come with me. I know I've been terrible and have just abandoned you, but please—''

''Of course I'll go with you,'' Beth said calmly. ''Now?''

Ginny shut her eyes and nodded.

Beth stood outside the stables while Ginny talked to Jacques, but she could hear everything they said. It wasn't pleasant. Ginny, in true Prentiss fashion, came straight to the point and refused even to let Jacques kiss her. "This isn't easy for me, Jacques," she said, "but I'm afraid we have to stop seeing each other."

"What! Ah, *ma chérie*, you can't mean it!" he protested, hurt and wounded at first.

"But I do, Jacques. We've been deluding ourselves. It's over. I'm so sorry."

"No, it cannot be as easy as that," he said sharply. "What has happened to you, Ginny? Tell me, eh? Two days ago, you were ready to defy your father and brother and run away with me, and now you are sending me back to the dogs."

"I never said I would run away with you, Jacques," Ginny said quietly. "I wanted to—I truly did—but neither of us would have been happy for long."

True, Beth thought, but Jacques LeBreque would have been richer.

"My Virginia, what has happened to you?" he asked, again trying his Continental charm. "Why have you changed your mind so quickly? Is it that friend of yours from New York?"

"No! Jacques, Beth had nothing to do with it. I—I've met someone else, that's all."

There was a long, heavy silence.

"Who?" he asked, his tone deadly.

"It doesn't matter. Jacques, please. I'm sorry if you're hurt—"

"I'm not hurt, Virginia Prentiss! No, no, not hurt. Don't you think you can throw me away like a doll you've grown bored with."

Beth stiffened, aware of how alone she and Ginny were. How quickly could she get help, if it came to that? She remembered Jared's warning about Jacques and felt her knees weaken.

Ginny rushed outside, and Beth thought she looked remarkably in control of herself. "Let's go," she said resolutely. "I'm sorry you had to hear all that."

Jacques stormed outside before they could get away, suddenly grabbing Ginny by the wrist and jerking her close to him. "I have not finished with you."

"If we both screamed," Beth said more coolly than she felt, "I'm sure we could attract some attention. I bet all those men watching the regatta are just spoiling for a good fight right about now."

Jacques released Ginny and turned his attention to Beth. She felt a chill run through her body at his searching look. "Jared Inman's woman," he said, almost spitting out the words.

"I am no one's woman but my own," Beth said icily. "Good day, Monsieur LeBreque."

Jacques spat on the ground between Beth and Ginny before spinning on his heels and stalking back into the stables.

Ginny burst into tears when he had gone, but Beth grabbed her wrist and urged her back toward the house. "Let's get out of here," she mumbled.

When they were clear of the stables but not quite back to the lawn party, Beth stopped and, holding both Ginny's hands, said gravely, "I don't think you should trust him. Please be careful, Ginny."

Ginny sobbed, tears streaming down her face.

"Be glad you got rid of him now instead of waiting," Beth said, trying to reassure her. "But he's very angry, Ginny, and I wouldn't—"

"Jacques wouldn't do anything to hurt me!"

Beth sighed and slipped an arm around her friend's thin shoulders as they proceeded toward the house. "Maybe not," she said, not expressing her own doubts, "but be careful anyway. Ginny, what does Jacques know about Jared?''

"I don't know. They—" She sniffled, regaining some control. "They seem to know each other. Perhaps they met out West or something. I don't know."

"Jared suggested I stay away from Jacques," Beth told her, making the demand sound eminently reasonable and kindly given. "So they couldn't be friends, could they?"

Ginny shrugged. "I don't even know why Jared came to Saratoga, Beth," she said, and smiled halfheartedly. "Not that anyone would tell *me*. They might be friends—or business partners. You never know whom business will bring together."

"Wiser words were never spoken," Beth mumbled absently.

This time Ginny stopped, turning to face her tall, dark friend. "You didn't like Jacques, did you, Beth?"

"No, I didn't."

"And you would have told me if I had asked you."

Beth nodded.

Ginny sighed. "Beth, ask me what I think of Jared Inman."

Beth lowered her eyes. "What do you think, Ginny?"

"I think you should be careful." She touched Beth's hand. "Very careful."

Beth didn't ask the reasons behind her friend's warning.

"I don't know why Father has allowed him to be a guest here," Ginny went on, her own troubles put aside now as she considered someone else's. "He's been nothing but kind and charming to me, and I haven't exactly brought up the subject of his reputation. But *you* know what it is, Beth! Oh, Beth, his world is so different from yours! He—he's a Jacques LeBreque with money."

"I'll be careful, Ginny," Beth said quietly.

Ginny smiled. "And so will I."

They rejoined the lawn party. The results of the regatta were in: Columbia first, followed by Wesleyan, Harvard, Williams, Cornell, Dartmouth, Princeton, Trinity, and, finally, Yale with its disabled rudder. The Intercollegiate Regatta of 1874 was over.

CHAPTER 7

Jared Inman didn't return in time for the College Grand Ball that evening, and for the first time Beth wondered if he ever would return. Perhaps, she thought, it would be best if she never saw him again.

But she knew she would, and even if she didn't, she wanted to know why he had been on the train from Chicago with Elijah Dobbs. Was it a coincidence, or were they planning something underhanded for their trip to Saratoga, when so many railroad executives, Dobbs's avowed enemies, would be in one place? And she wanted to know what Jacques LeBreque knew about Jared Inman and how they had happened, if indeed that were the case, to meet out West.

So many questions and no way to get the answers. Beth went up to her room, supposedly to rest, and wrote a long letter to her father. Perhaps he would have some answers for her.

Then, to give herself something else to do, she dressed carefully for the ball. Her gown was elegant and fashionable, yet simple, the low, clinging bodice of a deep rose silk moire that went tightly over her hips in a polonaise that looped up and back over her lace-trimmed bustle. The underskirt was white cotton voile, lightly trimmed with lace, and she wore white satin slippers. She left her thick chestnut curls tumbling to midback, swept off her face with the thinnest of velvet ribbons, a tone deeper than her dress. As an afterthought, she added a delicate silver necklace with a single amethyst stone and tiny earrings to match.

She laughed at her reflection in the mirror. "And whatever happened to prim and proper Elizabeth Harte?"

The Prentisses were pleased with her transformation, and, Beth thought, surprised. Even Ginny. Standing beside Richard Hoskins, her mouth dropped open when she saw Beth. "Why, you're gorgeous!" she exclaimed, clapping her hands together. "I didn't know you still had it in you, Beth."

"Neither did I," Beth said, and Ginny blushed at her own backhanded compliment.

The sun was still warm and shining when they rode to the village for the gala ball. Because the double postponements had put it on Saturday night there had been a huge outcry at the prospect of dancing early into Sabbath morning, so the time of the ball had been pushed up two hours, and now it would start at six.

Broadway, running through the heart of the village, was so crowded with people and carriages there was hardly room for the Prentiss carriage to let out its passengers. Beth was amazed. She had never been to a ball such as this promised to be. She was standing on the corner of Congress Street and Broadway in front of Congress Hall, a giant hotel of brick with brownstone trim, but across the street were the Springs's two most mammoth hotels, the Grand Union and the United States.

The Grand Union had been the Union Hotel for years—in Saratoga's less gaudy days, as Judge Harte would say—but Alexander Turney Stewart had purchased it two years earlier, spent a half-million dollars on renovations, and opened it for the 1874 season as the Grand Union. Its five-story brick contour sprawled over seven acres, with four-hundred-fifty feet of Broadway frontage, then folded back into two wings each nearly a quarter-mile long, with gorgeous gardens between. It boasted over eight hundred guest rooms, a dining room that could hold fourteen hundred, black walnut staircases, marble-tiled ballrooms and lobby, and a mile of piazzas. The promenade along Broadway was supposedly the biggest in the world.

"In the words of Judge Robert Lowell Harte," Beth muttered to herself, "gaudy, gaudy, gaudy."

But spectacular.

The ball itself was also to be the grand opening for the United States Hotel. The original had burned down seven years earlier, but now it had been rebuilt in true Victorian fashion. It was U-shaped, five stories tall, and, like the Grand Union and Congress Hall, occupied seven acres, three of them forming a park between the two wings. There were cottage suites, over seven-hundred-eighty guest rooms, a dining room that could serve a thousand, and, its most unusual feature, a thirty-foot veranda that overlooked Broadway.

Tonight the three largest hotels would be hosting the finest college oarsmen and the richest men and women in the country with simultaneous programs in each of their main ballrooms. Beth thought even her father would have to be impressed.

She followed the Prentisses into Congress Hall.

The ballroom glistened with gas burners, gems, and jewelry, and Beth immediately saw that her own elegant dress was subdued compared to what the other women were wearing.

"This would be a great place for a thief," she remarked to William.

He laughed and swept her onto the ballroom floor to dance the first waltz, Strauss's "Teorin." "You're beautiful tonight, Elizabeth, more beautiful than ever," he said. "I think I can even forgive you for your rowing escapade."

"I'm not asking you to forgive me," Beth reminded him.

"I know—and I don't care."

"You're just in a good mood because Columbia won the regatta today," Beth said cheerfully, and nodded at the Columbia flags swinging from the chandeliers and the huge blue banner on one wall with COLUMBIA in big, conspicuous letters. "Looks like a fraternity house around here."

"Elizabeth—"

But the music rose and drowned out his voice. When the waltz ended, William reluctantly gave up his partner to his father.

"I see you're behaving yourself," he said. Like all the other millionaires in the crowded ballroom, he was wearing a black tailcoat, trousers, and vest with white tie and white gloves. "You don't have any cigars tucked into your bodice?"

"I would like to know where there would be room!" Beth said with a grin.

The older man laughed. The informal, happy, indifferent atmosphere was contagious, and with the college oarsmen as the most prominent guests, everyone seemed to feel younger. Beth found herself laughing more and observing less, relaxing fully for the first time in months. She danced with anyone who asked, and many did, and she refused to discuss woman's suffrage or railroad corruption or any of the reforms she and her father were working toward. Even when someone teased her about the speaking engagements she had canceled to come to Saratoga or pointed to the stout, eighty-year-old Cornelius Vanderbilt and his second wife, a young belle from Mobile, Beth refused to take the bait.

And when she danced with William Henry Vanderbilt, the Commodore's principal heir, she didn't stray into talk of politics or corruption. Her father might have been disappointed in his daughter for not picking the brains of the man who controlled railroads throughout New York state and as far west as Chicago. But Beth didn't think the younger Vanderbilt would tell her anything of importance during a waltz, and so they talked only of the regatta and the weather.

When the Prentisses left Congress Hall for the ballroom of the Grand Union, Beth followed Ginny and Richard with William at her side. The elm-shaded grounds were decorated with several different college colors, and gas burners and a stunning calcium light lit their way. The Union ballroom was so crowded there was hardly room for dancing, but the orchestra was playing a Weingarten waltz, so Beth waltzed.

"Everyone's talking about you," William said, holding Beth close as they danced. "Those who know you are surprised you're the same serious, prim woman who lectures them on women's suffrage. Those who don't know you want to. Your father would be proud of you, Elizabeth.''

Beth laughed. ''On the contrary, William. My father would be disgusted. He hates balls. He hates anything frivolous.''

''But he's so like you, Elizabeth. He'll do anything—''

''On a dare,'' Beth finished. ''He likes adventures, but adventures aren't frivolous, you know. And, William, you have to get over your prejudices against suffragettes. We may be very serious about securing the vote for women, but we're not always serious—and we're certainly not always prim and ugly!''

''You've never been ugly, Elizabeth,'' William said, and Beth blushed when his eyes met hers. ''I hope I've never implied that you were. Elizabeth, would you ever give up your causes for the right man?''

''I wouldn't give up my causes for anyone,'' she replied and, not wanting to spoil her mood, changed the subject. She nodded to the huge allegorical painting that covered the west wall of the ballroom. ''Isn't that incredible? What's it called?''

She thought William sighed. ''The painting? 'The Genius of America,' I think. Stewart brought it in when he had the hotel renovated. Elizabeth—''

But the waltz ended, and someone else asked for a dance with Beth. Then the Prentiss party moved over to the United States ballroom, where the orchestra was playing the ''Blue Danube'' and Jay Gould was among the honored guests. Beth remembered her mission.

''What is Gould doing in Saratoga?'' she asked William.

''Enjoying himself, I should think.''

Beth frowned for the first time that evening. Gould had become more tame over the years as the government slowly began to clamp down on the excesses of corporate manipulators, but he was still no favorite in the Harte household. And Beth rather suspected Judge Harte was no favorite with Jay Gould.

"I wonder if I could talk to him," Beth mumbled, half to herself.

"Now, now, Elizabeth," William cautioned, "don't start worrying yourself about things that don't concern you."

Before she could respond, he swept her across the ball-room in yet another waltz.

And then Beth saw Jared Inman. She lost her footing and stepped on William's toes, but quickly regained her control. He was standing next to William Prentiss, Sr., with his jaw set firm and anger in his black eyes.

"What's wrong, Elizabeth?" William asked.

She shook her head. "Nothing. I—I'm just tired, that's all."

Across the room, her eyes met Jared's, but the anger in his didn't dissipate. She knew what those black eyes looked like as though they were just inches away. William led her off the dance floor, but he followed her gaze and stiffened.

"I thought I warned you about him, Elizabeth," he said darkly.

"I'm not—I don't know what to think, William," she said, her voice a panicked, hoarse whisper. "Why should you warn me about him? What's he done? William, please—"

"Ask him about Juan Correrro, Beth."

"What!"

He gave her a twisted smile. "Ask him," he said, and walked away.

Beth stumbled outside to the park between the wings of the hotel. Elms arched over gardens and a bandstand, and people crowded onto the landscaped acres, away from the heat and noise of the ballroom. All the benches were occupied, so Beth found a tree to collapse against. She leaned against the trunk and, still standing, looked up at the foliage against the darkening sky.

Juan Correrro had been a wealthy railroad builder in Sacramento, California. Beth knew his name, but little about him except that her father thought he was one of the few honest men in railroads.

He had made the comment two months ago when he read about Juan Correrro's death in the newspaper.

His murder.

Jared's tall, dark figure came around the tree. Beth caught her breath. He moved close to her, strikingly handsome in his formal black clothes. Not as fine and elegant as the other men, but always, Beth thought wryly, arrogantly masculine.

"Hello, Beth," he said, not smiling.

"Mr. Inman," she said with a polite nod.

"I see how patiently you waited for me."

Her violet eyes flashed up at his. "I never said I would wait for you at all, Jared Inman."

He fingered the lace trim of her dress along the neckline. "And whom did you dress for, Beth?"

"Myself," she snapped, and pulled away.

"If I had been here, you would have worn gray linen just to spite me." He gathered up her hair with one hand. "And you'd have tied your hair into a proper knot. But for William—"

"I don't intend to stand here and justify myself to you!" Beth said angrily, ignoring the weakness in her knees. "If you had been here earlier, you'd have tried to tell me what to wear, and so I would have done exactly the opposite. I don't like being told what to do, or what I would have done, or what I feel. If you want to know, ask me. Don't tell me. Don't assume."

His hand fell out of her hair, down to his side, and he

leaned against the tree trunk. "Did you miss me, Beth?" he asked quietly.

She spun around and saw that he wasn't laughing. She swallowed hard. There was nothing menacing about him, nothing to be afraid of. William was simply jealous.

"Did you, Beth?" he asked again, just as quietly.

"Yes."

She thought she saw a smile at the corners of his mouth. "You thought I wasn't coming back for you, didn't you?"

"Only when you didn't come this afternoon."

"And so you've been dancing all evening with William and playing at being the most beautiful woman here to drown your sorrow," he said sarcastically. "Don't play games with me, Beth. If you're in love with William—if you think he's more suitable than I am—say so now. I'll go away and you'll never see me again."

"That would be one way to get rid of you," she said with a small smile, "but I'm not in love with William."

Jared's eyes narrowed, and he stood silently looking at her for a full minute, but Beth didn't flinch under his scrutiny.

"Come with me now, Beth," he said, taking her hand. "You're sweating from all that dancing. Let's go for a ride together."

"But Mr. Prentiss—"

He drew her close and smiled into her eyes. "I dare you, Beth. Leave with me now."

Beth held up her chin and laughed. "You know I can't resist a dare. But I have to tell someone I'm going—"

"Now, Beth."

"Oh, my," she said lightly, and put out her arm for Jared to take. "You're on, Mr. Inman."

CHAPTER 8

"You think this whole thing's a joke, don't you?" Jared asked, his tone unamused, as they rode in a two-horse carriage down the wide boulevard toward Lake Saratoga.

"No," Beth said, and gave him her haughtiest smile. "Not entirely."

"Then why aren't you nervous?"

"Should I be?"

He paused, not looking at her. "You've been trying to find out about me, Beth. You've heard the rumors."

She said nothing.

"San Francisco is a different world from New York. It has different rules. What you could be hanged for in New York may very well be commonplace in San Francisco."

Beth stiffened. "Do you mean that literally?"

"In some cases, yes."

"*Now* I'm nervous," she mumbled lightly.

Jared grinned. "You *have* been listening to the rumors."

"Are they true, Jared?" she asked quietly.

"You'll have to make your own judgments about me, Beth," he said. "I'm not going to tell you how to feel."

"I'm not asking you how I feel. Jared, I want to know about you! What do you do for a living? What's your life like in San Francisco? Why are you here in Saratoga now? Why—why are you interested in me?"

He sighed deeply, not answering at once. "Forget about what everyone says about me," he said at last. "Judge me only by what I say to you. When I can, Beth, I'll tell you everything you could possibly want to know about me."

"Why not now?"

He touched her hand. "I've frightened you."

She tightened her fingers around his and shook her head. "Is this the hand of a frightened woman?" she asked with a laugh.

He almost smiled as he removed his hand from hers. "Don't ever be frightened of me, Beth," he said. "I would never do anything to hurt you."

But someone else? Beth decided not to ask. She looked at the moon rising on the horizon, giving off a glow to the clear night sky, and she knew Jared Inman did not scare her. Perhaps she was out of her mind, she thought, but she simply wasn't nervous. Her heart wasn't beating in her throat, she didn't have any chills running up and down her spine, and her mind wasn't conjuring up any dire prophesies.

And yet she didn't want to ask him about Juan Correrro

or Betty Bowman's husband or his reputation as an outlaw on the quiet, lonely road to Lake Saratoga.

She could, after all, be hopelessly wrong about this mysterious man from San Francisco.

He grinned down at her as the carriage turned into the Prentiss estate. "Having second thoughts about accepting my dare?"

Beth laughed. "On the contrary."

"You're a strange woman, Elizabeth Harte," Jared said as he leåped from the carriage.

Beth jumped down on the other side before he could help her. "So I've been told," she said, meeting him at the rear of the carriage.

He touched her hair above her ear. "Are you worn out from all that dancing?"

"Not especially, no."

"Then you'll walk with me down to the lake?"

She grinned up at him. "Is that a dare?"

"No, a request."

He took her hand, and they walked together toward the lake. When they came to the stand of birches on one edge of the lawn, Jared glanced knowingly at Beth and started into them. She followed, remembering that night seven years ago when, sick and angry, she had fled the billiard room to the quiet peace of the lake. She knew Jared was remembering, too. They crept silently through the brush, and in a moment were standing on the rock where Jared had sat watching her.

"You haven't changed so much since then," he said, taking her hand back into his. "Or have you?"

Beth shrugged and tried to turn away. She didn't want to be serious. But Jared held onto her hand, so she met his gaze. "You didn't know me then, Jared," she said, "and you don't know me now."

"I want to know you, Beth," he said quietly.

She darted away from him and jumped down off the rock. "I can't resist that water. I'll race you to that bank of rocks and back," she said, pointing to the opposite shore of the inlet some fifty yards away.

She ducked behind a staghorn sumac and began peeling off her dress, corset, bustle, stockings, and shoes, leaving on only a light cotton chemise.

"Beth, for godsake—"

"Chicken?" she challenged from behind her bush and, laughing, dove from the bank into the lake.

The shock of the cool water against her overheated body was momentary and, invigorated, she swam in even, strong strokes toward the opposite bank. Jared didn't catch up with her until she was touching the bank of rocks. In the glow of the moon, she could see the dark hairs glistening on his naked chest.

"Dammit, Beth, I've been riding all day. I'm exhausted—"

"Excuses, excuses," she chided and, laughing, kicked off for the return swim. She heard Jared curse and splash behind her, and he was beside her again in an instant. She grinned at him. "You can't do all the daring, Jared."

"You're outrageous, Beth."

He stayed beside her. She tried to outswim him, but he would just match her stroke. Unnerved by his naked chest so close to hers, she tried to ease up and let him pass her, but he stayed next to her. He was determined not to let her win or lose.

When they came to their starting point, Beth turned to him in the water. "Well, a race with no winner," she said brightly. "That's as it should be, I suppose. I'll turn my head while you get out—or don't you care?"

He grinned and stood up in the water, his chest rising up into the warm night air. "I don't care."

Beth remained discreetly below water, her cotton chemise wet and filmy against her skin. "As you wish, but I *do* care. I'll turn my head, and you'll do likewise when I get out." She pointed a wet hand toward the bank. "You first."

She turned her back to the inlet and looked out at the starlit sky above the lake, but there was no sound of Jared splashing his way onto shore.

"Jared?"

"What, Beth?"

His voice was near. Too near. "Jared, you're supposed to be on shore getting dressed." She turned around into his arms. "Oh—"

His mouth covered hers, hungrily, gratefully, and his hands caught her about the waist and pulled her long body against his, which, she suddenly realized, was entirely naked. Only her thin undergarment came between them. She let her arms go around his neck as he tasted her mouth, and she could feel the ache of desire mounting inside her. He kissed her cheeks and her wet throat, his fingers sliding up her waist.

"Jared—"

"I want you so much, Beth," he whispered.

She shut her eyes, lightheaded with her own passion and rapid breathing. "Jared, I've never—"

"I know, I know," he said gently, touching her wet hair. "You're so lovely, Beth."

He tugged at the chemise, and in a moment it was floating away in the current. Beth felt her body go rigid as she stood naked before Jared, but he smiled and kissed her lips, and the tenseness, the sudden awkwardness, vanished. She was conscious only of the yearning of her innermost being for the naked man before her.

"If you don't want this," he said quietly, "say so now and I'll leave."

She ran a dripping finger along the line of his jaw and

smiled into his black eyes. She had never made love before. There had been so little opportunity—so little time—to develop any romantic attachments during her long months of work. And there had never been any man quite like Jared Inman. She had long given up all hope of an early and lasting marriage, though she had never expected to remain a virgin for life.

"Please don't leave," she whispered.

Jared smiled, and together they made their way to the grassy shadow of the boulder. In the dim, soft light of the moon, Beth could see Jared's firm, nude body, virile, ready for her. She rolled against him, and he caught her about the hips. Nothing mattered. She didn't care who he was or what he was, she only wanted him. She gave herself up to the ache in her core as he kissed her neck, her breasts, her lips. His magic fingers and tantalizing lips awakened every inch of her flesh to new and glorious sensations. With a groan, she arched for him as he gently, slowly entered her. She wrapped her arms around his back and pulled him deeper into her, gasping at the melding of passion and a fleeting, exquisite pain.

"I could do this forever," Jared whispered.

She smiled up at his face, dark against the sky. "So could I."

And then their passion grew beyond anything Beth had imagined, and she clung to him, digging her fingers into the hard flesh of his back, knowing only the pleasure he was making her feel. When there seemed to be no escape from it, no end, she shuddered, then cried out his name and groaned with a sudden, overwhelming sense of peace. She felt his answering ecstasy and release. He rolled off her, against the rock, and smiled into her eyes. She smiled back and reached out a hand, covering his. "I want to get to know you, Jared," she whispered, exhausted.

"Not many people do know me, Beth," he said, and

twirled a lock of her hair around his finger. "Are you all right?"

"Yes!" she breathed.

"I wish we could stay out here all night, but we can't." He grinned suddenly. "I'll turn my head while you dress."

And then he slipped quietly into the water. Beth watched him swim, with strokes as strong and even as hers, across the inlet. She didn't want to leave. She would have slept naked in the shadow of the boulder, but it wouldn't do if one of her hosts found her that way on Sabbath morning. So she dressed, drying herself with one of her underskirts, and without a word left Jared to his solitary swim. She wondered if he were as confused and satisfied and happy as she, or if this were a perfectly ordinary experience for him.

She hoped it wasn't ordinary at all, and she smiled confidently to herself as she cut across the quiet, dark lawn. She had no regrets. Whatever their lovemaking had been to Jared Inman—and she was sure it had meant something—she had no regrets. Except, she thought as she slipped in the back entrance, that she couldn't have stayed out on the shore and slept beneath the stars and the moon. That was her one regret.

"My only one," she said to herself, laughing, as she ran up the back stairs to her room.

CHAPTER 9

Beth saw nothing of Jared Inman for the next week. It was as if, she wrote in her journal, their lovemaking had meant nothing at all to him. He wasn't staying at the Prentiss cottage. She wasn't sure where he was staying, and she didn't dare to ask. Her hosts were not pleased that she had disappeared from the College Grand Ball, and they were even less pleased when the gossip reached them that she had disappeared with the man from San Francisco. So Beth held back her questions and comments and decided to play the proper young lady for a few days. Until the dust settled. *Then* she would find out what had happened to Jared.

She couldn't, she told herself, afford to irritate her hosts enough to have them throw her out. With the racing season so near, she would never find a room in the village. So, while she waited for Jared to approach her, she watched for him at the casino, at dinners, at parties, at the mineral springs. She knew he was still in Saratoga only because William had said he was and warned her to keep away from him once and for all.

Meanwhile, she turned her attention to her father's task for her, but she was unable to glean much useful information. On Wednesday she received a reply from the judge to her letter. It was more than usually obtuse: "Jared Inman? I recall I sent him out with towels for you at that silly ball last time I was in Saratoga. Tall fellow, isn't he? Black eyes? I'm sure you can handle him, Beth."

And then he had gone on to discuss rate-fixing and the latest railroad bridge collapse and the outbreak of grasshoppers in the West. A train had stalled in three feet of the creatures at Kearney, and supposedly they had consumed every living bit of vegetation from the Canadian border to northern Texas.

"I don't care about the damned grasshoppers!" Beth had screamed in frustration.

On Saturday, July 25, opening day of the races, Jared Inman and Elizabeth Stanton Harte had still not crossed paths in the busy resort of Saratoga Springs. It was a warm, sunny day, and Beth was tired of waiting. Perhaps it was better that Jared had exited from her life rather than stand around gloating, laughing at her, thinking of himself as the conquering general, but she didn't think so. She had no regrets about their lovemaking, and she wanted to hear him say to her face that he did. Or say that he had gotten what he wanted from her and was finished with her so she could slap him.

"Or maybe shoot him," she muttered as she sat in the carriage with the Prentiss women on their way to the track. Richard Hoskins was driving.

"I'm so excited," Ginny whispered to Beth. "William is just so sure Louisiana is going to win today. We've never entered a winning horse. I just can't wait!"

"Louisiana is a beautiful animal," Beth agreed, but she couldn't share Ginny's enthusiasm.

The track occupied one hundred and twenty-five acres just east of the hotels along Broadway, and the Prentiss party was among the ten thousand spectacularly dressed men and women that filled the stands. Beth had worn her brown traveling dress without corset and bustle and had managed to slip into the carriage before anyone could demand she change. The Prentiss men were already at the track with Louisiana and Jacques LeBreque, who had been silent all week. A sixteen-year-old Irish boy was set to ride William's favored horse.

But when the Prentiss men joined the women in the stands, it was with angry, disappointed faces. William, Sr., related the bad news. "Louisiana won't be racing today," he said tersely.

Ginny grabbed her father's arm. "What! Oh, Father, it can't be. What happened?"

"Bruised leg. He'll be racing again shortly."

William sat beside Beth, and she could see he was taking his horse's injury hard. His face was ashen and sweaty, and his hands were shaking. He was clearly worried about more than his horse's health. "William," she said quietly, "how much did you bet on Louisiana?"

He refused to answer her. His expression wasn't simply of disappointment but of mourning, of nervousness bordering on fear. Beth wondered how a man as wealthy as William

Prentiss, Jr., could be so worried about losing money in a single race.

She and William looked up simultaneously when the stout, aging Cornelius Vanderbilt made his way to them. "Heard about your hard luck," he said to William. "Will we be seeing that horse of yours later this summer?"

"I hope so," William said dully.

"You take setbacks much harder when you're young, my boy. Just learn a lesson from this and you'll be all right."

William gave the wealthiest man in the country a fierce, angry look. "And what lesson would that be?"

Vanderbilt didn't take offense. "Oh, several I could think of, but if you can't figure them out for yourself, there's no point in me telling you." He started to turn away, but his eyes came to rest on Beth. He tapped her knee with the tip of his elegant cane. "Don't I know you, girl?"

Beth smiled and bowed slightly. "My name is Elizabeth Harte."

"Of course. Old do-gooding Judge Harte's daughter. How is the old fool?"

"Thirty years younger than you and doing quite well, thank you."

He laughed heartily. "You're as bad as he is, I hear. You'd both put the railroads out of business if you could, wouldn't you? Well?"

Beth held her head high, unintimidated. Cornelius Vanderbilt was used to having his own way and asking questions however he wanted. And getting answers.

"First of all," she said levelly, "neither my father nor I wants to put the railroads out of business. We only want them to run without corruption, safely, and with more than a passing interest in the people that use them. However, I am not concentrating my energy on reforming the railroads.

I am devoting most of my time to securing the vote for women." She smiled fetchingly. "At the moment, I am on vacation."

"Hartes don't take vacations," Vanderbilt said with a hearty laugh. "It's my guess, Miss Harte, that you'll write down everything you hear and see for your father to find what use he can make of it."

Beth managed to keep smiling, but she was amazed—impressed—at the way the old man had read her. Of course that was what she was doing. "And what could I possibly hear and see up here when everyone around me is vacationing?"

"Ha, ha! See! You're both like a couple of coon dogs with your ears up all the time." Still chuckling, he nodded to Ginny and Sophia Prentiss, clapped his hand on Prentiss's shoulder, and made his way back through the crowd.

To Beth's relief, the gun sounded for the Travers Stakes, the first race of the season. It had first been run on August 2, 1864, opening day of the new track, and was in tribute to the racing association's president, William R. Travers, a witty and rich New York stockbroker. Travers himself was in the grandstands now, and although that first Travers Stakes had been won by Kentucky, one of his own bay colts, this year was a different story. The strong, beautiful horse Attila dead-heated with Acrobat in the one-and-three-quarter-mile race, and Attila won the runoff.

William, watching the race mutely, muttered at his finish, "Louisiana could have beaten them both."

"He'll have his chance, William," Beth said tartly, irritated with his continual pouting. "Besides, it's only a race."

"Ha!" laughed a deep, familiar voice behind them. "That's very funny coming from you, Miss Harte."

Beth flew around. There stood Jared Inman, grinning. She recovered quickly from her surprise and smiled coolly, distantly. "Hello, Mr. Inman," she said politely. "I'm surprised to see you here."

"Are you now?" he said, and chuckled. "And I thought I had no more surprises left for you."

Beth turned away quickly and felt the heat of a flush overcome her. Damn, she thought. A week had changed nothing. His arrogance, his insolence, his rudeness, were all still there, but so were the odd tingling in the base of her spine, the rapid beating of her pulse, and the strange alertness—the heightening of her senses—that only he seemed to arouse in her.

But Jared Inman had dropped out of her life without a word for an entire week, and now he would discover that he could not drop in again as easily as he'd like to think. Beth turned back to the races and ignored his comment.

Jared didn't seem to care. "Well, William," he said, "I see Louisiana didn't make it to the Travers Stakes. I've heard rumors about a bruised leg. True?"

William nodded, his face sour.

"Was it an accident?"

Beth shot Jared a sharp glance. No one had yet intimated that Louisiana's injury had been anything more than bad luck. Leave it to Jared to fuel William's imagination. Or did Jared know something William didn't? Beth knew only too well that she had managed to learn very little about the man from San Francisco during the past week.

"I have no reason to think otherwise," William said, looking at Jared. "Do you?"

Jared shrugged, and to Beth it was obvious that he did. "No, not really," he said. "Sorry about your bad luck." He patted Beth on the shoulder. "Nice seeing you again, Miss Harte."

Jared left, and if anything, William seemed more sullen. Beth leaned toward him and spoke in a low voice. "You don't think he had anything to do with Louisiana's injury, do you?''

''I wouldn't put anything past Jared Inman, Elizabeth,'' William said dully.

''But why?''

The gun went off for the one-and-one-quarter-mile Saratoga Sweepstakes for horses of all ages, and Beth could get nothing further out of William. ''I think I'll stretch my legs,'' she said to no one in particular, and slipped away unnoticed.

She was looking for Jared Inman. She had let him skulk about Saratoga unimpeded for a week, but no more. She wanted to know who he was and what he was and what he knew about Louisiana. And what she, a suffragette in a dowdy brown dress, meant to him.

She saw him wandering toward the stables. She hung back, melting into the crowd, but as they approached the stables, there were fewer people and almost no women. Jared stopped in front of an open stable door. Not daring to move in closer, Beth hid in the shade of an elm.

Jacques LeBreque walked outside and visibly stiffened at the sight of Jared Inman. Jared gave him one of his offensive, arrogant smiles, but Beth couldn't hear what either said.

She saw the flash of the blade in the sunlight before she saw the knife that appeared in Jacques's hand. She started out of the shade with the vague idea of stopping any violence that was about to erupt, but Jared, with lightning speed, kicked the knife from LeBreque's hand, jerked him up by both elbows, and smashed him against the stable door. Beth didn't need to see Jared's face to guess what it looked like. She felt rather sorry for Jacques LeBreque.

Jared let Jacques drop and walked away. The wiry horse trainer scrambled to his feet and yelled, ''You're crazy!

Come near me again, Inman, and I'll kill you myself! And do you think anyone will blame me?''

He was still yelling himself hoarse, but Beth thought it best she beat Jared back to the crowd and fled from her spot in the shade.

Jared caught her by the arm and spun her around as she crossed over to the track. ''What the hell are you doing here?''

''Getting some air,'' she replied haughtily. ''Let go of me.''

''You followed me, Beth,'' he said, clenching her arm tightly.

''I did not,'' she retorted, but immediately was uncomfortable with the lie. ''And so what if I did? Obviously, I am no concern of yours.''

He dropped her arm and stared down at her. He was breathing hard, sweat dripping down his face, and Beth remembered he had just saved himself from a slashing. Even if, she added as she drew herself up to her full height, Jacques LeBreque ended up in worse shape.

''You are so wrong,'' he said quietly.

Then he turned and walked away.

Beth watched his retreating figure. He was heading away from the stands, and in the pit of her stomach she knew he wouldn't be back for a long time. She lifted her skirts and, free of bustle and corset, ran lithely after him.

''Wait!'' she called. ''You're not going to go strutting off and leave me again!''

She caught up with him, but he didn't stop or even so much as glance at her. She nearly had to run to keep up with him.

''Where have you been all week?'' she demanded. ''Why did LeBreque pull a knife on you? Did he have anything to do with disabling William's horse? Did you? Jared Inman, you are not going to outrun me.''

He stopped abruptly, and Beth nearly fell over him. "I should have waited until all this was over before I came for you," he said.

She stomped her foot in the dirt. "Until all *what* was over? Jared, please talk to me. I can't stand—"

"It's *not* your affair, Beth."

He started walking again, but she groaned, picked up her skirts, and ran after him. She tried another approach. "Why didn't you come to see me all week? I thought after the other night—"

He glanced down at her, his face softening. "I couldn't, Beth." But then he added impatiently, "I thought you might have used your brain and figured that out."

"Used my brain!" she yelled, indignant, throwing her hands on her hips. "Jared Inman, you haven't told me enough to figure out anything."

He turned full into her, and she could smell the dust on his clothes. "How much do I need to tell you for you to trust me, Beth? What more do I need to do?"

She fought a flush, but it came anyway. "You left without a word, Jared. What was I supposed to think?"

"You were supposed to think that I had things to do that don't concern you, Beth," he said quietly.

"Why, because I'm a woman?"

He didn't even hesitate. "No."

"Then because if you tell me, you know I'll turn you into the authorities?"

He grinned suddenly. "Maybe."

"Jared!" Beth yelled, exasperated. "You haven't answered any of my questions. What about William's horse? He's worried sick. I think he bet a lot of money on Louisiana—"

"So that's it," Jared said, the grin vanishing. "I was wondering why you were so cool when you saw me, but it was because your precious William was sitting beside you, wasn't it? Rich, handsome, proper William Prentiss." His face twisted in a bitter laugh. "You didn't exactly look *me* up either this week, Beth. What, is the thrill over now, and are you ready to settle down with someone benign and inane?"

Beth clenched her teeth angrily. "William is neither benign or inane, and he has nothing at all to do with us.'

But Jared wasn't listening. He had turned once more and walked away. This time Beth didn't follow him.

CHAPTER 10

Ginny was waiting at the corner of the stands for Beth to return. "Oh, there you are!" she called, relieved. "Father has sent William and Richard looking for you. Beth, you can't just run around on your own. Father will throw you out—"

"I know," Beth said. "I'm sorry."

"You didn't—" Ginny glanced around and lowered her voice. "You didn't follow Jared, did you?"

Beth nodded.

"Alone? Oh, Beth! Well, I won't tell Father if you'll

behave yourself." She smiled and squeezed Beth's hand. "You and Jared both have a wild streak, but I daresay Jared's is even wilder than yours."

"Ginny," Beth said seriously, "I have something to ask you. It's about William's horse—and Jacques. Do you think Jacques would hurt Louisiana to get back at you for ending your affair?"

The blood drained out of Ginny's face, and her body seemed to freeze. "What?"

"I'm just curious, Ginny. I don't have any grounds for my suspicions—"

"No, Beth, he wouldn't! Not Jacques. He loves Louisiana. He wouldn't do something like that to any horse, let alone a sure champion like Louisiana. He had nothing to gain by injuring Louisiana, only to lose. Why would you think such a thing?"

Beth shook her head and patted Ginny on the shoulder. "No reason, really," she said quickly. "Just forget I asked. Here, let's head back to our seats and watch—what is it now, the Flash Stakes?"

She started past Ginny into the aisle, but Ginny held her back, grabbing her arm. "Beth, there's something I wanted to talk to you about."

"Sure."

"Mr. Dobbs had invited us to dine with his family and the Vanderbilts this evening," she said, then licked her lips awkwardly. "The Prentiss family, that is. Beth, I hope you don't mind. Father said we wouldn't go if you objected."

"Of course I don't object!" Beth said, but she wondered why she had been excluded. Did Dobbs wonder what she might tell her father? Or did he merely consider that Judge Harte's daughter might inhibit their conversation and had therefore decided not to invite her? Beth smiled understandingly. "I will be perfectly delighted to spend the evening in my room. The pace of life in Saratoga can get quite outrageous!''

"Oh, Beth!" Ginny exclaimed, relieved, and hugged the taller woman. "I knew you'd understand. Father said he would arrange for your transportation back to the cottage."

"I don't mind taking the omnibus."

"Father insisted," Ginny said, and giggled, her fair cheeks turning pink. "He doesn't trust you as it is! People are so surprised that we're even friends, Beth."

Sometimes Beth was surprised herself, but she had always liked Virginia Prentiss. "You're an open-minded, tolerant woman, Ginny," Beth said. "You accept me for who I am, and I accept you for who you are. That's why we'll always be friends. Now let's go, before your father sends out a search party."

They rejoined the Prentiss party and watched Hunters and the Travers's two-year-old Olitipa win the half-mile Flash Stakes. Beth hardly noticed the race. She was thinking about Jared Inman and all the dubious things she had heard about him . . . and about their night together a week ago. She sighed and joined the crowd in a raucous cheer, but she could only see the look in Jared's eyes when he had kissed her, and then, suddenly, the quick, merciless way he had dealt with Jacques LeBreque. There seemed to be two Jared Inmans: one for his proper suffragette, one for men like Jacques LeBreque and women like Betty Bowman. Which, Beth wondered, was real?

She caught the mournful, pale look on William's face and decided she had to find out.

The transportation William Prentiss, Sr. had arranged for Beth was a two-horse carriage driven by Jared Inman of San Francisco.

"I'm surprised he trusts you with me," Beth said

coolly as she climbed onto the driver's seat next to Jared.

He grinned. "Actually, I'm surprised he trusts me with you."

"Don't you have more important things to do than escort the Prentiss's ugly-duckling guest?" she asked, her tone still cool as she folded her hands in her lap.

"Undoubtedly."

"You're maddening."

He coaxed the horses into the huge departing crowd, but he seemed oblivious to the crush of carriages. "So are you," he said quietly, a glint in his black eyes. "In many more ways than one."

Beth looked away quickly as she felt the heat of a flush. When she was near Jared, all she wanted to do was touch him, laugh with him, feel how much he desired her. Now she struggled to remember her father's mission and her doubts about this mysterious man.

"What is it, Beth?" he asked quietly.

She shook her head and bit her lip, not ready yet to speak, but Jared covered both her folded hands with his and squeezed them gently. She glanced sideways, trying not to acknowledge the rush of warmth his touch sent through her body. "I can't go on like this," she said as steadily as she could. "Who are you, Jared Inman?"

He sighed wearily and lifted his hand from hers, taking the reins in both hands and urging the horses forward.

Beth knew he wasn't going to answer her question. "William said I should ask you about Juan Correrro."

"Don't."

It was more of a plea than a command, but Beth plunged onward. "He was murdered two months ago."

"I know."

"William seems to think you had something to do with it."

"I know."

"Did you?"

He glanced down at her, no glint of amusement in his eyes now. "It's none of your business, Beth, and I don't mean that unkindly. Don't ask me about things that don't concern you."

She drew her knees tightly together and clasped her hands, almost wringing them. She rehearsed what she was going to say before she finally spoke. "I thought everything about you should concern me."

His face hardened. "You were wrong."

So that was where they stood. The carriage broke out of the crush along the track and speeded up as it headed down the wide boulevard to Lake Saratoga. Beth wished she had the nerve to jump out. Clearly, Jared had decided that all that should be between them was their physical attraction for each other.

"Beth."

His voice was low, gentle, but she refused to look at him.

"Oh, Beth, you're so very young in so many ways," he said softly, not mocking her.

She looked at him coldly, but tears burned in her eyes. "Why? Because I won't accept everything you say as if it were written in stone? Because I want to know more about you? You haven't told me what you're doing in Saratoga, Jared—"

"I have," he protested. "I came to see you."

"You did not! And why did the Prentisses have you as their guest if William depises you?"

He gave her a pointed look. "Ask him."

"Let's not start *that* again. You're not the type of man who would be jealous of someone like William, especially since you seem to care only about the physical side of our relationship," Beth said hotly. "So don't try to skirt the issue, Jared."

"Are you finished?" he asked, the amused glint back.

"No."

He couldn't suppress a laugh. "All right, what else do you want to know?"

"Why did you sneak off without a word after we—after last Saturday? Don't laugh at me, Jared Inman!" She unclasped her hands and slapped him on his upper arm, but he didn't budge. He did, however, stop laughing. "What were you up to all last week? What—what do you do for a living? Do you have a family? Parents, brothers, sisters? You're not a bum, Jared. You may wear scuffed boots, but you can afford to gamble in John Morrissey's private rooms."

"Anything else?"

"Why did Jacques LeBreque pull a knife on you, and did you have anything to do with the death of Juan Correrro?"

He didn't answer her. The horses plodded onward, and a cool breeze hinting of autumn blew. Beth knew Jared wasn't going to answer any of her questions. He hadn't before, and he wouldn't now. She wrung her hands together and stared at her blunt, even nails.

"I've told you before, Beth," he began at last, "that I will tell you everything when I can."

"Everything that concerns me, or everything?" she asked, still looking at her hands.

"That will all depend on—" he paused and touched her cheek, turning her face so that their eyes met, "both of us. Please, darling, trust me."

Beth closed her eyes, unable to speak.

"I missed you this week, Beth," he went on softly, his fingers brushing across her lips. "I can't tell you how many times I thought about you. I wish you could believe how deeply I care for you, but I do understand."

He took his hand away, and Beth opened her eyes

against the bright sun. They rode in silence. When the carriage turned onto the cobblestones of the Prentiss summer estate, Beth realized with a stab of panic that she and Jared were alone. The Prentisses were having dinner with the Dobbses. Only the servants were at their cottage. Beth wasn't at all sure she trusted herself alone with Jared Inman. She felt no remorse about their lovemaking last Saturday night, but too much had happened since then, too much still remained unexplained.

"How long do you plan to stay?" she asked cautiously.

The horses plodded slowly around the cottage toward the stables. "Oh, I didn't tell you?" Jared said. "Prentiss has asked me to spend a few days here."

"He knows William doesn't trust you?" Beth asked, trying to get information and to forget the trembling that had suddenly arisen in her fingers.

"I assume," Jared replied, then grinned. "I don't think Prentiss trusts me either."

"But you accepted his invitation in any case."

Jared brushed his hand along her jawline. "You're here, Beth, remember?"

She swallowed hard, the trembling descending to her knees. She was not, she told herself, afraid of Jared. She was afraid of herself and of what he meant to her. She was already too involved with him, and the sensible part of her warned her to get some distance between them. But Jared had other ideas. His hand eased down her throat and sent a shudder through her body when it skimmed along her breasts.

"Jared—"

But she couldn't explain. Even if he listened to her, she probably wouldn't listen to herself. She drew back from his touch and, in one swift motion, lifted her skirts and leaped out of the carriage. She stumbled on the cobblestones and fell onto her knees, but she quickly picked herself up and ran across the lawn toward the house. She didn't look back. She burst through the front door and raced up the stairs. A servant asked if anything was wrong, but she shook her head and kept running. She locked the door to her room behind her and sank against it. The only way to resist her passion for Jared Inman, she knew, was to lock herself in for the evening.

As she undressed and caught her breath, Beth glanced out the window. A solitary figure stood on a boulder on the shore of the lake. She walked to the window and pulled the curtains aside. Jared. Her throat tightened as she stared down at him. The lake was blue, still, the mountains beyond green, every leaf sharp against the clear sky, but Beth wondered what it was Jared Inman was seeing as he stood motionless on the boulder.

She watched him for a long time and turned away only when he did. She thought he looked up at her window, but she moved away too quickly to be sure.

CHAPTER 11

Beth had breakfast in her room and left only when she was
certain the Prentisses had gone to church. She was wearing
a functional riding outfit of breeches, jacket, and boots,
which would be sure to invite questions from her hosts that
she didn't want to answer. She had made her plans before
falling asleep last night, and now she meant to stick to
them.

Her first stop was the stables. To her surprise, Jacques
LeBreque greeted her. "Ah, Miss Harte," he said cordially.

Beth bowed slightly, wondering if Jacques would ever

pull a knife on her. "Mr. LeBreque," she said formally. "I heard about Louisiana's lameness. Will he be all right?"

He shrugged impatiently. "I think so. What is it you want, Miss Harte?"

"A saddled horse," Beth replied, hoping she didn't look or sound nervous. Perhaps she *would* have been better off if she hadn't seen the exchange the afternoon before between the horse trainer and Jared Inman. Perhaps Jared was right to keep her ignorant of his affairs. She shook off the thought. "I would like to go riding," she added.

"Of course."

"I can wait outside—"

"It will only be a moment."

He opened a stall across from Louisiana and led out a trim bay mare. "Marquita is very gentle, very agile," he said, stroking the horse. "She will give you a good ride."

Beth smiled appreciatively, hoping she wouldn't do anything to irritate Jacques. She already knew he blamed her for Ginny's retreat, and suspected he was just waiting for her to reveal her contempt for him or otherwise aggravate him.

"Monsieur Inman has gone riding today as well," Jacques added.

"Oh?" she said, wondering why he was telling her this. "Well, it's a beautiful day. Perhaps I'll run into him."

It was the very last thing she wanted to do, but Jacques handed her the reins without another word and deftly saddled the horse. Beth thanked him politely and left.

She did not take the trail around the lake, as the Prentisses no doubt would have expected her to, but instead headed to Union Avenue and rode straight into the village of Saratoga Springs. The mare had a steady gait and gave Beth an easy, comfortable ride: agile but gentle, as Jacques had promised. She wouldn't have put it past him to mount her on a fidgety horse she couldn't control. Perhaps, she thought, her first impression of William's horse trainer was wrong. She wondered if Jared had done something to *deserve* having a knife pulled on him.

She turned up Broadway, not too crowded on a Sunday afternoon, and rode past the Grand Union and the United States hotels, then the Adelphi and Clarendon and several smaller hotels. She avoided the eyes of anyone she thought she might recognize, or who might recognize her, and urged Marquita further up Broadway, then down a narrow side street. She dismounted at a freshly painted white Gothic Revival house, a sprawling building with towers and turrets and gingerbread fretwork, nothing like the clean, classic lines generally preferred in the Harte household. Beth purposely avoided the stable and slipped the mare's reins over a post.

Then, swallowing hard, she strode up the brick walkway to the mahogany front door. She bit her lip and glanced over both shoulders as she knocked.

Betty Bowman herself answered the door. Even on a Sunday afternoon, she was dressed in black satin. "Why, Miss Harte," she said, smiling, totally in control of herself, "what a surprise. I hope you're not looking for work?"

"Oh, no," Beth, said and glanced again over her shoulder. "I'm afraid I wouldn't do anyway. No, Mrs. Bowman, I was wondering if I might take a few minutes of your time to talk to you."

"To me? Why, darling, I must be coming up in the world! A respectable judge's daughter wanting to talk to me." She laughed off the remark, and Beth didn't take offense. Betty opened the door wide and motioned Beth in. "You won't faint, now, will you?"

Beth laughed. "Of course not. I'm not the fainting type, Mrs. Bowman."

The older woman gave her a frank, appraising glance

from head to toe. "I think I'm going to have to start liking you after all."

They walked from the small foyer to a dim parlor, furnished with thick, flowered carpets, red velvet chairs and sofas, marble-topped tables, and a giant mirror above a gleaming grand piano. A maid was cleaning up the remains of a late-night party. A mix of smoke and perfume still hung heavily in the air. Betty Bowman eyed her guest for any signs of nervousness, but Beth smiled nonchalantly and ignored the stiffness in her spine. This was her first venture into a bordello. She wondered if she would tell her father about it.

"Busy night last night," Betty said, and winked at Beth. "I expect it'll be busy for a while with all these railroad men coming to town. They're big spenders, and they like my kind of ladies. Here, we'll go into my private parlor."

They went through french doors into a carpeted hall, and when they came to another set of french doors, Beth stood aside while Betty unlocked them and pushed them open. The room was small and delicately furnished in Queen Anne style, in contrast to the Victorian front parlor. Beth sat gingerly on a chair upholstered in pale blue. Betty's skirts rustled as she plopped on a love seat and tucked her feet up beneath her. "Not what you expected?" she asked, smoothing her black satin skirts.

"To be honest," Beth replied, "no."

"Yes, well, I'm a woman of contrasts." The madam smiled and leaned over a tiny chest of drawers for a silver cigar box. She watched her guest as she opened it and withdrew a slender cigar. "And surprises," she added, sticking the cigar in her mouth and lighting it. She exhaled a mouthful of smoke. "Now, Miss Harte, what can I do for you?"

"Well—"

"Don't hem and haw, honey, just come out with it."

Beth swallowed and folded her hands in her lap, aware of the road dust on her boots and breeches. "Mrs. Bowman, when we met you offered to tell me what you know about Jared Inman. That's why I'm here."

Betty Bowman stuck her cigar in her mouth and studied the young woman across from her. Beth met her gaze. Without rouge on her cheeks, the older woman looked tired, and closer to fifty than forty without bows and ribbons in her graying black hair. Her life, Beth thought, couldn't be easy, even if of her own choosing.

"You're still seeing Inman?"

"I—well, we—" Beth wrung her hands and gritted her teeth. "That's irrelevant."

"You snuck out with him from the College Ball," Betty observed, flicking her ashes into a crystal tray. "That's not what a proper judge's daughter should be doing. What happened?"

Beth sat with her spine very straight. "My relationship with Jared has no bearing on the information I want from you," she said carefully. "Mrs. Bowman, I only want to find out what you know about him."

"And why should I tell you if you won't even answer a few simple questions?" Betty asked reasonably. "What happened after the ball, honey?"

"He drove me back to the Prentiss cottage," Beth replied primly, deciding that her need to find out what this madam knew about Jared was more important than her sense of privacy.

But Betty Bowman wasn't satisfied. "And?"

"Nothing."

"He dropped you off nice and pretty and you went off to your separate rooms in that great big empty house," Betty said sarcastically. "I'm a woman of the world, remember, honey?"

"We took a walk along the lake," Beth said, avoiding her hostess's look. "You can—assume what happened."

"You lost your virginity," Betty guessed.

Beth flushed to the roots of her auburn hair.

"I know, I know, I'm a blunt woman," the madam said with apology. "Are you in love with him?"

"I don't know."

"Is he in love with you?"

"I don't know that either."

"All right, I've got about ten minutes to talk some sense into you, honey, and you'd better hope I do." She dropped her feet to the floor, her cigar stuck on her lower lip. "He's no good."

Beth nibbled on her lower lip and listened.

"Look, I can see why you picked him for your first time—will you quit blushing? Your secret's safe with me. Inman's a handsome bastard, I'll agree with you there. How much do you know about him?"

"Assume I know nothing about him," Beth said quietly, still recovering from her embarrassment.

Betty Bowman grinned broadly. "Honey, you know more about Jared Inman than I ever will. All right, all right, no more teasing. Look, Beth—do you mind if I call you Beth?"

"No, of course not."

"Good. I've got a daughter about your age, and let's just say I'm a good enough mother that I wouldn't want her falling in love with Jared Inman. I wouldn't even want her near him. He's trouble, honey."

Beth saw that her knuckles were turning white and loosened the grip her fingers had on each other. "Why?"

Betty kicked off her shoes and stretched her legs out on the couch. "Let me tell you a story," she said. "About five years ago, I knew a woman, about my age. She and her husband and daughter had just moved out West, to

Sacramento. The husband was a gambler, but he wasn't a bad man. In fact, he was a damned good man. Better than most." She looked up at Beth and stubbed out her cigar. "Better than Jared Inman."

Beth pursed her lips. "Go on."

"Well, one day the husband and wife were both in a saloon—you've never been to a saloon, have you? No, you'd never see anything like it in sweet, civilized New York. Anyway, the husband got into a poker game."

"Was Jared playing?" Beth asked.

"No, watching with the wife. A friend of his was playing, a big, tough-looking man like Inman. The bet came down to Jared's friend and this woman's husband. The husband won with a clean, fair bluff on three-of-a-kind. The friend had a full house. He'd lost fair and square, but the friend started tossing out accusations about cheating and whatnot. Next thing you know, they've got guns out. But does Inman let the two of them settle it on their own? No. He stood there like a rock, and as quick as lightning—that fast—he pulled his own gun and shot the husband down dead."

Beth swallowed hard in her dry throat and wondered if she was suddenly going to turn into the fainting type.

"I watched Jared Inman kill my own husband, Beth," said Betty Bowman. "He left me with nothing, nothing at all."

"Was it—was it a fair fight? Was Jared shooting in self-defense? Was—"

"It wasn't even his fight."

"But—"

"And let me tell you something else. The night before Inman was in town—the night before, mind you—there was a train robbery right outside of Sacramento. The men who did it were never caught."

Beth sank her forehead into her hands and tried to think.

"The West is populated with men who would like to take something out of the hide of Jared Inman, and I'm one woman who would," Betty went on. "As I said, he's trouble. End it now, honey, while you still can. You might have nothing left when he's through with you."

"I was wondering," Beth said, struggling to get the words out, to stay in her seat and not flee. "Mrs. Bowman, I was wondering if you know anything about his background, his family?"

"Not a thing. I'm not sure I want to."

"I see," Beth said, and stood up, the blood rushing from her head. She thought for an awful moment she *would* faint, but she rallied. "Thank you, Mrs. Bowman. If I can ever return the favor—"

"You can return it right now by telling Jared Inman to go find himself some other sweet young thing." The madam smiled kindly. "Go on, honey, cry your heart out. Then get rid of him."

Beth thanked her again and, mumbling that she could find her own way out, fled, bumping into doors and walls, nearly knocking over the maid. Finally, she was outside breathing in the warm afternoon air. She mounted Marquita and made her way back to Union Avenue through a maze of side streets, avoiding Broadway, where someone—even someone she didn't know—might see her tears and offer help that would do no good.

Jared Inman had killed a man in cold blood.

A man? How many men? How many women like Betty Bowman had he left to find their way in the world? She coughed and choked on tears and road dust the four miles to the Prentiss estate.

She wiped her tears with a dusty hand and guided the horse into the stables. Betty Bowman was right. Beth would have to keep her distance from Jared Inman. She would have to be careful. But before she rid herself of him

entirely—the very thought made her choke with despair—
she would find out what he was doing in Saratoga Springs
and what it had to do with Elijah Dobbs and William's
horse and Jacques LeBreque. If Jared Inman was a corrupt
and despicable criminal, if any charges could be leveled at
him, she, Elizabeth Stanton Harte, intended to bring him
to justice.

William was waiting in the stables for her, and he
dragged her off Marquita himself. "Where the hell have
you been?" he shouted, holding her harshly by the shoulders.

"What? William, I left a note. I—you're hurting me."

"Dammit, Elizabeth," he said, his breath hot on her
face, "I've been worried sick about you."

He pulled her hard against his chest, crushing her shoulders in his hands. His face was purple, and he smelled of
drink and sweat. His eyes were badly bloodshot, his blond
hair matted, his white shirt damp. Beth put her hands
firmly on his chest and tried to push away, but he held her
fast. Her tears of misery turned to ice as cold fear crept up
from her spine. Was Jacques LeBreque around? Would he
help her—

"Where have you been?" William demanded hoarsely.

"William," she said softly, her voice a strangled whisper.
"William, get hold of yourself."

"Don't, Elizabeth. Don't lie to me," he warned in a
tortured, angry tone. "You've been with Jared Inman,
haven't you?"

Beth shook her head. Was this LeBreque's doing, or
only William's drunken mind at work? "No, William, I
haven't."

"Dammit, you have!" he shouted.

"William, please!"

He cupped her face in his hands and covered her mouth with
his in a hard, fierce kiss. Feeling only distaste, Beth beat
against his chest and pushed him away with all her strength.

"William, stop it! You're drunk. Stop it now, before you do something worse."

He dropped his hands to his sides and stepped back, releasing her. His face drained of color as he stared at her. "Oh, my God," he sobbed, and covered his face with his hands. "Oh, my God, what am I doing? Elizabeth, forgive me. I—"

"There's nothing to forgive, William. You're not yourself," Beth said, her voice shaking but kind. "Please go. We can talk about this later, when you're feeling better."

She turned away, fingering Marquita's reins, giving William the opportunity to exit gracefully. She heard his heels dig into the dirt floor, then his running footsteps. When she knew he was gone, Beth collapsed against the horse, but she had no tears left.

"My, my," Jared's voice said from the other side of the mare. "If that had been me, you'd have had me hung from the nearest tree."

Beth froze as Jared came around the horse to her. He was wearing riding clothes, a short, close-fitting, double-breasted jacket over skintight trousers, and despite everything Betty Bowman had told her, despite everything she suspected, Beth threw herself against his chest and sobbed.

He caught her about the waist and found her lips. "You taste like dirt," he said sardonically, then studied her face. There were smudges around her eyes and cheeks, even on her mouth. He touched one still-wet cheek with his fingertips. "You've been crying," he said gently. "Why? Beth, where have you been?"

"Just out riding," she said evasively, and turned to Marquita. She shouldn't have collapsed against him like that. This man was a cold-blooded killer, and she was pursuing him in the same methodical way her father pursued corrupt politicians and businessmen. "I have a lot to think about."

"I don't wonder. Playing two men in love with you off each other must not be easy."

She flashed her violet eyes at him. "You can think as you like, Jared Inman. It serves you right for spying on me."

"Spying on you? Beth, I was peacefully unsaddling my horse when William stormed in here, not seconds before you rode in. I would guess he was watching for your horse. How romantic of him, don't you think? But, suddenly and in all innocence, I was forced to witness a rather sordid, intimate scene."

Beth spun around angrily, then whirled back around at him. "In all innocence! Jared, why didn't you help me? I was afraid—"

"He was drunk, Beth, but hardly violent."

"Hardly violent! He yanked me around like a side of meat, kissed me against my will, accused me when he had no right—and you stand here and act as though it were nothing at all."

He shrugged and grinned. "Well, I hope you never have to deal with me drunk and angry."

"I hope not," Beth echoed and suddenly froze. "Of course, in your world, William probably didn't seem violent at all," she mumbled.

"What?"

She stood her ground and raised her face to his. "I have gathered, Jared, that you are accustomed to witnessing much more sordid scenes than the one between William and me. You're used to a far greater level of violence in your life than I am."

Jared tapped her nose with the tip of a finger and grinned. "That is precisely what I've been trying to tell you for days now," he said. "Look, William's jealous, and I would say he has reason to be."

"No, he doesn't," Beth snapped back. "He's nothing to me, and I have never once led him to believe otherwise. If he's jealous of you because of me, then that's his problem."

"No, Beth," Jared said lightly but pointedly. "It's your problem, too. Or do you want him dragging you off your horse and smothering you with kisses?"

"Jared! Of course not," Beth groaned, angry and confused that she was caught between two men, trapped in a dilemma she hadn't asked for. "Look, I'll talk to William. I'll tell him I'm not in love with him and he has no right to be jealous of you or—"

"Why, Beth?" Jared probed. "Because you're not in love with me? Are you going to tell William there's nothing between us?"

Beth remembered her vow to keep this man at a distance, her tears, her anger. Who was he? What did he want from her? And why, above all else, why was she still so attracted to him? She felt her knees weaken at his mocking smile. He was no better than William. At least when William hauled her off her horse, she knew where she stood and why.

"What's between us is no one's business but our own," she replied steadily. "If you'll excuse me."

She started out the stable, but Jared caught her by the arm and turned her back around to face him. His grip wasn't harsh. "Why are you so angry?" he asked, jibing at her. "I thought you were happy to see me."

"I was *relieved*," she corrected frostily.

He stepped toward her and cupped her cheek with the palm of his other hand. "I'm not buying your sophisticated judge's daughter act anymore, Beth," he said thickly. "So be forewarned."

She opened her mouth to answer, but Jared wasn't waiting for answers. He kissed the smudges on her eyes, then her cheeks, then her lips, pulling her tightly to him as his mouth covered hers. She tried to keep her lips firmly together, but the feel of his tongue warm and moist against her mouth made her gasp.

It was the only invitation he needed. His tongue circled hers, probing, placating, enticing, as he gathered her up in his arms. Beth let him support all her weight and gave herself up to the magic of his kiss. In his arms, with his body a rock against hers, she knew only that she wanted him. She wasn't at all confused about that. Her whole being melted at his touch, dissolved at his kiss. His hands slowly coursed down her back, then around the curve of her scantily covered hips and back up her spine.

"Beth, Beth, Beth," he whispered, "if only I could take the time to be with you more, if only I could explain—oh, darling." He pulled her head against his chest and stroked her arms as she placed her hands on his shirt, felt the hardness beneath them, and breathed in his male scent. He touched her hair. "I would never have let William hurt you."

She raised her head from his chest and nodded. "I know, Jared."

He gave her that little smile again. "You'd better go. I—um, I can't trust myself here with you much longer, and, darling dear, this is neither the time nor the place."

"I agree wholeheartedly," she said, grinning, not blushing now. She wanted Jared Inman. She was confused about a thousand other things, but about that there could be no doubt. She laughed at herself and her tears as she drew away from him. He was standing beside the horse, looking strong and kind. "A rough character indeed," she muttered, and headed quickly from the stables.

Behind her, Jared called out, "A what? Beth Harte, what are you talking about? Has someone—Beth!"

But she was still laughing as she walked up to the house. Perhaps there *were* two Jared Inmans, she thought, but she would lay odds in John Morrissey's betting parlors that the real Jared Inman of San Francisco was the man who had just kissed the smudges off her face.

And if she were wrong?

She stopped dead in her tracks. If she was going to do any betting on Jared Inman, she should confine it to John Morrissey's game parlors. But she knew she wouldn't. She had a gnawing, terrifying suspicion that she was going to bet everything she *was* rather than everything she *had* on Jared's being the kind of man she could love. If she lost, what would there be left?

She shook off the thought. No. Jared was an unsavory character, unsuitable for anything more than a midsummer's deflowering, as Betty Bowman would say. Her—what was the word she was looking for?—acquaintance. Yes, her acquaintance with him was thrilling, exciting, and adventuresome. It might even land the rascal in jail. But it was not going to ruin Elizabeth Stanton Harte of New York.

Her gait grew steadier and more resolved as she approached the Prentiss cottage. When she pulled open the front door, she was almost laughing again.

Jared Inman may be rough and tough, she thought, but he has never dealt with a Harte on a Harte's terms!

She raced upstairs for a hot bath and to clean the last of the smudges off her face. Had her father, she wondered, anticipated such a vacation for his educated and mature suffragette daughter?

CHAPTER 12

Beth guessed that if William had worried about her absence, regardless of her note, it had made his father furious. William Prentiss, Sr., after all, considered Beth his responsibility as long as she was a guest in his home. So when the clouds rolled in and the rains came on Sunday afternoon, Beth relegated herself to the drawing room with a George Eliot novel. With dinner still two hours way, she found herself blissfully alone. She had no idea what had happened to Jared and William. She told herself she absolutely couldn't care less and started on the first chapter of *The Mill on the Floss*.

Did Jared really kill Betty Bowman's husband in cold blood? Surely there had to be more to the story. Why would anyone—even a reckless westerner—gun down a man for cheating at cards? Beth couldn't understand it. The West, she supposed, lived by a different code.

But not that different. Murder was murder.

So why wasn't Jared in jail? Hung? Why didn't Betty Bowman avenge her husband on the spot and shoot his killer, or at least turn him in to the authorities?

Beth had read three pages of her book and not remembered a word. She went back to the first sentence and tried again: "A wide plain, where the broadening Floss hurries on . . ."

What was Jared's connection with Elijah Dobbs? Judge Harte had said Dobbs bore watching, and Jared had journeyed to Saratoga with him. What did that mean? And *was* Dobbs up to anything illicit?

Beth leaned back against the heavy upholstery of the sofa and listened to the rain pelting against the windows. She closed her eyes and sighed. She wasn't learning anything for her father—or herself—by sitting around in a drawing room reading!

Perhaps her father simply expected too much of his sole offspring. She was a woman, and the men he had sent her to investigate weren't the kind who discussed their business, much less their underhanded dealings, in front of the so-called fairer sex.

She would have to write her father and tell him she was failing miserably at her mission.

When Beth opened her eyes, she found Ginny Prentiss sitting by the fireplace. "I didn't want to disturb you," Ginny said, smiling, her hands folded on her lap. She was wearing a low-bodiced evening dress of gray and garnet piqué with a glittering gold and diamond necklace and a delicate white mohair shawl over her round shoulders, in direct contrast to Beth's staid beige linen, a dress she had chosen to remind Jared—and William, if necessary—that she had other things to do besides worry about men. The adventures of the day had reminded Beth that she was twenty-four, Vassar-educated, a respected suffragette, not some wild and daring girl.

"I've hardly seen you at all today," Beth said. "How are you?"

Ginny answered with a radiant blush.

"Ah, in love," Beth ventured, and laughed. "Happily in love, I see. Where is your Mr. Hoskins?"

"In the billiard room with Father, William, and—" She hesitated, but only for a moment, as she glanced up at Beth. "And Jared."

"Well, I imagine that will be an interesting game," Beth said lightly. "How is your brother feeling?"

Ginny knit her brows, confused and surprised. "Fine, as far as I know. Why?"

"I saw him briefly earlier this afternoon, and he wasn't entirely himself. But never mind that, so long as he's fine now." Beth shifted in her chair and closed her book on her lap. She would start it again another time. "I suppose your father is delighted I'm safely ensconced in the drawing room with George Eliot."

"Oh, yes, but you know he can never stay angry with you for long, especially after what happened with Jacques." Ginny lowered her eyes shyly. "Father thinks you got me to break off with Jacques and fall in love with Richard."

Beth frowned and said dryly, "He doesn't give you much credit, does he?"

"He thinks I'm easily led," Ginny admitted. "I suppose I am, but—I'm serious about Richard, Beth. I love him as I never loved Jacques."

"And how does Richard feel about you?"

Ginny looked up at Beth, tears welling in her big blue

eyes, but she was smiling. "He's asked me to marry him," she said quietly.

Beth jumped up, ran over to her friend, and threw her arms around her. "Ginny, that's wonderful!" she exclaimed, delighted. "Congratulations! Have you told anyone yet? Do your parents know?"

Ginny shook her head.

Beth knelt on the floor beside her friend and waited for Ginny to explain.

"He wants to wait a few days," she said, sniffling, then laughed as she wiped the tears out of the corners of her eyes. "He says Father might not believe two people could fall so much in love after knowing each other for just one week."

"When one of the people is Virginia Prentiss, I'm sure he would believe it," Beth teased, and tugged gently on one of Ginny's fair ringlets. "A few days isn't very long in the broad scheme of things, Ginny, especially a few days in Saratoga."

"I know," Ginny admitted, still smiling. "But I've been in love enough times to know that it *is* different with Richard. Oh, Beth, I've been waiting for this moment for so long!" She stopped herself and laughed. "Here I go getting sentimental again. With you, of all people!"

"Your severe and serious friend," Beth said, her tone mockingly prim.

"Well, you're not the most sentimental person I know, Beth, but you're certainly not serious! Father tells the story about your taking the boat out during the regatta as though it were all a big joke from the beginning. He says a Harte is always good for a party. Of course, he also says you have a dangerous sense of humor, which is probably true." Ginny paused and refolded her hands in her lap and studied them. "Beth, what *have* you been up to these past few days?"

"What do you mean?" Beth asked, genuinely confused.

Ginny looked at her seriously. "I mean Jared Inman."

Still kneeling, Beth sank onto her heels and shrugged. "Oh," she said. "What are the rumors?"

"That he's after you and you're too dumb to know it."

"I would have to be very dumb *not* to know it," Beth mumbled dryly. "Ginny, what do you think of Jared?"

"I don't know.. Beth, no one else would have helped you sneak in here the way he did—"

"So he's sneaky. Deceitful."

"Kind and generous. It all depends on the way you look at it."

Beth raised her eyes to her friend. "And how do you look at it, Ginny?"

"He's always been a perfect gentleman to me, and my father thinks he's worthy enough to be a guest in his house," Ginny said. "But I've heard the same rumors you have, Beth. He comes from a different world than we do."

"I know," Beth said, but her mind was already on another train of thought. "Ginny, how did Jared come to be a guest here? Did your father invite him, or did he more or less invite himself?"

Ginny shrugged, confused at Beth's sudden intensity. "I don't know. I'm not sure—I thought Father invited him."

"From San Francisco?"

"No one's ever said," Ginny replied, her brows knit. "I was so preoccupied with Jacques at the time. Jared just sort of—turned up."

Beth licked her parched lips. "He couldn't have found out about your letter to me, could he?"

"What?" Ginny was more confused than ever now. "Beth, what are you talking about? You don't mean—"

"Jared has suggested that he came here expressly to find me," Beth said quickly. "I don't believe him, of course, but—"

"Beth!" Ginny's face paled. "Beth, are you saying Jared Inman came all the way from San Francisco to see you?"

"That's what *he* says."

"My God!"

"Look, Ginny," Beth went on, regretting taking her friend into her confidence, "I'm just trying to figure out what Jared *is* doing here. I don't believe he came expressly to find me, but I have to be sure. He couldn't have learned of your letter?"

"I don't think so," Ginny said thinly. "Beth, are you sure you can handle him? I mean, I don't have any reason to distrust him, but he—well, he is from the West, and I'm sure he—he must have a lot of experience with women."

Beth laughed, suddenly and unreasoningly, and patted Ginny's hand. "I've told my father about him, and he's certain I can handle one Jared Inman of San Francisco."

"He would be," Ginny said, relaxing. "But has he ever met Jared?"

"At that ball here seven years ago."

"The night of the cigars," Ginny put in, remembering the incident fondly. "And that's when you met Jared."

"We hadn't seen each other since—until that day he carried my trunk up the stairs."

Ginny's blue eyes flashed, then she shook her head, impressed. "I never even guessed any of this, Beth. You're always so cool!"

"Not always," Beth admitted wryly.

"I suppose you want me to keep this a secret?"

"You have to, Ginny!"

"There are already so many rumors about you two," Ginny said, shaking her head. "Well, at least it's not me this time. Melissa Dobbs has done her share of rumor-mongering."

"I haven't even seen her," Beth said.

"I think she finds Jared tempting, perhaps in the same way I found Jacques so tempting," Ginny mused. "Of course, Jared moves in the same circles we do, but he's hardly suitable for someone like Melissa Dobbs."

"Or Beth Harte?" Beth quirked an eyebrow in inquiry.

"I don't know. That's for you to decide."

Beth laughed and hugged her. "That's why we've been friends all these years, Ginny."

Ginny smiled, pleased. "Do you want me to find out what I can about Jared?"

"Without being obvious," Beth said. "Right now I'm interested in where he gets his money—evidently he has plenty of it—and what kind of family he comes from. No one seems to know much about him beyond the usual dirty rumors."

"Maybe he likes it that way, Beth."

"Maybe."

There was a short, heavy silence. Beth rose abruptly, smoothed out her skirts, and winked at Ginny. Her violet eyes flashing, she said, "But if he does, that's just too damned bad!"

They laughed and, arm-in-arm, headed in to dinner.

The Dobbses were guests for dinner, but Beth reminded herself that she had visited a bordello today and should probably listen instead of asking questions. Someone might decide to ask *her* a few questions as well. She found herself seated between William and Jared and directly across from Melissa Dobbs, who was clad in an elaborate dress of coral-red flowers, fringe, and bows. Beth was delighted with her own carefully achieved dowdiness.

Beth, however, not Elijah Dobbs and his business in Saratoga or Jared Inman and *his* business in Saratoga, became the topic of conversation during the soup course.

"I understand you went riding today, Miss Harte," William Prentiss, Sr., said.

Beth was certain Jared and William both stiffened beside her. William, she had noticed, hid his paleness in his elegant clothes. There was nothing at all Jared could do about his arrogance.

"Yes," she said obtusely.

'Where did you go?"

Beth despised lying—the world was already too filled with lies—but she could hardly tell the truth. Melissa might faint, she thought, and almost giggled. She quickly wiped her mouth with her napkin. "I ended up riding into the village," she said. "It was such a lovely afternoon."

She thought the conversation would end there, but Elijah Dobbs said, "I heard one of the Prentiss bay mares was seen in town today with a young woman in the saddle. Do you always ride alone, Miss Harte?"

Her host answered for Beth. "Miss Harte is not accustomed to my strict rules," he said amiably, turning to her. "Elizabeth, you understand that you are my responsibility as long as you are in Saratoga. In the future, you will not ride into the village unescorted."

William seemed to relax beside Beth. At least he knew she hadn't been with Jared, not that that should matter to him. Beth smiled complacently at the senior Prentiss.

But Elijah Dobbs, spooning soup into his mouth, added, "Did you have business on Caroline Street, Miss Harte?"

"Business?" she asked dumbly.

"You were seen on Caroline Street," he went on. "I was just wondering if you were visiting anyone there."

Beth placed her hands on her lap and looked directly at Elijah Dobbs. She could feel Jared's black eyes on her. He knew Betty Bowman's bordello was on Caroline Street as well as she did, but did Dobbs? And why should he care what she had been doing there?

Had she "been seen," as he so vaguely put it, knocking on Betty Bowman's door?

All eyes were on the young suffragette. Beth picked up her spoon and flashed her dark-fringed eyes with a frank smile. "I was doing an errand for my father," she said boldly, and not altogether untruthfully. She had been gathering information about Jared Inman that might possibly interest Judge Harte. "I had some questions I had to ask Mrs. Betty Bowman."

As Beth had expected, all eyes turned away and the subject was quickly and deftly changed. Betty Bowman was not a woman one discussed at dinner, Beth thought gleefully. She almost laughed. William was probably more upset with this news than he had been when he thought she had been off with Jared, and Jared himself had visibly tensed beside her. Well, she thought, let them fume. She had talked to Betty Bowman, and she might as well admit it. She had always been willing to take the consequences of her actions.

But the consequences, she knew, would come after dinner, not during. Beth could almost see the purple cloud of rage hanging over her host's head. She did Ginny a favor by not even glancing at her.

During the main course, someone mentioned railroads. Beth, determined to be a help to her father and resigned to everyone's disapproval, drank some mineral water, set down her glass, and said, "I understand Saratoga is crawling with railroad executives."

"That's none of your affair," William muttered beside her.

Beth ignored him. "I know Saratoga is the watering spot for the rich and the dandy," she went on boldly, "but I do think it a bit odd that so many railroad men would be here the same week, don't you, Mr. Inman?"

He raised his glass and glanced down at her. "No."

"Neither do I," William concurred sourly.

"Well, I do," Beth said, as though anyone cared what she thought. "I wouldn't be surprised if they all get together somewhere and plan how they can tighten the noose around their passengers' necks."

"Miss Harte," William Prentiss, Sr., interrupted darkly, "these things are better not discussed over dinner."

"Over cigars in the billiard room instead, Mr. Prentiss?" She smiled her most fetching smile. "We women are passengers as well, and we, too, pay the exorbitant rates."

"What makes you think anyone wants to raise the rates?" Elijah Dobbs asked, ignoring the furious look from his host. "Maybe these railroad executives want to get together and look after the best interests of their passengers."

"That would be a first!"

"Elizabeth!" William pleaded in a strangled whisper.

Beth took her fork in hand. "What I wonder, Mr. Dobbs, is if they are planning a meeting and mean to tell the public, or if they will simply fix the rates behind our backs."

William Prentiss, Sr., huffed angrily, but he had already lost control over the dinner conversation.

"What makes you think the public has a right to know anything?" Elijah Dobbs demanded.

"My sense of justice."

"Bah!"

Beth stabbed a piece of beef with her fork and lifted her knife, pointing it absently at Dobbs across the table. "I thought you weren't interested in railroads, Mr. Dobbs. Isn't your business steamboats?"

Their host shifted in his chair. "Miss Harte—"

"Just curious," she said innocently.

Dobbs rested back in his chair, his face ruddy, perspiration glistening on his forehead. Beth popped a slice of meat into her mouth. Arguing railroads with an outspoken suffragette made Elijah Dobbs break out in a sweat?

"Are the railroads hurting your business, Mr. Dobbs?" she asked pointedly.

He threw down his fork and knife, and for a moment Beth thought he would leave the table. "I am sick to death of people thinking the railroads are going to ruin me!" he spat furiously. "In fact, I am sick to death of hearing about railroads!"

Beth wiped her mouth with her napkin and readied her next comment, but Jared made it before she could. "So soon, Elijah?" he said calmly. "I would say the railroad age has only just begun."

"It won't begin on my north-south route on the Mississippi," Dobbs vowed.

"But you aren't completely against railroads, are you, Elijah?" Jared asked smugly. "I've heard you're thinking of putting in your own line west out of St. Louis."

Dobbs's ruddy face paled. "Where did you hear such nonsense?" he demanded.

Jared shrugged, obviously not planning to answer.

"Well, that's what it is!" Dobbs insisted. "Nonsense."

"The St. Louis Western it will be called," Jared added indifferently. "Supposedly."

Beth bit her lower lip and listened carefully. This was what her father meant when he said Elijah Dobbs bore watching! How much had the judge heard? Not this much, surely, or he would have told his daughter before he packed her off to Saratoga.

Beside her, William gave a little laugh. "What difference does it make to you, Jared? Will this mythical railroad interfere with your own investments?"

So Jared Inman did have a stake in the railroads! Did he also, Beth wondered, have a stake in some massive stock manipulation with the St. Louis Western Railroad?

And why the sudden animosity between Jared and Dobbs? Hadn't they come to Saratoga together?

Or merely on the same train?

"Well, it's all nonsense," Dobbs sputtered before Jared could answer William's question. "I'm not involved in starting up any railroad called the St. Louis Western or anything else. I'm a steamboat man."

Even Beth knew when not to press a point. Everyone but Jared was willing to leave it at that. "Even the Commodore got into railroads, Elijah," he said, his tone easy and unruffled.

Beth and every other dinner guest knew that Cornelius Vanderbilt had made his first fortune in steamboats.

Sophia Prentiss and Beatrice Dobbs were looking distinctly uncomfortable. Melissa Dobbs listened quietly, fascination on her pretty features. Ginny Prentiss and Richard Hoskins talked quietly at the end of the table. Beth thought she noticed Hoskins glance up at Jared and assumed he was only listening to his fiancée with one ear.

William Prentiss, Sr., changed the subject without so much as looking at the dark scowl on Elijah Dobbs's face. The weather, Prentiss said emphatically, was lousy.

Dinner ended peacefully.

Beth had developed quite a long list of people she needed to avoid, but it was composed only of men. So she glued herself to Ginny and Melissa and followed them into the drawing room. The men retired to the billiard room.

"Beth, how could you!" Ginny whispered. "Father will be furious. He *is* furious. Oh, Beth, I think he might ask you to leave—"

"Please don't worry," Beth said reassuringly.

Melissa came between them. "Have you two noticed William? He doesn't seem himself."

"Yes, I have noticed," Beth replied archly. "I don't think he's feeling well."

Melissa wasn't as discreet. "He's drinking too much!" she exclaimed angrily, but she lowered her voice, concern in her pretty eyes. "I'm worried about him."

"Oh, please, Melissa," Ginny interrupted.

"I am," Melissa said firmly, quietly. "I think something's wrong with him. He hardly talks to anyone anymore."

Beth smiled with the realization that Melissa Dobbs was more than naturally concerned with William Prentiss, Jr. "He'll be all right, Melissa," she assured the young woman, wishing she were as confident as she sounded.

"Do you think so?" Melissa asked hopefully.

"Of course he will!" Ginny insisted, disgusted, but she broke into a smile when Richard Hoskins entered the room. "If you two will excuse me—"

When Ginny joined her fiancé, Melissa sighed sadly beside Beth. "She's so beautiful, isn't she?" the younger woman said rhetorically. "Beth, do you think I'm at all pretty?"

"Melissa, how could you wonder such a thing?" Beth asked, baffled. "Of course you're pretty! Very pretty, in fact."

"Really?" Melissa beamed. "I'm not used to being around so many beautiful, elegant women as there are here in Saratoga Springs. St. Louis is no hick town, but Saratoga—I don't know."

"It's the watering place for the best and the worst people in the entire country," Beth suggested. "Those of us who lead conventional lives can seem out of place."

Melissa gave Beth a long, curious look. "Your life is hardly conventional, is it?"

"Well—" Beth had to laugh. "No, I guess it isn't."

"I mean that with your father being a judge—"

"And with me a suffragette," Beth added frankly.

"Beth," Melissa said, her voice dropping, "did you

really visit Betty Bowman? What's she like? What—what is her—her establishment like?''

Beth recalled the opulent living room, the dainty sitting room, the thin cigars, Betty Bowman's warning. And her story about Jared Inman. She smiled at Melissa. "It was very understated," she said. "And Mrs. Bowman is a very caring woman. She's had a hard life."

"But why did you go there!"

"Just doing an errand for my father," Beth said, knowing that she wasn't telling the entire truth and hating herself for it. Why didn't she admit to all what she had learned about the Prentiss's guest from San Francisco? But perhaps, she thought, everyone already knew what kind of man Jared Inman was. "Really, Melissa, it was quite innocuous."

"Do you think Mr. Prentiss is going to ask you to leave?" Melissa asked, clearly loving the adventure.

"He might."

"Will you?"

"I'll leave the cottage," Beth said, "but I won't leave Saratoga. I have things to do."

Melissa dared not ask what. She wished Beth luck and quickly excused herself. Beth, finding herself standing alone, looked around to see who would accost her next. Sophia Prentiss and Beatrice Dobbs were studiously avoiding her, and no doubt Richard Hoskins was warning his impressionable fiancée about her dangerous friend. Jared Inman, Dobbs, and the Prentiss men were still in the billiard room. Beth decided to retreat before they joined the ladies.

In her room, she let her body go limp. Suddenly, she was exhausted. She slipped off her dress, unpinned her hair, and lay naked across her bed.

She would have to write her father at once. The information she had learned at dinner flooded her mind, and she had to close her eyes and will away the tide. She couldn't think about that now. She had to concentrate on how to pacify her host and prevent him from putting her on the morning train back to New York. She couldn't go home now. There was still so much to learn!

She heard her door creak and reached wildly for her nightgown, sitting up in bed and covering her front with it. "Ginny?" she whispered, panicked.

Jared Inman strolled into the room and shut the door behind him. "So, Beth," he said casually, "what did Betty Bowman tell you about me?"

Beth clasped her nightgown over her breasts and sat very still. "Jared, please get out of here! I'm in enough trouble as it is."

"That, my darling Beth, you can be sure of," he said, and walked slowly over to the bed. "No one saw me."

"I don't care!" She drew her knees sharply away as he moved toward her. "We can discuss this another time—"

"You could have avoided this if you'd wanted to, Beth," he said, huskily. "You knew I wouldn't let you sleep tonight without your telling me about your visit with Betty Bowman."

"I did not know any such thing!" Beth exclaimed, her voice a fierce whisper. "Please leave, Jared. *Please.*"

She drew her feet up on the bed and shrank away, the nightgown still clenched over her breasts, leaving her legs and shoulders exposed to his penetrating look. He sat down at the foot of the bed and covered her small foot with one hand. "Tell me, Beth," he said quietly.

"And if I don't?" she queried, her voice stiff and hoarse.

Even in the dim light, she could see the passion in his black eyes. He ran his fingertips across the top of her foot to her ankle, sending a warm quiver through the rest of her body. Beth jerked her foot away, but he held it fast and pulled her leg out straight. She inhaled sharply.

"She said you killed her husband in cold blood," she said quickly, panic creeping into her words. Was she afraid? Her knuckles were white as her fingers tightened around the thin fabric of her nightgown. Her ankle ached in Jared's rough grasp. "You're hurting me," she said in a small voice.

He released her at once. "Darling," he said, his voice thick and soft, "That's the last thing I want to do, not that you don't deserve a good flogging."

Beth put her feet flat on the bed, her knees up, the gown covering not nearly as much as she wished, but her fear was gone. "Did you kill him?" she asked.

"Yes, but hardly in cold blood."

"Will you tell me about it?"

"Not now," he said simply, without expression.

"But—"

"Darling Beth," he whispered, and kneeled beside her. His hands covered hers, still clinging to the nightgown, and the warmth of his touch loosened her grip on the cotton fabric. "Don't ever be afraid of me, Beth. Please, don't ever be afraid."

"Jared, I don't know what to think," she whispered back, her voice hoarse, strangled with confusion and a sudden, rising passion. "Except when I'm around you. Jared, when I'm around you, all I can think about is how much—" she released the nightgown and intertwined her fingers into his, her violet eyes gazing into his softening black eyes, "how much I want you."

He drew the nightgown away and gazed at her naked figure, not touching her. Beth took his hand again in hers and laid it flat on her stomach. She knew he could feel in her warm skin, see in her already taut breasts, how much she wanted him.

"We shouldn't, Beth," Jared said quietly, longing in his gaze. "I came here to talk to you, not to seduce you."

"You're not seducing me."

He smiled and leaned over to kiss her lightly, but she opened her mouth against his lips and let him taste her desire. His lips parted, his tongue circling hers, and as she lifted her hand off his, she could feel his fingertips travel slowly up her stomach, between her breasts, around them, then, finally, brush her erect nipples.

"Beth, Beth," he whispered, pulling his mouth from hers, "I should stay away from you—at least for now. Darling, there's so much I can't tell you, and if we let our desire for each other—oh, darling, you do know how much I want you?"

"I only know that I can hardly breathe, much less think, when you touch me," she said, lifting his hand from her breasts and kissing the palm, then replacing it over one breast. "Please love me—"

His mouth covered hers and he pulled her against him, cupping her naked buttocks in his hands as he probed and tasted every sensitive corner of her mouth. She could feel his hardness against her, his desire, and wrapped her arms around him, pulling them even more tightly together. He stretched his entire length against her, then rolled her back down on the bed as his kisses descended to her throat, to the warmth between her breasts, then across her breasts until he took each of her nipples between his teeth and teased them until she thought she would explode with pleasure.

"I want you so much, Beth," he rasped, kissing a flaming trail to her navel. "God, how I want to love you!"

She dug her hands into his hair, arching beneath him, wishing away the clothes that kept him from her. "Then do, Jared," she begged. "Do!"

He kissed a searing path back to her mouth, but lingered there only for a moment before he kissed each of her eyelids. "Darling, we can't."

Before she could gasp her answer, he had rolled off the bed. He picked the gown up off the floor and spread it over her naked body. "I should have known better than to try to talk to you alone up here," he said wryly. "You have a fine way of avoiding the issue, my darling."

"We both do," she whispered. "Jared, I—"

He placed a finger over his lips. "No more, Beth," he warned. "I don't think I could stop myself a second time, and if I stay here any longer—"

He let the sentence dangle and turned sharply on his heels. Beth sat up and opened her mouth to call him, but she resisted. He didn't so much as glance around him before the door opened and closed again behind him.

Beth fell back onto the pillows and groaned at the ceiling. It was frightening! Her desire for Jared—the ache in her body that even now made her tremble—was so overwhelming, so overpowering, that when she looked at him, when she touched him or he touched her, she couldn't think beyond her need for him.

She couldn't even remember Betty Bowman's warning or the rumors of her own good, Harte common sense.

"What common sense?" she muttered aloud, and laughed.

But it was a long time before she fell asleep.

CHAPTER 13

In the morning, Beth stood at her window and watched the clouds roll out over the mountains. She had risen at dawn and written a long letter to her father, mentioning Jared Inman in the most businesslike fashion: "Rumors concerning him abound, Father, but I have been unable to discover the most basic facts about him. William did insinuate that Jared has investments in the railroads and possibly would be hurt by this St. Louis Western system." She had noticed on rereading her letter that she had referred to him as Jared, but to go back and write Mr. Inman above it would only fuel her father's suspicions. And, at the moment, Beth wanted to keep her relationship with this mysterious man her own secret.

The sun appeared in the blue sky between two billowing clouds and glistened on the still-wet grass. Beth wondered what Jared was doing now, what he was thinking. She had wanted him so much last night! Even now, she could feel the heat of a flush as she recalled her reckless pleading. Yet she admired Jared for his restraint. It made her wonder if it possibly meant that there was more than a physical bond between them.

Did she want a man like Jared Inman in love with her?

Suddenly, her eyes narrowed at a figure crossing the lawn toward the stables. She recognized the stout frame and the blond hair blowing in the wind. William.

Behind him followed Jared, in William's shadow.

Beth didn't think. She gathered up the skirts of her practical day dress and raced out of her room. In a few minutes, she emerged from the back door and ran across the dew-soaked lawn in the wake of Jared and William.

She slowed as she came to the stables and dropped off the path, edging her way carefully to the open doors. She could hear the two men talking. Not breathing, she leaned against the cool stone of the stable.

"I suppose you have a handy sum tied up in him," came the deep voice of Jared Inman.

"Enough," William answered.

"How much, William?"

"I don't have to answer that, Inman."

"No, you don't," Jared said easily, but when he went on, his tone darkened. "I know the trouble you're in, William."

Beth flinched when she heard someone kicking something, probably a stall door.

"Stay out of my affairs, Inman," William warned.

"You're hoping Louisiana's lameness won't keep him out of the races for the season, aren't you, William?" Jared persisted. "That could be a mistake, you know."

"Is that a threat?"

"An educated guess."

Beth flattened herself against the wall and suddenly wished she hadn't followed them. She edged her way away from the door lest one of the men inside stomp out and find her eavesdropping.

"I can take care of myself," William snarled.

Beth could envision Jared's smirk. "Can you, William?"

"Look, Inman, stay out of my way!" There was the scuffling of feet, then a sharp, painful inhalation. "Damn you, Jared," William coughed.

"Don't ever try anything so stupid on me again, William," Jared said, biting out each word. "And while I've got you about the throat, don't ever let me catch you laying a hand on Beth Harte or I just might break your stinking, cowardly neck."

Beth heard something fall on the floor, William probably, she thought, and crouched in the shadows, frozen.

"You're the one who'll hurt her, Inman," William sneered. "Not me."

"Get out!" Jared roared, his smug control gone. "Go on, before I—"

He didn't finish, or if he did Beth didn't hear him. She scrambled to the other side of the stable and, tripping on her skirts, fell headlong into the tall grass, but she knew she was out of sight and didn't move. She prayed William had the sense to do as Jared ordered and leave.

She lay motionless and began counting. She reached a thousand and still heard nothing. They had both gone. When in her blind panic she stumbled out of sight of the door, they had left together, or at least soon after each other. Slowly, she crawled to her knees. She could hear the snorting of the horses, the chirping of birds in the fields, the rustle of the wind in the leaves. She rose, still in the shadow of the stable. Her brow was perspiring, her dress grass-stained, her hair disheveled. She smoothed her skirts and caught her breath. With any luck, she could get back to her room without being seen.

She stood at the corner of the stable and peered around. The sun was bright now, beating down on the cobblestones. Tentatively, Beth stepped out into the brightness.

Nothing happened.

She tucked a few loose strands of hair behind her ear and walked more confidently out into the sunlight, onto the cobblestones.

Two strong hands settled around her waist and hauled her swiftly into the stables. Beth choked, unable to scream, but the hands spun her around, into the chest of Jared Inman.

"How much did you hear?" he demanded, his square jaw set, his black eyes half-closed.

She raised her eyes innocently to his. "Of what?"

His fingers dug into her waist. "How much?" he ground out.

Beth didn't want to lie, but neither did she want to tell him the truth. She pushed out of his grip, daring him to abuse his physical superiority, daring him to crush her to him.

He did, fiercely, and Beth cried out in shock and anger. "How much?" he repeated.

"Not a word—"

She felt his thumbs press hard into her ribs just beneath her breasts. "As I recall, you don't want to be lied to," he snarled. "Well, dammit, neither do I!"

"I don't know how much I heard!"

His hands dropped to his sides, and with an agonizing

twist of his mouth he turned away and sank against the door of Louisiana's empty stall.

Beth drew back, fighting her sobs, covering her mouth, trembling.

"I'm sorry if I hurt you," Jared said, his voice dull, thudding. He didn't turn around. "Beth, you've got to leave here. This isn't just a political scrabble. I can't—I can't do what I must with you near."

Slowly, a frightening calm crept into her body. She recalled the jeers and threats she had faced during so many suffragette speeches and marches. Always she had been able to divorce herself from what she felt—her betrayal, fear, loneliness, anger—and concentrate on what she had to do.

"What kind of trouble is William in?" she asked levelly.

Jared turned around, weariness dulling his eyes and cloaking his rugged face. "You never give up, do you?"

"What would you have me do, Jared?" she asked calmly. "Take the next train to New York and forget about you?"

"Yes!" He took two long steps toward her, but the sudden intensity in his eyes vanished, replaced by a warmth and passion that made a shambles of Beth's sudden calm. He touched her hair. "Yes—and no," he said softly. "I don't want you ever to forget me, Beth."

She brushed her curved fingers along his wrist. "How could I?"

He brought his other arm around the small of her back and the hand on her hair swept to her neck, cupping her head as her face lifted toward his. Her lips parted as their mouths joined, their tongues sweetly, gently mingling. Jared's arm tightened around her middle, and for a moment her feet left the dirty stable floor. The sudden rush of desire made her forget his harshness, his furious interrogation, and she clung to him longingly, wishing for an even deeper loss of memory.

"You know I can't go," she said into his mouth. "I just can't, Jared."

"You won't," he corrected, and stood back. He smiled and twisted one of her stray locks of hair around his finger. "My darling, outrageous Beth."

"Jared—"

"I'd better go now before we—" He cut himself off with a leering grin and let go of her hair. "Forget what you overheard, Beth. It was nothing. And don't ever let me catch you eavesdropping on me again!"

"Or you will do more than kiss me?" she asked boldly.

His grin broadened lecherously. "You can be sure of it!"

Beth couldn't suppress her own grin as she watched him leave, but gradually it withered and left only a lingering glint in her violet eyes. Jared Inman was a volatile, strange, mysterious man. She couldn't leave Saratoga, and she couldn't forget him. Whatever Jared was to others, he would always be her first lover, and perhaps her only lover.

With any luck at all, she thought, he *would* be her only lover.

William Prentiss, Sr., did not ask his suffragette guest to leave. Instead, he wired her father with a long list of his daughter's transgressions and suggested the judge come immediately to Saratoga and escort her back to New York. In so doing, Prentiss absolved himself of all responsibility for Beth's behavior.

"I know he won't come," he told Beth in the drawing room after dinner that evening. "He trusts you far too much, Elizabeth. If you were my daughter, I'd keep you under lock and key at all times."

"My father approves of my behavior," Beth told her host.

Prentiss shook his head dismally. "I know. You're an interesting pair, you two. Amusing and infuriating. I don't suppose you're going to tell me why your father had you nosing around that bordello?"

William Prentiss was speaking frankly, more frankly, Beth knew, than he ever would have with his own wife and daughter present. "It doesn't concern you," she replied, and thought she sounded very much like Jared Inman. "I promise I won't go there again."

"And do you promise you won't start another argument at my dinner table?"

"I promise I won't start one intentionally," Beth vowed, her eyes flashing, but she lowered her voice and said sincerely, "I hope I haven't embarrassed you, Mr. Prentiss."

"Everyone knows you're a Harte, Elizabeth," he replied gruffly. "That alone explains you. You're impetuous and naive, my dear, but you're a good-hearted woman."

Beth smiled. "Thank you, Mr. Prentiss."

He reached over suddenly and took her hand in his. "That's why I worry about you and Jared Inman, Elizabeth. Don't think I haven't guessed what's going on. I want you to be careful, not because I'm worried about being embarrassed or having you flaunt my rules, but because I'm worried about *you*, my dear." His voice was quiet, sincere, his words quickly spoken. "I invited Jared Inman here for reasons of my own, but that doesn't mean I believe he is the kind of man in whom a respectable young woman should take an interest."

"Why, Mr. Prentiss?" she breathed. "What's he done that no one trusts him?"

"I didn't say I didn't trust him, Beth," Prentiss said carefully. "I do, but that's because I know what he is."

"And what is he?" Beth persisted.

"Just look at him, Elizabeth. He does as he pleases, dresses as he pleases. He can be charming when it suits him, but his life in San Francisco has hardened him. I admit that he can fit into our level of society as easily as we can, but that isn't what he's used to."

She averted her eyes, and Prentiss took his hand off hers. "Is he used to robbing trains and killing people?" she asked bitterly.

"He might be," Prentiss said quietly. Then he added, closing the subject, "Please be careful, for your own sake, Beth."

"Thank you, Mr. Prentiss," she said. "I will."

CHAPTER 14

By Tuesday night, Beth realized she must have given herself away Sunday at dinner. Elijah Dobbs, William Prentiss, Sr., and Jr., and Jared Inman all knew now that one Elizabeth Stanton Harte hadn't come to Saratoga Springs merely to discourage her friend from running off with a horse trainer or to drink mineral water or to luxuriate in the mud baths. Beth Harte, suffragette and reformist judge's daughter, had come to Saratoga to spy for her father.

She was certain everyone knew it.

Jared was clearly avoiding her. He didn't come to her

room and never said what he was doing or where he was going. He simply disappeared on Monday afternoon and all day Tuesday. Only Ginny's whispers told Beth he was even still a guest at the Prentiss cottage. He was purposely, stubbornly staying away from her and her questions.

And William withdrew further into his own private world. The more he sulked and drank, the more Beth wished she had interrogated Jared more closely. William was in deep, serious trouble. She was sure of it! Was Jared causing his problems? Aggravating them? Or trying to help? Beth remembered the scene she had overheard and doubted that Jared was interested in helping William, or that William was interested in receiving his help.

What was wrong with William? Could he have so much money tied up in one horse that he would become this withdrawn and irritable when Louisiana turned up lame? *Did* Jared have anything to do with Louisiana's lameness?

And where did Jacques LeBreque fit into William's difficulties?

And what about the St. Louis Western Railroad?

And all the railroad executives streaming into Saratoga?

In frustration, Beth finally did go to the mud baths, and there she was delighted to meet some of the wives of the railroad executives. They, however, only wanted to discuss their health and glowing skin. Disgusted and bored, Beth went about making herself as beautiful and tempting as she possibly could.

At dinner that evening, she was positive no one noticed. Her skin was soft and milky, her cheeks rosy, her chestnut hair gleaming and curling down her back, her nails sparkling. She wore a violet dress that matched her eyes, with a small but convincing bustle, and a gold and amethyst necklace and matching earrings.

Jared Inman hardly glanced at her, and William only stared.

But Ginny, a true friend, whispered in her ear, "Beth, you're lovely! Even Richard said so."

Richard Hoskins, Beth knew, did not approve of her, but she smiled in appreciation. "I'm glad someone noticed."

"Oh, Beth, believe me, everyone's noticed."

She didn't even try to hide her pleasure at Ginny's compliment. "Thank you, Ginny."

"Will you be going to the Club House after dinner?" Ginny asked.

"I don't know—"

"Oh, please do! It would be such fun, especially after the first time when you went in that gray dress. I can't wait to see the look on Old Smoke's face when he sees you in violet!" Ginny tugged her friend's arm. "Please say you'll come."

Beth grinned broadly. "With an invitation like that, how could I resist?"

This time, however, Beth wasn't asked to ride with Jared Inman. William, Sr., invited her to ride with his family, and she found herself sitting close to William, Jr. She wondered if he thought that she had changed her image for any particular reason, and if he suspected that reason was Jared Inman, or even himself. Beth had assumed she had acted out of boredom and, more than anything, was being obstinate. But now she wondered. *Was* she reacting to Jared's indifference?

Was that what Jared thought?

She wriggled uncomfortably in the carriage and began to regret her imprudent if rather spectacular dress.

John Morrissey's Club House dining salon was as crowded as Beth or, they said, the Prentisses had ever seen. It glistened with jewelry and bright costumes, all more spectacular even than Beth's, and throbbed with high-pitched laughter and the gossip and chatter of women who were offered little else to do. Beth observed that tonight there were few men in the salon.

The Prentiss men didn't stay long, and Ginny was having little luck persuading her elegantly clad Richard Hoskins to remain. "Oh, Richard," she pleaded, clinging to his arm, "won't you stay with me just a while?"

He smiled, rather patronizingly, Beth thought, and extricated himself from her grasp. "Now, Ginny," he said, patting her hand, "You know I promised your father and brother."

"I know," Ginny said, pouting. "But is it wrong of me to want you to stay here?"

Beth quietly moved into the crowd so that Ginny and Richard could settle their disagreement in private, but she heard her name and turned to see Rachel Shaughnessy, exquisitely dressed in an emerald-green silk crepe tunic over a dark blue underskirt with a huge bustle and train covered with beads and ribbons. Beth counted three diamond rings, a diamond necklace, and a gold hairpin inlaid with tiny diamonds.

"Hello, Miss Shaughnessy," Beth said politely. "You look very nice tonight."

Rachel smiled coquettishly. She wasn't any older than Beth, a dark-haired woman with ivory skin, wide blue eyes, and a dimply smile. The multitude of cloth and accessories seemed to weigh down Rachel's tiny frame. Beth could have worn every jewel and bead and square inch of cloth and still have looked tall and slender.

"I daresay no one looks as nice as you this evening, Miss Harte," Rachel said. "You're turning heads tonight."

"Thank you," Beth replied awkwardly. "How—how is Mr. Shaw?"

Rachel laughed heartily. "My uncle?" she asked with a lewd look in her blue eyes. "He went back to New York last week."

"Rachel's with me now," Betty Bowman said as she came between the two young women and put a dimpled arm across Rachel's shoulders. "And how are you this evening, Miss Harte? Not so dowdy-looking tonight, I see. Expecting someone?"

Beth shook her head and wondered who would report to her host that his suffragette guest was talking to prostitutes. Again! "No, I'm not," she said quickly and firmly, aware that the madam was referring to Jared Inman. "I dress for myself."

"Do you now?" Betty said skeptically, and eased herself into a red velvet chair. She was wearing her usual black satin with a white gardenia in her hair. A single look sent Rachel back into the crowd. Betty sipped on a glass of mineral water. "You aren't taking my advice, are you?"

Out of the corner of her eye, Beth saw Richard squeeze Ginny's hand and pass through the guarded doors into the gaming rooms.

"Don't worry," Betty said mildly, reading Beth's mind. "If you don't want to be seen talking to me, I won't be offended."

Beth's spine stiffened. "I'm not afraid of gossip, Mrs. Bowman."

"Betty," she corrected with a twist of a smile. "I've told you to get rid of the man you love, so you might as well call me Betty."

"I'm not in love with Jared Inman," Beth maintained.

A heavy black eyebrow rose. "No? All the more reason to send him packing, honey." She leaned back in her chair and eyed Beth steadily as she stuck a finger into her mineral water and licked it. "You told Jared you came to see me."

"What?" Beth said, caught off-guard. "Well, no, not exactly—at least not the way you're implying. Someone saw me in the village, and I was forced to admit where I had been.''

"And I suppose you were forced to tell Jared I told you about my husband?'' Betty asked levelly.

Beth stared at the older woman. "Has he been to see you?'' she asked breathlessly.

"Honey, that's the understatement of the year,'' Betty said with a world-weary sigh. "If he could have gotten away with it, he would have chopped my head off and kicked it all the way down Broadway.''

"Did he threaten you?''

Betty shrugged nonchalantly. "He knows what I know about him.''

"If he murdered your husband, why didn't you have him arrested?'' Beth asked, her voice just above a whisper. "Why don't you have him arrested now?''

"What happened in Sacramento five years ago would hardly interest the Saratoga police,'' Betty said bitterly. "It interested the Sacramento authorities little enough at the time. I did go to them, Beth, and they did nothing. That's the kind of power a man like Jared Inman has out West.''

Beth sank into the chair beside Betty Bowman. She wanted to ask difficult, suspicious questions and trip the madam up in a lie, but all she could do was think of how right Betty Bowman must be. Why else would she bother to interfere?

"Jared Inman wants you to think he's the kind of man for a smart judge's daughter like you,'' Betty went on. "At first I couldn't understand how you could get under his skin like that, but looking at you now, I can see why. You're a beautiful woman, Beth. I don't expect you realize just how attractive you are, and maybe you're flattered by Inman's attentions.''

"Mrs.—Betty, Jared has paid me very little attention of late,'' Beth said crisply, her tone giving away her anger.

Betty shook her head and smiled knowingly. "You *are* naive," she said. "You have no idea just how much under Inman's skin you are, honey. Take my word for it—I know about these things."

Beth lowered her eyes and felt her face going red. Did she deep down hope Betty Bowman was right?

"So if you do take my advice and get rid of him," Betty said, "I wouldn't hang around to find out what he has to say or do about it. I'd be on the next train out of Saratoga."

Beth looked up in disbelief, but she saw that the plump, middle-aged madam was very serious. "You don't mean—"

"You'd better find someone else to chat with," Betty interrupted in a low voice. "Your friend and mine is coming through the door."

Beth rose quickly. "You don't miss anything, do you?"

"Not that wears pants," she said, and flashed a bawdy grin. "It's my business."

Beth thanked her and retreated, making her way toward Ginny as she searched the crowd for Jared. Finally, she saw him talking to one of the bouncers. He was more finely dressed than usual in brown linen trousers and double-breasted coat, but not anything equal to William's black silk broadcloth coat and striped trousers. Beth expected Jared would head straight upstairs to the gaming rooms, but instead he began searching the crowd with his eyes. For her, perhaps? She maintained her route to Ginny.

As she approached her friend, Beth turned and saw Jared grin broadly. He made his way to Melissa Dobbs. Melissa beamed with pleasure.

"So much for smart suffragettes who ask too many questions," Beth muttered, too angry to be hurt.

"So," Ginny said, breaking away from her mother and taking Beth's hand. "You see what I see. I'm sure Jared isn't interested in her."

"She's so pretty—and feminine."

"And she has nothing between her ears but empty mountain air," Ginny added uncharitably. "Not that you wouldn't be better off without Jared, from what I hear."

Beth sighed. "Perhaps you're right."

"The gossip about him *is* terribly imprecise," Ginny said, trying to be helpful. "I can't find out anything concrete about him, at least not by being discreet. Beth, maybe it doesn't matter what he is, so long as you love each other. Love can change people."

"Oh, Ginny, please!" Beth said, laughing in spite of herself, but one eye was watching the tête-à-tête between Jared and Melissa. "She doesn't seem to think he's anything special," she said idly.

"Melissa is flattered by any man's attentions," Ginny said confidently. "I'm sure she likes the idea of having the roughest, toughest-looking man around pick her out of the crowd. She's getting a thrill."

A thrill, Beth repeated silently. Was that what Jared Inman had gotten from her? Maybe he had always wanted to bed a judge's daughter, and now that he had done it—

No, that was the rumors and gossip talking, not what Beth herself knew about the man from San Francisco. Surely there had to be someone in Saratoga who knew Jared Inman better than Betty Bowman! Someone Beth could talk to in confidence, someone who would tell her the truth.

The two parted, and Melissa headed for Ginny and Beth while Jared walked straight to the gaming rooms. He paused before he went through the doors and turned abruptly, catching Beth's eyes on him. She flushed crimson when he grinned broadly. She could almost feel his strong hands on her back, but he turned away sharply and went through the doors.

"Well, good evening, Melissa," Ginny was saying. "I hope you're enjoying yourself?"

"Oh, yes! I'll be sorry to leave Saratoga," Melissa cooed, her ringlets bouncing as she spoke. "Everyone here looks so splendid! Even you, Beth—oh, I didn't mean—I'm sorry."

"It's all right, Melissa," Beth said, reassuring her.

"I only meant you don't usually dress up. You always look lovely."

Ginny rolled her eyes, but Beth laughed.

Melissa smiled at Beth, but her eyes lingered nervously on the disapproving Ginny before she gestured vaguely to the other side of the salon, where she and Jared had been talking. "Um, I just spoke to Jared Inman, and he asked me to give you both his regards."

"How nice," Ginny said, politely cool.

"Thank you, Melissa," Beth said warmly. "Did he say anything else?"

"Oh, no, not really. He was just asking about Daddy's plans to return to St. Louis." Melissa smiled again, this time through her awkwardness. "I should join my mother."

"What a nitwit," Ginny muttered when Melissa had moved away.

"I think she was embarrassed—"

"Embarrassed! Beth, she loves throwing it in your face that Jared slighted you to talk to her."

Beth scoffed cheerfully. "I'm no more to him than Melissa is, and he's nothing at all to me."

Ginny stared at Beth in disbelief, but they both burst out laughing.

And then the railroad men began to arrive.

The Vanderbilt party came first: the Commodore, aging but still elegant in his black suit and white tie, and two of his sons, William Henry, the tough leader of his father's railroad empire, and Cornelius, Jr. John Morrissey greeted them personally and led them to the gaming rooms.

They were followed by J. H. Devereux, president of the Atlantic and Great Western Railroad, Thomas Scott of the Pennsylvania Central, H. J. Jewitt of the Erie, and Amasa Stone of the Lake Shore Railroad.

"Crawling with railroad executives is right," Beth mumbled. She pointed to a group of elegantly black-clad men that followed the first group by less than five minutes. "I'd be willing to bet a few of these gentlemen have money tied up in our great American railroad system," she said dryly.

"Doesn't everyone?" Ginny said cheerfully.

Beth raised an eyebrow. "Do you know who they are?"

"E. W. Woodward, president of the Indianapolis and St. Louis Railway," Ginny said, bored, "William Bliss of the Bangor and Aroostack—"

"And James Joy of the Michigan Central," Beth said, as yet another black-clad man entered the dining salon. "I suppose the gentlemen accompanying them are assorted underlings?"

Ginny giggled, amused at her friend's obvious suspicious train of thought. "Only vice-presidents and treasurers!"

Beth clenched her fists at her sides. "What I would give to be a fly on the wall in one of those upstairs rooms!"

"Oh, Beth."

"You don't suppose there's a way?"

Ginny shook her head adamantly. "Women have been trying to get into the gaming rooms for years, Beth, but none has ever gotten past Old Smoke. He doesn't want to fuel any fires of the antigambling forces around town, and letting women play poker—"

"I don't want to play poker. I just want—" She stopped and grinned, her violet eyes flashing. "I just want to spy on all those great gents of the railroads! They all adore my father, you know, especially since he's begun to get vocal about instituting government controls to protect the people from railroad excesses."

"His heart's in the right place," Ginny said wryly.

Beth raised an eyebrow at her friend and was instantly ready for a political argument. How she missed her work! "You believe the railroads will regulate themselves when they have their passengers by the throat?"

"I think most of these men are honest and well-meaning," Ginny put in lamely.

"And don't want to build unsafe bridges because they won't spend the money on good materials, and don't want to suck hard-earned dollars from their passengers' pockets with unfair rates, and don't want to do a disservice to the farmers and small businessmen who rely on the railroads with the games they play with the rates!" Beth's hands clenched even more tightly at her sides. "I know these men, too, Ginny, and they'll do whatever they can get away with to make a bigger profit, even if it means bringing their country to the brink of ruin."

"Oh, Beth," Ginny said, shaking her head, caught in a subject she didn't want to talk about. "There's nothing wrong with making a profit—"

"I agree, but fairly and not at the expense of the interests of the general public," Beth countered. "My father and I believe the government's role is to protect the interests of all the people, and as such it should step in and mediate on behalf of both sides before there's violence."

Ginny paled slightly. "You don't think there will be violence, do you, Beth?"

"The farmers are beginning to organize into granges," she replied steadily. "They've been taking everything the railroads have thrown at them, but for how long? No, the federal government *has* to step in. Railroad systems cross state and territory lines, and it's the only place where regulations with any teeth can be made."

"No wonder the Commodore wishes you and your father would stick to women's rights," Ginny muttered.

Beth's eyes gleamed. She wished her father were here now, so at least he could be in the private gaming rooms arguing and spying! She would have to wire him at once. "Well, you know Father. A finger in—"

"Everyone else's pie!"

They both laughed.

But Ginny seized the opportunity to change the subject and begged Beth to walk with her onto the trim grounds of the Club House. "It's too nice a night to roast in here the entire evening," she said, tugging on her friend's hand.

In seconds they were out of the overly perfumed room and on the casino lawns. The moon was rising over Saratoga. Beth breathed in the cool night air, but it didn't soothe her impatience. She wanted to get into those gaming rooms!

Ginny pointed to the couples walking arm-and-arm beneath the wineglass elms. "I wish Richard thought a stroll through the park with me was more exciting than a poker game with my father and brother," she said, pursing her lips in a pout."

"Ginny!" Beth said in disbelief. "You two are practically inseparable as it is!"

"You think so?" Ginny asked, blushing, as they started across the lawn. "Oh, Beth, I'm so happy I can't believe this is actually happening to me. I keep thinking something awful will go wrong and ruin everything."

"What could possibly happen?"

Ginny shrugged her thin shoulders and spread her hands helplessly.

Beth hugged her quickly. "Quit worrying. I don't think I've ever seen anyone as much in love as Richard is with you."

"Except Jared Inman with you?" Ginny asked devilishly, giggling.

"Hardly."

"Oh, how I do love Richard!"

Suddenly, a young man hurried between them and took both Ginny's hands in his. "Virginia Prentiss! I heard you were in town. You beautiful child, how are you? I just arrived last night myself, and I'm already stone-cold broke. I'm such a sucker for the roulette wheel."

"Oh, Benjamin, it's so good to see you!" Ginny exclaimed, still holding his hands as she turned to Beth. "This is my good friend, Elizabeth Harte. Beth, this is Benjamin Wood. He's an actor—"

"A Shakespearean actor," he amended, and gave Beth a slight bow. He was slim, slightly taller than Beth, and had fine, chiseled features and a mass of dark curls on his head. Even in the moonlight, Beth could discern huge, round hazel eyes. He smiled beautifully. "A flat-broke Shakespearean actor."

"I'm sorry to hear that," Beth said politely.

He shrugged good-humoredly. "It makes my trip to the Springs that much shorter, I'm afraid." He smiled broadly and winked. "But I could win all my money back if I just had another fifty dollars—twenty, even. What about you, Virginia Prentiss, my wealthy patroness?"

"Benjamin Wood, you're incorrigible!" Ginny chastised affectionately. "If Father knew how much money I've already given you—"

"To further my artistic career," he said loftily, then put his hand on his heart and moaned. "This is for the rabid capitalist in me, the money-hungry, starving—"

"Save the performance, Ben. I haven't a nickel on me."

"Worthless child," he snorted.

"You're a year younger than I."

He shrugged again, an engaging mannerism. "And worth even less than you."

Beth cleared her throat. "I have money."

"Ah-ha!" Benjamin said, pivoting elegantly to face Beth squarely. "Always trust those with beautiful chestnut curls! Am I a sorry enough case for you? Would you like me to kneel and beg? Anything for a dollar! I'll repay every cent when I've cleaned out Mr. Morrissey—"

"You won't have to repay me," Beth said, cutting him off. "I want to make a deal with you. I have an idea."

"Uh-oh," Ginny interrupted. "Watch out, Ben!"

"You want me to sell you my soul. Fine, you can have it—"

Beth grinned, her eyes sparkling in the moonlight. "No, just your clothes. And I only want to rent them for a few hours—probably not even that long. We're almost the same size."

"Do I want to know more?" Benjamin Wood asked himself, and shook his head profoundly. "Absolutely not. I have a suit that would look lovely on you. I'm staying at Congress Hall, which is just a hop, skip, and a jump from here. I'll be back in three minutes. You have the money ready, dear woman, and tell me nothing. Aah—not a word more."

He slipped behind an elm, but Beth followed. "Wait," she called in a whisper. "I have to go with you. I can't very well change in the women's powder room."

Benjamin groaned. "Don't tell me. Just come along and tell me nothing!"

"Beth," Ginny called hoarsely, coming around the tree. "Beth, you're crazy. You're not going to—"

"Oh, yes, I certainly am!" Beth confirmed with a broad grin. "It'll be fun. With a little luck, I might last a full minute before I'm discovered."

Benjamin moaned as if he'd been shot.

"I'm with Benjamin," Ginny said, holding up a palm. "I don't want to know."

The arms of Benjamin Wood's shirt and coat were too long, his shoes were too big, and Beth hadn't thought about pins for her hair, but, she thought, at least the pants fit relatively well. She tied her hair up as best she could with her ribbon and hoped it would stay under the hat.

"You look like Elizabeth Harte dressed in men's clothes," Benjamin said unfeelingly.

She sighed. "I do, don't I?"

"Yes, and I'm an idiot, but here." He dragged a battered cloth bag from his closet and opened it up on the floor. "I'm an actor, so I have such things as straight pins and hairpins." He thrust a box of each at Beth. "Here, put up your hair properly and turn under your sleeves."

Beth obeyed, trying not to grin too broadly.

Benjamin dug around in his bag some more, muttering to himself about his idiocy, and when Beth turned around, sleeves and hair properly pinned, he had a wealth of paraphernalia lined up on the floor.

"When you're caught," he began, "you don't mention me. You don't sneak back here with this stuff. You wait until you get back to New York and you mail it to me, or you buy it from me here and now. As beautiful as you are, dear woman, I hope never to see you again."

"You're taking this all much too seriously," Beth told him.

"John Morrissey was the heavyweight champion of the world and outweighs me by a hundred-fifty pounds," Benjamin pointed out, and held up a wig of thick blond curls. "Put it on."

Beth seized the hairpiece and raced to the mirror.

Benjamin stood behind her with a bushy blond mustache. "I could be a splendid confidence man if I wanted to be," he said, and glued the mustache just beneath her nose. "There, now don't you look ridiculous? No, no, put the hat down! Just pray those chestnut locks don't start poking out all over the place. Look at you, you're not even sweating! I'm drenched, and I'm not even involved. Am I?"

"No, not at all. I don't even know who you are."

"Good. Come sit on the bed and I'll do your face."

Beth looked at him with curiosity, but he snapped his fingers and she did as he said. Then, from a series of mysterious glass jars, he powdered, painted, and dabbed at her face. When he was done, he stood back and appraised his work. "Not bad," he said, "not bad at all. I'll tell you what will give you away, though."

"What?"

"Your eyes. Men just don't have violet eyes. Here—" He bent over and dug into his bag once again, coming up with a pair of glasses with gold wire rims. He put them on her face, pushed them high up on her nose, and stood back to study the effect. "You still have violet eyes, but those should help. Now. Do you want some advice?"

"I would love some advice," Beth said, and walked over to the mirror. "Wait, Ben, who's this in the mirror?"

A fair, thin young man with thick blond curls, glasses, and a big bushy mustache, so incongruous as to be totally convincing, stared out of Elizabeth Harte's violet eyes. She looked closer. Even her eyebrows were lighter.

"Oh, heavens, yes, a name! Something simple, but not suspicious."

"Abraham Wood," Beth said, turning. "Your brother from Chicago."

Benjamin paled. "No, uh-uh, no."

"You've got dark curls, I've got blonder curls, we're just about the same height and weight, and if I went in with someone I'd be less likely to be caught right off and—"

"I can't, I can't, I can't!"

"Oh, yes, you can. You're an actor—"

"Don't appeal to my ego, Elizabeth," he warned. "That's not fair."

"You're an actor, Ben, and you're broke. I'll pay you one hundred dollars if you'll go through with this."

He groaned and fell against the wall with his hand on his heart. "You're a hard woman. Brutal, unfair—one hundred dollars, you say?"

Beth nodded.

He straightened up. All right, I want you to listen carefully. You're Abraham Wood of New York, not Chicago— the accent is wrong—but only if someone asks. If no one asks, you remain quiet and anonymous. We just walk into the gaming rooms together and separate immediately. Do you understand?"

"Yes."

"No. You don't talk if you can help it, but when you do, you don't disguise your voice. That will only draw more attention to you. I know it will be tempting, but don't do it. Understood?"

Beth nodded.

"And watch your hands. Try to keep those delicate, slender fingers out of view." He turned to the mirror and straightened his tie. "Idiot," he said to his reflection.

Beth smiled to herself. "Anything else?"

"Bet small and lose small. How much money do you have? Don't worry, I'm not going to rob you."

"Five hundred dollars."

He nearly choked.

"I have a generous father, and I've hardly spent a dollar since I arrived here," she explained demurely.

"You carry it with you?"

"What else are corsets for?" she said, and grinned, digging into her trouser pockets for her white satin purse.

Benjamin Wood snatched it out of her hands. "Good

God,'' he said, paling. "You can't go in there with this! Thank heavens I mentioned it. Here—'' He opened the purse and shoved the wad of bills back at Beth. "Put that in your inner jacket pocket. This—'' he held the purse with his fingertips as though it were something foul, "stays with your corset."

"I feel stupid," Beth admitted.

"And so you should. Stupid enough to change your mind?''

She grinned. "Too stupid to change my mind."

"So I feared," he said, and sighed with resignation. "Come, we'll practice our act on the way."

They started out of his Congress Hall room. Beth wondered what her father would say if he could see her now. Probably nothing, she thought. He wouldn't recognize his own daughter!

And it was all, she thought, for a good cause.

"Benjamin, do me one more favor," she said as they came to the elegant lobby. "Tell me the rules of poker."

"Oh, don't worry about poker, dear," he said. "Just stick to the faro and roulette tables. Most of the poker games are high-stakes games played upstairs with all the big shots, at least tonight."

Beth looked at him. "Yes," she said cheerfully, "I know."

He turned marble white. "No!"

She nodded and said nothing.

"You're Abraham Lincoln and I don't know you."

"Abraham Lincoln is dead, and I'm your brother Abraham Wood from Chi—from New York."

He shook his head in desperation.

Beth laughed. "Cheer up, Ben! This will be fun, I promise, even if I don't last ten seconds."

He looked at her sharply. "No, don't smile!"

"What?" she asked, confused.

"Your smile, your laugh—people will recognize it."

"I'm not planning to come into close contact with people who would recognize Beth Harte."

"If you're going upstairs," Benjamin said, his tone very grave, "you are bound to run into people who know Elizabeth Harte." He turned to her as they went out onto the street. "Namely William Prentiss, Sr., and Jr."

Beth smiled courageously. And Jared Inman, she thought as they crossed Congress Street to the Club House.

CHAPTER 15

Benjamin Wood and his brother Abraham simply walked through the guarded Club House doors into the public gaming rooms. Without so much as an encouraging glance at his newly found brother, Benjamin abandoned him for the roulette table. Abraham Wood, alias Elizabeth Stanton Harte, stood awkwardly in the middle of the spacious, carpeted room and knew that the woman beneath the blond wig and mustache was on her own.

Out of the corner of one eye, Beth could see John Morrissey towering over one of the roulette tables next to a tall, elegantly draped window. The room, crowded as it was, seemed strangely quiet, almost muffled. Civilized, Beth thought and, keeping her back to the proprietor, edged toward a faro table. She observed the four players and dealer without the slightest idea of what was going on, but quickly picked up the game.

Faro was played on a felt board on which an entire spade suit was pasted. The player would place a chip on one of the pasted cards and make his bet. The dealer would then begin turning up cards in the deck. If neither of the first two were the bet card, the bet was still unsettled. If the first card turned was the bet card, the player would lose. If the second card was the bet card, the player would win. That would complete a turn, bets would be laid, and the new bets would be made.

It was, Beth thought, frightfully simple. She smiled to herself, careful not to show any teeth, and wondered if that was why men were so intent on keeping women away from the betting tables. She supposed the impulse to cheat could get overwhelming, but she couldn't see that winning and losing at a silly game of cards was so very important. And if she caught someone cheating? It would depend, she supposed, just how daring and ingenious he had been. Beth thought she would admire someone who could fool a table full of watchful, distrustful men. What a wonderful prank!

Of course, men were shot and beaten and maimed regularly for cheating at cards. Jared Inman, Beth reminded herself, had killed a man for cheating at cards.

"You've never played?" a deep voice suddenly beside her asked.

Beth, startled out of her concentration, spun around and faced John Morrisey. She remembered not to smile. "No, I haven't," she admitted. Her voice sounded high-pitched, but it was clear and strong. Her mustache tickled, and she fought an urge to shove her glasses higher up on her nose. "Faro is not my game," she added, hoping that what she had been observing was indeed faro.

"I don't know you," Old Smoke boomed.

"Wood," she said automatically. "Abraham Wood."

"John Morrissey," he said, and extended his hand. Beth took it reluctantly, her own hand not even half the size of his. Her nails still glowed from her afternoon of pampering and mud baths. "Well," Morrisey went on, "would you care to try your luck?"

Beth cleared her throat, terrified that her mustache was going to fall off and land on Old Smoke's gleaming black shoes. "Actually," she began casually, "I am looking for the Prentiss party."

Actually, she thought, she was looking for the dozen railroad men who had shunned the public gaming room for the private ones upstairs, but Beth guessed that where railroad men went, so went the Prentisses.

Morrissey's black eyes narrowed, and he studied her closely, looking gravely down over his black beard.

"I'm not with them," Beth offered, and accidentally let a smile slip across her face. She caught it with a bite of the lip. She always smiled when she was pulling a prank! "William Prentiss asked me to look him up when I was in town—young William Prentiss."

"Is he expecting you?"

"I should think so. I sent him a message this afternoon."

Old Smoke's eyes were still narrowed at his thin young client, and he crossed his massive arms on his chest. "Abraham Wood, you say?" He snorted. "I'll have one of my men find out if Mr. Prentiss wishes to see you."

Beth's heart sank down to her oversized shoes, but she nodded confidently.

John Morrissey started toward the door, but he was intercepted by one of his smartly dressed bouncers. Beth edged her way, as subtly as she could, past them. The bouncer was waving his hands as he spoke. Morrissey lit a cigar as he listened, concern knitting his heavy brow. The young man with the bushy blond mustache seemed momentarily forgotten.

Beth pulled her lower lip all the way under her top row of teeth, causing her mustache to tickle her chin, but she didn't pause to think. While ex-heavyweight champion, brawler, and politician Morrissey answered his bouncer, his suspicious, skinny client, a suffragette in disguise, quietly tiptoed up the carpeted stairs. Beth felt absurd when she reached to lift her nonexistent skirts. She almost laughed aloud, but a glance at Morrissey stopped her. He had sent his bouncer off and was now heading for the stairs.

The private gaming rooms were guarded. Beth's heart raced. Morrissey was right behind her, would see her, would guess Abraham Wood had no business upstairs, and toss him out. Perhaps he would even recognize the violet eyes behind the glasses.

She stopped next to a guard. "Excuse me, this is the Prentiss room, is it not?"

The guard, twice the size of Beth, shook his head.

"I must have gotten turned around," she said lamely.

He pointed nonchalantly across the hall. "Over there."

Beth strutted to the specified door and ignored the guard there as she raised her fist and rapped on it once. The guard caught her by the wrist before she could get off the second knock. "Name?" he growled.

"Abraham Wood," she said condescendingly, her voice deep and throaty with tension.

The guard still had her about the wrist when the door opened. They both looked up at Jared Inman's tall figure. Beth inhaled sharply. She didn't know if she was turning white or red, but she could feel the sweat soaking Benjamin Wood's linen shirt.

"What's going on here?" Jared demanded, glaring at the guard. "We're trying to—" He stopped and stared at the thin blond-haired man still in the guard's grip. "You!"

Beth winced and said quickly, "Abraham Wood, Mr. Inman."

"I know who the devil you are!" he shouted.

"Would you like me to show Mr. Wood out?" the guard asked.

"No, unhand him."

The guard obeyed immediately, and Beth began rubbing her bruised wrist. She couldn't bring herself to meet Jared's eyes. He had recognized her at once. Surely the rest of the Prentiss party would see through her disguise as easily.

"Come in, Mr. Wood," Jared said, a grin twisting at the corners of his mouth, the teasing lilt in his voice so subtle that only Beth, who knew whom she was, would hear it. "I've been looking everywhere for you."

Beth couldn't speak or move.

"Come in, come in," Jared urged impatiently. "We have quite a poker game going on. As I recall, you don't play, do you?"

"I intend to learn," Beth replied tartly, and stepped past the guard into the opulent gaming room.

"Do you now? Well, that should be entertaining." Jared grinned over his shoulder and stood behind his chair at the big, polished table. Beth was aware only of the pairs of male eyes studying her impatiently. "Gentlemen, I would like you to meet Abraham Wood. Mr. Wood, may I introduce you to William Prentiss, Sr., William Prentiss, Jr., Richard Hoskins, Elijah Dobbs, and—" he paused dramatically, "Judge Robert Lowell Harte."

Beth met her father's eyes. Judge Harte cocked his head politely. "Mr. Wood, it's my pleasure. Won't you join us?"

Beth had no idea if her father recognized her. He would never publicly humiliate her if he did, but that did little to comfort her. Her self-control was shattered. What was the judge doing in Saratoga? When had he arrived? Why hadn't he wired her he was coming?

Beneath her vest and shirt, the perspiration dripped down Beth's naked breasts. She swallowed hard and collected her wits. "I—I would like to watch, if none of you mind," she mumbled.

"No, no, of course not," the judge said amiably, assuming the rest of his party was as good-natured and accommodating as he. "Have a seat. Not a poker player, eh?"

Beth shook her head and reluctantly sat at the chair Jared had pulled up between himself and Judge Harte. She nodded politely at the other men around the table and kept her hands in her lap. She refused to look at Jared.

The cards were gathered up and dealt, the skinny intruder forgotten. Beth watched closely. Her father wasn't a poker player, at least not that she knew, but he snatched up his cards and eyed them with the acuity of a veteran. She twisted her fingers together. Jared's knee touched hers, and she glared up at him and caught his small grin behind his cards as he slumped back in his chair. She wanted to ask who was winning, but she didn't know if that would be naive or rude or both, so she kept quiet.

She wished she had asked for J. H. Devereux's party.

William opened the betting. Beth saw that he was red-faced and sweating profusely. He gulped at a glass of whiskey and gnawed on the corner of his mouth as one by one the other men responded to his bet. Richard Hoskins raised it. Jared dropped out. The judge muttered that he would stay in for the hell of it. William raised Richard. Prentiss dropped out with a curse. The judge shrugged and met the raise. Elijah Dobbs tossed his cards face down on

he table without a word. Richard rolled his tongue around
is mouth and called.

William laid down a low club straight. The judge scoffed
and tossed his cards face down on the table. Richard
ighed and shook his head. "I'm sorry, William," he said,
and laid down a medium heart straight.

William groaned as if in pain. "That does it," he said,
aking his blond hair, damp with sweat. "I'm cleaned out.
Goddammit—"

"Why don't we take a breather?" Jared suggested quietly.
He turned to the young blond man with the mustache and
tartling eyes. "Would you care to join us in the next
and?"

Beth almost smiled, but caught herself in time. "I'm not
ure I can afford your stakes."

"You're not supposed to say so," Jared said, laughing.
"They'll run you up on the first hand now and clean you
out of what you do have."

"Well, we have a novice in our midst, I see," William
Prentiss, Sr., said, and chuckled to himself. "Where are
you from, Mr. Wood?"

"New York."

"And what do you do for a living?"

"I'm an actor."

The elder Prentiss roared with laughter. "And you're
riends with Jared Inman?"

Beth stiffened. "Actually, we hardly know each other."

"If you'll excuse me," the judge interrupted, rising,
"I'm going to have another look for my daughter."

Beth lowered her eyes and studied the edge of the cherry
able.

"Have you asked Ginny?" William, Sr., suggested.

"Yes," Judge Harte said. "She said she left Beth out-
ide on the lawns, but I didn't see her there."

"Well, ask Ginny again and see what she tells you this

time. If your daughter is up to something, mine probably knows about it. If you don't mind my saying so, Judge Harte, your daughter has a dangerous wild streak. Supervising her has been no easy task.''

Judge Harte smiled lightly and shrugged. ''That's why I don't bother,'' he said.

Jared squeezed Beth's thigh beneath the table, laughed at the flash in her eyes, and quickly followed her father out. Beth almost went after them both, but stayed in her seat. Would Jared tell her father where he could find his missing daughter?

Prentiss and Dobbs left together to spend a few minutes with their wives and daughters. What would they do when they still couldn't find Beth Harte? Beth/Abraham rose abruptly and walked to the small bar where Richard Hoskins and William were pouring drinks. She nearly tripped on her oversized shoes, but the two men weren't paying attention to their unexpected guest. She poured herself a glass of whiskey, which she hoped she didn't have to drink, and nodded at them. They still didn't pay any attention to her. She sat in a velvet-cushioned chair, half-hidden by the bar, and stared at her whiskey.

''You know Father won't lend me any more money!'' William was saying, desperation choking his voice.

''We can discuss this in private—''

''There's no one here.''

So William hadn't even noticed the slim intruder. Richard nodded to him and whispered his name. Beth forced a bit of whiskey down her throat and pretended to be uninterested in their conversation.

''Oh, who cares?'' William whined. ''By tomorrow morning, everyone will know I'm in debt up to my neck to you.''

''You're a compulsive gambler,'' Richard said mildly. ''Compulsive gamblers are easy to beat, because they never know when to stop. You think every hand's going to be your big winner, so you overbet. I just keep matching your bets and have better hands than you.''

William groaned. Peeping around the corner of the bar, Beth saw him prop his elbows upon his knees and sink his head into his hands. "But you never run out of money!" he moaned. "I keep expecting you to run out, and you never do. Who the hell are you, Hoskins? What do you want from me?"

"You know who I am," Hoskins said quietly, "and you know what I want."

"Dammit, I won't even be at that meeting tomorrow!"

"Shut up, will you?" Richard hissed. "Look, I *know* what you are up to—"

"But that has nothing to do with that damned meeting! They're just going to discuss freight and passenger rates and try to tone down some of the competition that is hurting everyone. It's Garrett's own damned fault if he doesn't like what they do. He could be here and throw his weight around if he wanted to."

Beth sipped her whiskey, feeling it burn down her throat, and pretended not to listen. John W. Garrett was president of the Baltimore and Ohio Railroad.

"This whole thing is Vanderbilt's idea, and you know as well as I do that he wants to control as many trunk lines as he can," Richard said, still speaking in a hushed, controlled voice. "He won't get the B and O, and he won't twist our arm into doing anything. We make our own decisions."

William sprang to his feet. "What the hell does that have to do with me?"

"You know, William. Don't play games with me." Richard paused and looked at William's back. "If you dump your B and O stock, especially with business off the way it is this year, you'll hurt us. It's that simple. Don't dump your stock, William. You owe me too much money. You haven't told your father how much, have you? Don't bail out on us and we'll just forget the debt, how's that? You don't put any pressure on the B and O, and I won't put any pressure on you."

William whirled around, smirking, desperation still clouding his eyes. "So you're getting your money from Garrett. I should have guessed. You're a spy for the B and O, Hoskins. I'm sure my sister will be glad to hear it."

Hoskins leaped up and clamped an arm on William's shoulder. "Don't try to threaten me, William," he snarled bitterly, his cool control suddenly gone. "My relationship with Ginny has nothing to do with this business, and you know it."

"I'll pay you back," William said, drawing himself up, but not looking very impressive with his sweating red face. "Every cent. Louisiana will be ready to race on Saturday—"

"I want my money tonight, William, or your promise to keep the B and O stock," Richard said, calming himself.

"Dammit, you know I can't pay you back tonight!"

"That's right, William."

William gulped down the rest of his whiskey. "I'll get the money for you, Hoskins. Even if I have to steal it, you'll have your damned money."

He slammed his empty glass on the bar and stalked out. Richard Hoskins calmly sipped his own whiskey and walked over to Beth.

"Do I have to pay you," he said quietly, "to keep what you've heard to yourself, or are you a gentleman?"

"I'm an actor," Beth replied. "I have no interest in business dealings."

Richard sighed, but Beth avoided his gaze. "That wasn't very pleasant," he said, more to himself than to Abraham Wood, and turned back to the card table.

The men returned, even William, who looked as though

he had splashed his face with cold water. Beth took her seat at the table and was looking forward to her first game of poker. It seemed simple enough, and she still had four hundred dollars.

John Morrissey, however, marched into the room behind Elijah Dobbs and snatched Abraham Wood from his chair. "I'll see Mr. Wood out," he said to the men at the table.

All but Jared Inman looked confused. He grinned at Beth and shuffled the cards. "What a shame you couldn't try your tricks on us, Mr. Wood," he said mildly, amused with himself. "Of course, you know I don't suffer men who cheat at cards."

Morrissey had her by both elbows, but Beth still managed to twist back around and glare at Jared. He was the cause of this humiliation! "No, you kill them instead!" she snarled.

With one tug, Morrissey spun Beth around and shoved her out the door, but not before she had seen Judge Robert Lowell Harte's mouth drop open and the worry on his gentle face vanish.

Morrissey dropped one elbow and muttered darkly, "I'm glad you're not my daughter."

Beth felt her face grow pale.

"We are going to walk down the back stairs and out, Miss Harte," Old Smoke informed her before she had a chance to deny anything. "And if you tell me you're Abraham Wood, I'll pull off your wig and that mustache of yours and toss you back into that room. Just go quietly."

He marched her down the back stairs. Beth doubted she could have spoken even if she'd had something to say. She concentrated on not tripping over her big shoes. When they reached the back door, John Morrissey released her and opened it for her.

"Benjamin Wood is waiting in his room for you," he

said. "Go straight there, get yourself dressed, and march your little rear end back here. Be quick about it, and have an explanation ready for your absence." He squeezed her shoulder just enough to let her know how much he could hurt her if he chose to. "No one needs to know a woman dressed as a man got past John Morrissey."

Beth flashed a smile. "I agree wholeheartedly!"

"As I said, Miss Harte, I'm glad you're not my daughter."

He turned away, but Beth stopped him. "But how did you find out?"

He growled at the delay and Beth's audacity, but turned halfway around and answered her. "I knew you'd snuck upstairs, so I got suspicious. I watched Benjamin Wood and got to wondering where he found himself another hundred dollars to lose. Then Jared Inman came downstairs, and when I asked, he told me you'd crashed the game. So we talked to Benjamin together."

"Poor Benjamin," Beth mumbled.

"He admitted everything after I offered to bash his head in."

"And then you and Jared decided to brand Abraham Wood a card-cheater and throw him out?" Beth asked.

Morrissey grunted in agreement. "There'd better be no next time, either, Miss Harte," he growled. "Now get going. Wood'll be meeting you in his hotel lobby, if he has any sense. If he's not there, come get me."

Beth nodded, thanked him, and scrambled out.

Benjamin Wood was waiting for her in the lobby of Congress Hall as promised. "You lasted longer than I thought you would," he said cheerily.

Beth scowled. "No thanks to you."

"Every thanks to me, dear woman. You should be grateful. John Morrissey didn't offer to bash your head in, did he?"

"Nice point," Beth said, smiling. "What about Jared Inman?"

"He would have stood quietly aside and watched me beaten, I'm sure," Benjamin said, "although I do believe he knew who you were from the beginning."

She snorted angrily. "He probably loved every minute of it!"

"I do believe he did."

"Well, I've got about ten minutes to get dressed and back there as prim-and-proper Beth Harte."

"That's all you need," Benjamin said, and led her up to his room.

Beth pulled off all her men's clothing and scrubbed her face and combed her hair, then pulled on her dress, smoothing out what wrinkles she could.

"I never would have considered doing this if you hadn't stopped to say hello to Ginny," she told Benjamin when she was finished. "But there you were, and there I was—and, well, the idea just presented itself." She flashed a smile that told him she had no regrets. "I couldn't resist."

"The world should be glad you don't have a criminal's heart," Benjamin said dryly. "Now go. Out of my life, woman."

Beth grinned, thanked him, and was gone.

CHAPTER 16

"Oh, Beth, there you are!" Ginny said, spinning around when Beth appeared behind her. "Everyone's been looking for you. Beth, your father's here. He arrived on the evening train—"

"I know," Beth said.

Ginny paled. "Then you did go through with it. Beth, You weren't discovered? How? Oh, Beth, I want to know everything!"

All the pleasure went out of Beth's face. How would

she tell Ginny about Richard Hoskins? "Of course," Beth said evasively. "Have I been missed?"

"Have you ever!" Ginny exclaimed. "Father could kill you, I'm sure. He's so embarrassed. Here your father shows up, and my father, who thinks he's responsible for you, doesn't have an idea in the world where you are. I did my best, Beth, but I think they all know you've been up to something. Did anyone recognize you? Did you make it upstairs?"

Beth grinned, her eyes dancing devilishly. "I actually sat through a game of poker with your father, brother, Richard, Elijah Dobbs, Jared, and my father," she said, keeping her voice very low as John Morrissey's eyes caught hers from across the salon. He looked away, satisfied. "Jared recognized me instantly, and my father did eventually, but neither said anything."

"My father would have had your head!" Ginny said merrily. "He didn't recognize you?"

Beth shook her head.

The Prentiss party entered the salon in a group. William, Sr., led, then Richard Hoskins, Elijah Dobbs, and Jared and the judge, talking together, Beth noticed. William trailed a few yards behind, looking like a very bad loser. Prentiss ignored his unpredictable guest and asked his wife and daughter if they were ready to leave.

Beth remembered she was supposed to be seeing her father for the first time in weeks. She broke into a wide grin and threw her arms around him. "Ginny just told me you were here," she said for the benefit of the Prentisses. "What a surprise! I thought Saratoga was much too gaudy for you."

"It is," he said dryly, kissing his daughter perfunctorily on the cheek, "but it's amusing in its own peculiar way. One never knows who will pop up in the most unlikely of places. Besides, New York is stiflingly hot in August."

Beth smiled affectionately, noticing Jared hovering behind her father. "It isn't August yet, Father. It couldn't be, could it, that New York is stiflingly boring without your daughter around?"

"You egotistical little thing," he said, laughing. "I gather you haven't been having a dull vacation."

"Not at all," Beth said, feeling her cheeks redden as she caught the lecherous glint in Jared's black eyes. She looked away and took her father's hand. "Where are you staying? Should I join you—"

Prentiss interrupted, proper host and friend that he was. "I've been trying to persuade your father to come out to the lake and stay with us."

Judge Harte held up a silencing hand before Beth could open her mouth. "I have a small, very civilized room at the Clarendon, and I'm perfectly content to stay there," he said, inviting no arguments from his daughter. "I'm just staying a few days. If you would like to walk over with me, Beth, I would be happy to have a cup of tea with you."

"Father, I'd love to, but I don't have any transportation back to the lake—"

"That's already been arranged," the judge said. "Mr. Inman here has graciously offered to wait for you and take you back in his carriage."

Beth glanced at Jared, who bowed with mock nobility, no doubt proud of his maneuvering to get her alone again in his carriage. She knew he would grill her about her Abraham Wood adventure, but she also desperately needed to talk to her father.

"How nice of him," she said dully.

William Prentiss, Sr., opened his mouth, but closed it again and shook his head. Beth guessed he wanted to warn Judge Harte about the man he had just agreed to leave alone with his daughter and spell out all the rumors about their relationship, but, like Beth, Prentiss knew there was little he could do. Judge Robert Lowell Harte had responsibility over his own daughter now.

The Prentiss party began to leave. Ginny was hanging on the arm of Richard Hoskins, who looked decidedly smug and victorious, while William, deflated and miserable, followed his family out.

"Miss Harte," Jared was saying, "I'll meet you in the Clarendon lobby in twenty minutes. Will that be enough time?"

Beth nodded, distracted.

"Thank you, Jared," the judge said for her.

"I assure you," Jared said politely, "it's my pleasure."

As Beth left with her father, she glanced back and saw Jared making his way to Elijah and Beatrice Dobbs. Melissa, who had been talking to a group of young women, immediately hurried across to her parents and Jared. Beth sighed. Melissa Dobbs, she thought, wasn't as empty-headed or disinterested as she pretended to be.

At the door, John Morrissey thanked them for coming and said good night. Beth made a point of giving him her best smile and thanking him for an interesting and informative evening.

Saratoga was still brightly lit with hundreds of people walking about the wide, elm-lined main street of Broadway and crowding the huge piazzas of the major hotels. The air was cool, soothing, and Beth could feel her muscles beginning to loosen. She hadn't been aware of how tense she was until now that she had begun to relax. Neither spoke as they walked up Broadway toward the Clarendon Hotel. It was tiny compared to the Grand Union and the United States and, since it had been built in 1860, had refused to modernize. Still, it was the *grand dame* of the Saratoga hotels, the favored spot of the social elite, and the only hotel in the spa Judge Robert Lowell Harte even considered. It was a lovely, statuesque building with classic columns and shutters, known for its pictuesque green shutters and gleaming white woodwork.

"Well, Beth," her father said as they entered the lobby, "are you going to tell me about everything?"

Her eyes flashed. "Of course."

"Including Jared Inman?"

Beth felt her face redden. She couldn't speak.

The judge raised his eyebrows and drew down the corners of his mouth. "I see."

He waited to pursue the subject until they were in his room with a pot of tea on the way. The room was small, elegant, and charming, with a sitting area of a Windsor chair and two smaller chairs upholstered in deep maroon velvet. Beth took the Windsor. The judge settled into one of the velvet chairs and lit his pipe, studying his daughter though the cloud of smoke. She was more than willing to leap up and answer the door when the tea arrived. She poured two cups and avoided her father's eyes. He was in a serious mood now.

"There's to be a meeting of railroad executives tomorrow," she said.

Her father accepted a cup of tea from her. "You're in love with him."

"I think they're going to discuss rates and ways to control competition," Beth went on, pretending not to have heard the judge.

"Infatuated?"

She sat down in exasperation. "Jared Inman doesn't favor the vote for women."

"Is that so?" her father asked, smiling. "Have you asked him?"

"I don't need to ask him. A man like that wouldn't favor advancing the rights of women."

He puffed on his pipe. "Being in love isn't a bad thing, Beth. I was in love once, you know. I still am."

Beth swallowed hard, the tightness returning to her throat. Her mother had died when Beth was twelve. She had been a Quaker, active in both the abolition and suffrage movements during the explosive 1850's. She had died during the War Between the States, catching influenza from the soldiers she nursed, unreconciled to the violence her own rhetoric had played a role in bringing about. She had been a dedicated, tireless reformer, and the only woman Robert Lowell Harte had ever loved. Beth had long ceased hoping to find anyone who could be as devoted to her as her father had been to her mother.

"I just don't know, Father," she said, fighting back tears. "I can't trust him."

And she told her father everything but the extent of their lovemaking. Then, before he could comment, she launched into her report, beginning with the names of the executives in the spa and ending with a recounting of the conversation between Richard Hoskins and William Prentiss, Jr.

"I'm sure Jared knows about William's problems," she added. "And I think Louisiana was prevented from running the race so that William couldn't get money to repay Richard."

"Do you think Hoskins paid LeBreque to injure the horse?" her father asked, his attention focused on the problem at hand.

"It's possible," Beth said. "Or he and Jared could be working together against William."

"Why?"

"Richard seems to have a limitless supply of money. He could have paid Jared to handicap Louisiana, or Jared could have gotten LeBreque to do his dirty work."

Judge Harte chewed on the end of his pipe. "What's the connection between Hoskins and Inman?"

"None necessarily," Beth replied. She sipped her lukewarm tea. "Inman could simply be a—a gun for hire, so to speak."

"He's been William Prentiss's guest," her father pointed out.

"So has Richard Hoskins."

"Jared Inman seems to be the odd man out in this entire affair. He is involved, yet he is not involved. He has no visible connection to anyone." Judge Harte smiled at his daughter. "Is that what you're saying?"

She nodded.

"And that is what makes you so nervous?"

"Yes."

"What about Elijah Dobbs?"

Beth sighed and finished off her tea, setting the cup and saucer on a small table. "Wait!" she said suddenly. "That's the connection! Elijah Dobbs and his St. Louis Western Railway. William wants to dump his B and O stock and jump with both feet into Dobbs's scheme, and Jared— Jared came to Saratoga with Dobbs. I bet—Father, I believe Jared Inman is a spy for Elijah Dobbs the same way Richard Hoskins is a spy for John Garrett."

"Inman's from San Francisco," her father said mildly.

"So? Maybe he spies for a living. That's why he moves in and out of high society so easily." Beth sprang from her chair and paced back and forth across the small sitting room. "And that explains his secrecy."

"Beth, I think you're jumping to conclusions before all the facts are in. I have none to offer, but I think you should discuss this with Jared before you make any hasty decisions."

Beth eyed her father closely. He sat puffing on his pipe, his long, thin legs crossed at the ankles. His advice was impartial and sound. It usually was. But there was something—a fleeting hesitancy to meet her eyes squarely—that made her suspect he wasn't telling her all he knew about the troubles in the Prentiss household and how they involved Jared Inman.

"You and Jared seemed to get along quite well," she said suspiciously.

Her father cocked his pipe at her. "He recognized you in that ridiculous disguise right away," he said. "I didn't, and I'm your father. I suppose I wanted to know why."

Beth flushed red. She flew around and looked out a window, her back to her father. "William insinuated that Jared was involved with the murder of Juan Correrro."

"Juan Correrro's death was ruled an accident."

"You know better than that, and so do I!" She whirled around, wild-eyed, her skirts swirling about her ankles. "Father, I can't stand it! I know so little about him, and he won't tell me anything! Maybe Jared isn't a spy. Maybe he wants to be one of the principal investors in Dobbs's railroad and is trying to force William out. Maybe—oh, Father, he could be anything for all I know!"

"That he could, that he could," her father replied, his tone casual and steady.

Beth collapsed into the other maroon velvet chair. She could feel her frustration and anger draining out of her body. "Why are you here?" she asked.

"Oh, you know me, Beth," he said mildly. "I'm just a nosy old man who likes to be on the fringes of all the excitement."

"Whom are you trying to fool?" Beth said, scowling. "You're not old, and you're no innocent—and you've never been on the fringes of anything in your life. You happened to turn up in Saratoga the very day before a secret meeting of railroad executives."

"So I've heard."

"Father!"

He set his cup and saucer squarely on his knee and rested back in his chair. "You've kept me well informed, Beth," he said, "and you've worked hard. I don't believe that meeting tomorrow will amount to much, but we can't be sure until it's over. I never can understand why those men insist on such secrecy. It makes those of us listening for rumors that much more suspicious."

"What are we going to do?"

"We are going to let the railroad executives meet and discuss what they will and try to find out what they've decided," her father said, rising. "And we're going to try to rescue William from that hare-brained scheme of his. I hope he will learn a lesson!"

Beth shook her head drearily. "I don't see that there's anything we can do—"

"If we pay off his debts, he will go through with this nonsensical deal with Dobbs, and if we don't pay off his debts, he'll drink himself into oblivion." Like his daughter, Judge Harte shook his head. "Well, let me think about that overnight. I am sure the Prentiss family and the world will go on if William can't find a way out of his dilemma."

"What about—" Beth stopped herself and rose beside her father.

He touched her cheek affectionately. "What about Jared Inman?"

She nodded, smiling.

"We'll tackle him tomorrow as well—perhaps."

Beth looked into her father's eyes and knew that he was still not telling her everything. "After what I've told you, do you trust me with him alone?" she asked with a devilish glint in her eyes.

"I believe the question should be if I fear for poor Jared alone with you." He laughed and hugged his daughter.

"Don't drown the man with your questions and accusations."

"Father, you're impossible!"

"I'll come by for you on the omnibus in the morning," he said. "We'll find out what's going on around here, one way or the other."

Beth squeezed his shoulders. "It's so good to have you here, Father! I've missed you."

He kissed her cheek. "And I've missed you, Beth. You've done a good job. I'll see you tomorrow. Now have a good ride home."

She scowled at him, and he laughed loudly as she left.

Beth was still laughing when she walked into the lobby, but her face grew serious and rigid when she saw Jared waiting there, his back to her as he studied a painting on the wall. He had his hands stuffed in his pockets, but he seemed interested in the painting, a beautiful, eerie landscape. Beth hung back a moment and watched him. His dark hair was tousled, his clothes neat but casual, incapable of concealing the breadth of his shoulders and the thickness of his thighs. His rugged features and nonchalant air only added to his mysteriousness and aura of arrogant masculinity.

He would look at ease, Beth thought tartly, riding alongside Jesse James or studying a painting in the lobby of the Clarendon Hotel. Jared Inman seemed to be comfortable wherever he happened to be.

She walked up to him and stood at his side. "I'm ready."

"My carriage is right outside," he said, his eyes lingering on the painting, his mouth a straight line.

He didn't glance at Beth, but turned on his heels and walked outside. She hesitated, then followed reluctantly. Jared was already leaping into the driver's seat. Beth grimaced and climbed up beside him. She didn't say a word. If Jared wanted to sulk, that was fine with her.

She crossed her arms over her breasts and pulled her shawl close. What did *he* have to sulk about? He had seen to it John Morrissey threw her out! He had flaunted Melissa Dobbs before her! He had ignored her all day! She huffed and refused even to look at him.

The carriage turned down Congress Street and was past the racetrack and on the wide boulevard of Union Avenue before Jared broke the tense silence.

"I was surprised to see your father," he said evenly.

Beth didn't look at him. "So was I."

"You've been spying for him, haven't you, Beth?"

"And for myself and the good of my country," she replied airily, holding her chin high.

"Dammit, you're both incorrigible idiots sometimes!"

"One can't be incorrigible sometimes," Beth replied, still using her haughty New York society accent. "One either is incorrigible or is not."

"Beth," he growled, his voice a low warning, his mouth hardly opening.

She waved a hand dismissively. "I suppose you are irritated only because Father and I are hot on your trail, as it were."

He grabbed her between her wrist and elbow before she could return her hand safely beneath her shawl and almost jerked her onto his lap. "I am irritated, Beth Harte," he ground out, "because you're an overconfident damned fool! Will you listen to me for once?"

Her eyes flashed, then narrowed as they focused on her arm in his. "That arm has been bruised quite enough for one evening. Do you mind?"

He released her with a loud huff. "You two had better not come crying to me when you get yourselves in over your heads."

"My father and I have managed quite nicely to take care

of ourselves all these years without you, Jared," Beth
said, wincing at the gentle way she said his name. She
looked away from him. "I thought you and my father were
getting along."

"That doesn't mean I don't think he's foolish for
coming," Jared muttered.

"Why should you care if Judge Harte is in Saratoga?"
Beth asked. "Are you worried what he'll tell me about
you? Or are you afraid he will stop you from ruining
William Prentiss?"

Jared whirled around, confusing the horses, but he calmed
them and himself before he spoke. "What the hell do you
know about William? Dammnit, Beth—"

"One never knows what one can learn masquerading as
an actor from New York who can't play cards," Beth said
lightly. "William is in debt to Richard Hoskins, who is a
spy for the Baltimore and Ohio and prefers that William
does not dump his B and O stock and go in with Elijah
Dobbs on this secret St. Louis Western Railway. I also
assume that Richard will spy on the meeting taking place
tomorrow morning among various railroad executives, since
John Garrett has refused to attend."

"Good God Beth," Jared said dully. "I knew I should
have hauled you out of there the minute I recognized those
violet eyes of yours."

"But you didn't, and now I know," she pointed out
crisply. "Will you explain your involvement in all this?"

"No."

"Why not?"

"Because it's not your affair!"

Beth pursed her lips and stared out at the two horses
clattering along.

"Beth, darling," Jared said, his voice softening but
frustration still at the edges, "can't you please trust me?"

"Virginia Prentiss trusted Jacques LeBreque," Beth said

evenly, "and she trusted Richard Hoskins, blindly and willingly. I have learned, Jared, that there are very few men left in this world I dare to trust. Richard Hoskins had nothing at all against him, and look what he's turned out to be. You, Jared Inman, have a long and sordid list against you. I would indeed be an incorrigible idiot if I trusted you blindly."

Jared tightened the reins on the horses, and the carriage stopped off to one side of the avenue. Beth stopped breathing. He touched one shoulder, then the other. Slowly, he turned her toward him. Then he placed one finger under her chin and raised her face to his. She inhaled sharply at the look of unbridled passion in his black eyes.

"What are you going to do?" she mumbled.

"If I were the wild frontiersman you think I am, what do you suppose I would do?" he asked, still holding her chin with that single finger. "What would I do, Beth, to a woman who drives me mad with just one glance from those deep violet eyes?"

"Jared—"

The finger slowly traveled across her jaw, behind her ear, and into her hair. His entire hand dug into the chestnut locks at her neck and kept her face tilted toward his.

"Jared, don't do this."

"Don't do what, Beth?" he asked patiently, and lowered his head, with his free hand pulling the shawl from her low-cut bodice. He fingered the curve of her breasts. Beth shut her eyes tightly when his lips caressed the white swell of her breasts and slowly traveled upward along her throat. His tongue darted in and out against her night-cooled skin and left in its wake a trembling warmth. His mouth suddenly exploded against hers as his arms went fully around her and pulled her against him, his tongue tasting every sweet crevice her mouth offered. The shawl fell to Beth's waist as she wrapped her arms around his broad shoulders and moaned deep in her throat, responding to his plundering kiss. She ran her teeth over his tongue and pulled herself more tightly against his hard body. He tore his mouth from hers and kissed her from her cheek to her ear.

"Tell me what you want from me, Beth," he whispered.

"Jared, please, I can't think when you touch me," Beth said, groaning, kissing his tough cheek, refusing to let the fire in her veins die. "I don't want to think. I just want to—" She stopped suddenly and lifted her face from his, searching his eyes. The passion was there, lingering, but she knew nothing would come of it. She lifted her hands from his shoulders and gathered her shawl up, turning away from him. "I don't know what's happened to me," she said quietly. "In New York two months ago, I no more would have disguised myself as a man to get into a gaming room than I would have changed my mind about the vote for women. I—I've been behaving like—like—"

"A wild-eyed girl of seventeen?"

Beth glared sideways at Jared. "I've told you before, Jared. I am not the girl you found swimming naked in Lake Saratoga."

One eyebrow arched, and a grin found its way across his face. "No? Try telling that to John Morrissey, Beth," he said. "Maybe you're discovering you're more like that impulsive girl than the mature and prim young woman you think you are."

"Which would you prefer?"

He smiled and touched a strand of hair that had fallen across her brow. "Whichever you are, Beth."

"Perhaps I'm both," she said quietly, and looked away. "But who are you, Jared?"

"A wild frontiersman who would like nothing better than to haul you off into the bushes," Jared replied, refusing to be serious. He laughed heartily when Beth angrily clamped her mouth shut. "Oh, my sweet-tempered, outrageous Beth, I'm sure it will be only a matter of time before you find out more about me than you'd care to know, or have you already?"

Beth drew her knees together and her shawl about her shoulders, lifted her chin high, and watched the horses resume their course down Union Avenue. Jared chuckled beside her and began to whistle merrily. What, Beth wondered, did he think he had accomplished? She wouldn't ask him. She wouldn't ask him or tell him anything at all. He would only laugh at her now. She had told him what she had learned during her brief stay in the Club House gaming rooms, he had vented his anger, and he had kissed her. Now he was relaxed, amused with himself, amused with her.

She stiffened, not breathing.

Jared Inman was relaxed and smug because Beth hadn't uncovered his role in the Dobbs-Prentiss-Hoskins scheme.

She whirled around and glared at him, but he was busy guiding the carriage to the Prentiss's front door. "I'm not finished with you yet, Jared Inman," she told him in her best deadly voice.

He grinned at her. "I certainly hope not, because I've hardly even begun with you," he said easily, his eyes exaggeratedly traveling up and down her figure.

Beth leaped out of the carriage, but her enormous skirts got hung on one side. Jared reached over and pried them free. Beth snatched the fabric from his hands and twisted it back down where it belonged. He was trying to suppress another grin.

"Swine!" she snapped, and stalked off.

She could hear Jared's roar of laughter as he brought the carriage around the house to the stables. In spite of herself, a smile slipped across Beth's face. So very few men thought Elizabeth Stanton Harte was amusing.

Not, she thought, that she wanted Jared Inman to think everything she did or said was something to laugh about!

CHAPTER 17

Beth awoke to Ginny's screams for help. She sprang out of bed and was on her feet racing down the hall before she had even realized she was awake. Had she been dreaming? Ginny screamed again, sobbing wordlessly, and Beth pushed through the half-opened door.

"Ginny! My God, what is it?" Beth yelled frantically, but then she saw her friend standing frozen in the middle of the room. Her thin satin nightgown had been torn at the shoulders, revealing the smooth white curve of one breast.

Beth put her arms around Ginny. "It's all right, Ginny, it's all right."

"Oh, Beth," she sobbed, sinking against the taller woman. "I was so scared. He—" She sobbed again, unable to get the next word out.

"You're all right now," Beth said in as soothing a voice as she could manage through her own tenseness. Ginny had been badly frightened, but as far as Beth could tell, she hadn't been hurt or raped. "What happened? Who? Ginny, it wasn't Richard—"

Ginny cried out loudly, burying her face in Beth's cotton nightgown. "Oh, Beth, what's Richard going to think of me now? He won't want to marry me—"

"Ginny, this isn't your fault."

She pulled her face off Beth's shoulders, and the moonlight streaming in the window caught her tear-streaked face. "It was Jacques, Beth," she said, and closed her eyes as they filled with tears.

"Oh, dear."

"He—he said this was his revenge for the way I treated him," Ginny said, and sniffled as she flicked the torn nightgown with the tips of her shaking fingers. "He said there would be more. He—he's not finished yet. Oh, Beth!"

But the men of the house burst in, and Beth was unable to gather further facts from Ginny. Richard, in trousers and a nightshirt, reached her first, crying her name in alarm and scooping her up. Beth scowled. For all she knew, Richard Hoskins had paid Jacques LeBreque to terrorize Ginny.

Ginny's parents and brother followed. William was paler even than his mother, but Sophia Prentiss immediately took charge of her daughter and dispatched the men to find LeBreque. Beth backed out of the room. Jared Inman was not around.

She slipped down the hall. His door was closed, no sound coming from within. She didn't knock. She turned the knob and pushed it open.

His four-poster bed was still neatly made.

Beth frowned and closed the door again. Jared Inman hadn't been to bed. Jacques LeBreque had terrorized Ginny, but he had claimed that was only part of his revenge. More was to come.

How could he get back at her?

Louisiana.

Jacques blamed Ginny's brother in part for her decision to end their affair. Jacques had access, unquestioned access, to the thoroughbred.

Jacques also blamed Ginny's friend from New York for influencing Ginny's decision.

Beth's frown deepened.

Somehow she didn't think Jacques LeBreque would get as much satisfaction from wreaking his revenge on Beth as he would on William.

Suddenly she lifted the hem of her nightgown and dashed down the hall, down the back stairs, and out the kitchen door. The dew-soaked grass was cool on her bare feet, and her long body and flying hair cast a shadow across the moonlit lawn, as she ran, lifting her nightgown above her knees.

She slowed as she came to the open stable door. Perhaps the Prentisses were ahead of her—

There was no light inside, but, creeping toward the opening, Beth could hear Jacques LeBreque's quiet accent.

"Ah, my beautiful creature," he was saying, "I would rather kill ten men than you, but I have no choice."

Beth swallowed hard and peered into the stable. Now she could see a small kerosene lamp burning on Louisiana's stall door, but William's champion horse was standing in the middle of the stable, his coat gleaming in the glow of the lamplight.

Jacques LeBreque sighed and cocked his rifle.

"No!" Beth screamed, bursting through the door, leaping toward Jacques.

He looked up sharply, startled, and raised his rifle at her. She dove into a pile of hay on the other side of the huge horse. A shot went off, then another. The horse screeched in fright, and rolling onto her side, Beth could see him rise up onto his hind legs. She knew she was going to be trampled to death.

With another terrified scream, Louisiana dropped onto all four hooves, just missing Beth's legs, and was off. She watched his sleek body race through the open stable doors into the moonlight. Slowly, she rolled onto her back, expecting to see the barrel of Jacques LeBreque's rifle aimed at her.

Instead, she saw Jared Inman's big body looming above her. He grabbed her by the wrist and hauled her out of the hay.

"What in the name of hell did you think you were doing?" he demanded, his hand still clamped on her wrist.

Beth was too shocked, still too terrified herself, to answer.

Jared hissed furiously, "You could have been killed, you little fool!"

She glanced down at the wrist caught in his grip, but her eyes riveted on the huge, ugly revolver hanging from his other hand. She swallowed hard. "What's that?"

"A gun, what does it look like? Don't look so horrified, sweetheart," he said bitterly, "if I hadn't had this, you would be dead right now."

Beth couldn't take her eyes off the gun. "Jacques?"

"Don't fret, dear, I didn't kill him."

"But there were two shots—"

"One was from him for you, the other from me," Jared said, his tone still harsh and unsympathetic. He dropped her wrist and stepped back. "I think I wounded him in the arm, but that won't stop him from being fifty miles from Saratoga by morning." He kicked at the strewn pile of hay. "Damn!"

Beth had never seen him so angry, so out of control. She hesitated, not sure what she should do. "He—he was going to shoot Louisiana."

"I know that, damnit!" Jared shouted. "And when you pulled your stupid Hercules routine, he was going to shoot you. Damn, Beth, don't you ever think? You risked your life to save a horse. A horse!" He groaned, incredulous, angry, and kicked more hay, but then he stopped still and narrowed his black eyes at her. His fists were clenched at his sides. "William's horse," he said heavily.

Beth stared at him. Her body was trembling, and it was taking all her energy to remain standing and proud against Jared's scrutiny. He had shot a man. Right here in front of her, he had shot a man. And she was certain he was furious with himself and her because he hadn't managed to kill him.

Jared threw down his gun and took her by both shoulders, his fingers digging into the flesh beneath the thin nightgown. "Is it William, Beth?" he asked harshly. "Are you spying for him, too? Maybe I've been wrong to trust you. You risked your life for pretty William, but you won't even trust me. Tell me now, Beth. If it's William you want, you can have him."

"You'd let me go that easily?" she asked hoarsely.

He pulled her close to him, his hands lightly running down her arms. "No."

His arms slipped around her waist, his touch gentle,

soothing. Beth felt her body relax, and her lips parted and
met his willingly. She threw one arm around his neck and
with the other touched the muscles of his chest with her
flat palm. They kissed again and again, hungrily, passionately, the terror of the last moments dissolving into the
abandon of their want. Tears of relief and confusion sprang
up in Beth's eyes and washed down her cheeks, and when
Jared tasted their salty wetness, he drew her even closer.
She could feel his heart racing beneath her palm.

She laid her head on his shoulder and let him caress her
hair. "I can't go on like this," she whispered.

She could feel his chest heave against her. "Neither can
I, Beth," he said quietly. "I let Jacques get away because
of you. I had to be sure you were safe. What you do to
me, darling! I—I just don't know." He sighed again and
didn't go on.

Beth lifted her head off his shoulder and looked at him,
his black eyes narrowed at her, half his face a shadow, his
jaw set firmly. His gun at his feet. Her voice wasn't even a
whisper when she spoke. "Jared, tell me everything. Where
were you tonight? How did you get here in time to rescue
me? Why—why do you have a gun? Jared—"

He pulled away from her and turned.

Beth bit her lip and said nothing. His answer was the
broad back of his shoulders. She lifted her chin and started
toward the stable door.

"Beth."

She stopped, not turning around.

"I'll explain to the Prentisses what happened here."

"As you wish," she said crisply.

"We'll talk, Beth," he said. "But not now."

She was all the way to the stable door before Jared
spoke again.

"Is it William, Beth?" he asked again, his voice hushed,
toneless.

She turned, one hand on the doorjamb, the moonlight gleaming on her chestnut hair. "No," she said starkly, "it's you."

Beth didn't get any more sleep that night. Few in the Prentiss household did. William and Jared captured Louisiana, William, Sr., called in the law, and Richard Hoskins comforted Ginny. When the law arrived, all the men retired to the billiards room to discuss their strategy. Sophia stayed with her daughter. Beth went to bed. She knew if she stayed up any longer, she would tell Ginny the truth about her lover, and she didn't want to. Not yet. Ginny needed to recover from the shock of her attack before Beth gave her another shock, one perhaps even more horrible.

But Beth didn't sleep. She hung up the robe a servant had brought down for her, changed out of her damp and filthy nightgown, and sat up in bed drinking a glass of wine. She examined everything she knew and everything she felt about what had happened since she had arrived in Saratoga Springs. When the light of dawn rose over the mountains, she had come to only two conclusions.

She was in love with Jared Inman, and she must leave him.

She slipped out of bed and, without a robe, tiptoed down the hall. The door to Jared's room was closed. She turned the knob carefully, and pushing the door open just enough for her to squeeze in, she entered the room without looking first to see if he was there.

He was, standing in front of his window in just his trousers with his big, ugly gun pointed at her.

"Awfully handy with that thing, aren't you?" she asked fearlessly.

He set it on the nightstand. "You should knock before you enter a gentleman's room," he said dryly.

"I thought you would be asleep—or don't you ever sleep?"

He shrugged. "Occasionally." He appraised her, raking her with his eyes from head to toe. Then he grinned. "I slept Saturday night after that ridiculous ball."

"I should hope so," Beth said, refusing to flush. She moved toward him. "Would you like to get some sleep tonight?"

She stopped at the foot of his bed. She had changed into a filmy gauze nightgown with a drawstring neck. Already her naked breasts were straining against the translucent fabric. Jared slowly walked toward her and caught the end of the drawstring between his thumb and forefinger.

"It's already morning," he said.

Beth could feel a strange tingling in her mouth as she stared at Jared's dark, muscular chest, so broad and weather-worn, so much a part of his impossible masculinity. Tentatively, she reached out and brushed his manly nipples with the backs of her fingers. "I've been thinking about you for hours," she whispered.

He smiled wryly. "Then you haven't slept either?"

And with that, he pulled the drawstring and let the nightgown fall to her feet. She lifted her arms to his neck and let her bare, straining breasts rub against the rough hair on his chest. He ran his palms from her shoulders to her elbows and kissed her gently on the lips. "You're beautiful in daylight or moonlight," he said huskily.

Beth smiled against his mouth and drew herself harder into him, so that his arms went around her. He stroked down her shoulders and back to the silky curve of her buttocks. She boldly ran the tip of her tongue along his lips, moaning with delight when he seized it with his teeth and drew it into his mouth. His fingers dug into the flesh of her hips as he lifted her so that he could stand straight and they could kiss. Eagerly, they plundered the sweetness of each other's mouths.

He gently pushed her down on the bed and kissed her throat down to her breasts, capturing first one pebbled nipple in his mouth, then the other. Beth spread her arms above her head and closed her eyes against the onslaught of her senses. Jared concentrated on one breast, circling it with tiny kisses, then teasing it with darting flicks from the tip of his tongue. One hand slowly caressed a smooth thigh, and Beth groaned aloud when his fingertips brushed across the sensitive spot between her legs.

He stood up abruptly, and in one swift motion had his pants off and tossed them aside. Beth raised up on her elbows and looked at his strong, naked body, straining against his own desire. She sat up and kissed his hard stomach, wrapping her arms around his buttocks. Slowly, she brought him down to the bed with her, searching his eyes.

They kissed again, drinking deeply of each other, and she carefully guided him into her, gasping with delight when their bodies joined. Their desire was already near its peak, and Jared thrust into her as she arched for him, and for herself. She clenched his shoulders and lay still, tensed against his blinding thrusts, then she moved and met his rhythm until they reached the height of ecstasy. Their muffled cries came together, and afterward they lay in each other's arms for a long time.

When Beth heard Jared's quiet breathing, she untangled her arms and legs and sat beside him. Never had she known such pleasure, such abandon. She kissed his shoulder, and a hot tear fell on his dark skin. She brushed it away with her fingertips and slipped out of bed. She put on her nightgown and looked at Jared's sleeping figure again, wanting to remember every detail of this special dawn. Then, the tears flowing, she tiptoed back down the hall to her room.

CHAPTER 18

Beth slept for two hours, but her head was clear the minute she awoke. She was leaving Saratoga today. She threw her things into her trunk and washed. Then she put on her brown linen traveling dress, braided her hair and wound it high on her head, and placed a small brown velvet hat neatly atop it all. Her reflection in the mirror was of a determined, clear-headed woman. There were no signs of her twisted, jittery insides.

She found Virginia Prentiss sitting on a marble bench in the rose garden looking remarkably calm. "Well, good morning,'' Beth said, sliding beside her. "Did you get some sleep?"

"Some," Ginny said with a placid smile that vanished when she noticed Beth's hat and traveling dress. "What's this?"

"I'm leaving today," Beth announced. "Father is coming over on the omnibus, and I'm going back with him. I'm going to try to talk him into taking the afternoon train back to New York."

Ginny turned sideways on the bench and took her friend's hand. "Beth—but why? You don't have to leave. Is it because of last night? They'll find Jacques, and even if they don't, I'm sure he won't be back. Beth, I know you were nearly killed but—"

"It's not Jacques, Ginny," Beth said quietly. "I simply need to get back to New York. Please don't blame yourself. I've had a wonderful vacation. Tell me, have the men gone into the village yet?"

"Yes—but how did you know? They were so secretive. Father didn't tell Mother until the last minute, and Richard didn't want to tell me until I cornered him." Ginny's blue eyes bore into Beth's, and she pulled her hands sharply from her chestnut-haired friend's. Her fingers trembled. "Beth, what do you know that you aren't telling me?"

"Ginny—"

"Beth, please! I'm not a child. You don't have to protect me. Is Father—Beth, I know you've been gathering information for your father. I don't mind! Without your help, I'm sure I would never have given up Jacques—"

"I doubt that," Beth said sincerely.

Ginny was not easily distracted. She folded her hands on the lap of her sage-green lawn dress, her eyes on her feet. "What don't you want to tell me, Beth?"

Beth sighed. She wanted to leave and let the Prentisses solve their own problems. Richard Hoskins could explain himself to his fiancée as he saw fit. William could get out of the mess he had helped create. Beth sighed again, more heavily. Perhaps Ginny had been protected from reality for far too long. But what business was it of Beth's to tell her about Richard and her brother?

She wrung her hands together. How could she not tell her?

She began calmly, matter-of-factly. "Ginny, did you know the Commodore has called a meeting of the owners of most of the trunk and western railroad lines for this morning, here in Saratoga?"

Ginny shook her head. "I don't pay much attention to that sort of thing. Father doesn't own a railroad."

"No, but he's a major stockholder in several railroads," Beth said. "And so is William."

"Oh, only in the Baltimore and Ohio," Ginny said dismissively. "Daddy still controls everything else."

Beth smiled wryly. She hadn't expected Ginny to know even that much. "And no doubt your father is trying to teach his son some sound business tactics before he gives him any more control over the Prentiss empire," Beth speculated.

"I've listened to more than one fight over that very subject," Ginny admitted. "But what does that have to do with this morning's meeting and your leaving?"

"Your brother's a compulsive gambler, Ginny."

"I know that," she said quietly, looking at her hands. "He's been drinking too much as well." She turned just her face, nearly just her eyes, toward Beth. "He's in some sort of trouble, isn't he?"

Beth bit her lip and nodded.

"How bad?"

"He's overextended himself, and your father has refused to cover any more of his gambling debts, I'm sure in an effort to curb his excessive betting." Beth stared for a moment at her hands folded in her lap. "I do think your father would come to William's aid, if William asked him to, in this particular case. William has been very cleverly and maliciously exploited by a man secretly working for the B and O."

"What!"

Beth pretended not to hear Ginny's outburst, or the horror in her voice, and went on. "That man wishes to pressure William into not dumping his B and O stock, and he has done so by lending William enormous amounts of money—"

"So he could keep on gambling."

"Exactly."

"How dreadful!"

Beth nodded dully and wished she had never begun. "Now that man is calling in his loan when he knows William can't pay."

Ginny knit her brow and shook her head in commiseration with her brother. "Poor William. Oh, Beth, is there anything we can do?"

"Wait, there's more—speculation on my part, actually." Beth sighed at the sky and suddenly felt exhausted. It *would* be good to get back to New York. "The things I've just told you I learned last night while I was masquerading as Abraham Wood. Ginny, William has been counting on Louisiana to win him enough money to pay his debt, but first Louisiana was injured so he couldn't race on opening day, and then last night—"

"Jacques tried to kill him," Ginny said, going white. Suddenly, she whirled around, her eyes blazing. "Beth, are you trying to tell me Jacques is this spy? That he's the one doing this to William? Oh, Beth, how could I have been so badly duped myself! Father will disown William and me both for being so stupid!"

Beth looked at the roses, bright and red and alive in the

summer sun, and she felt a warm breeze against her cheek. How could she go on?

"Jacques may have been hired by this spy for the B and O, but that's not who it is," she said quietly. "The spy was in the poker game with William last night. William would never go into debt to someone like Jacques."

"Then who?" Ginny whirled around and grabbed Beth by the shoulders. "Jared? Oh, Beth—"

Beth shook her head. "I don't know what his role in all this is, but, Ginny—" she hesitated, closed her eyes briefly, then spoke—"Ginny, it's Richard."

Her hands dropped away from Beth's shoulders and she sat, pale, frozen with shock. "He's a lawyer from Baltimore," she said in a hushed, choked voice. "He works for a private firm."

"He works for John Garrett."

Ginny turned her back to Beth and refused to speak.

Beth sighed and touched her friend on the shoulder. "I'm sorry, Ginny," she said quietly.

Ginny didn't acknowledge her presence or her touch. Beth rose wearily and walked softly through the grass back to the house. She asked a servant to bring down her trunk and set it in the foyer. Then she sat in the drawing room and read her George Eliot novel while she waited for her father to arrive.

He was, she thought, rather late.

Fifteen minutes later, she heard a clunk in the hall. She held her place with her forefinger and went to see what was going on. Ginny, in a neat maroon traveling dress and a black velvet hat, was directing a servant as he set a second trunk beside Beth's. Her face was pale, her hair twisted into a severe chignon, but there was determination in her blue eyes. She smiled feebly at Beth.

"Mother has gone to the village for a luncheon with the Episcopal women," she said. "I left her and Father a note. I thought you wouldn't object if I rode to New York with you and your father."

Beth dropped her book on the floor and ran from the doorway to her friend, hugging her silently. She knew they both held back tears.

They broke apart at the clatter of a carriage at the front door. Beth peered out the window and saw her father's lanky figure jump lightly out of the two-horse open carriage. A breeze caught his thick iron-gray hair and sent it waving in every direction. Judge Harte didn't seem to notice.

"Omnibus, my foot," Beth said, delighted. "The old elitist rented a carriage. Well, that should make our departure that much easier." She opened the door for him. "Hello, Father."

He grinned at his daughter. " 'Morning, Beth, or is it afternoon already? Why on earth are you dressed like a sourpuss dowager?" He came inside and saw the two trunks. "Ah-ha, planning a trip, I see.

"I thought I could persuade you to take the afternoon train with us."

He raised both eyebrows, first at his daughter, then at Ginny. "I only arrived yesterday."

"I should think twenty-four hours of Saratoga Springs would be more than enough for you," Beth said affectionately, but her face grew serious. "We have to leave, Father. Ginny and I. You don't have to come with us—"

"Nonsense, nonsense," he said. "As you say, I get my fill of Saratoga within five minutes of arriving at the train station. And, fortunately for you two, my reasons for coming up here seem to be well taken care of." He held up a silencing hand at his daughter. "If you won't ask me questions, I won't ask you. It's better to exit now and demand explanations later, wouldn't you agree?"

Ginny nodded briskly. "Yes, please, can we leave now?"

"Just as I thought," the judge said dryly. "You are

leaving a note for your parents, aren't you, Miss Prentiss?"

She nodded reluctantly.

"You told them you would be in my care? They would worry about such things."

"Yes, sir," she said quietly.

"And if I tried to persuade either of you to stay put instead of running off like a couple of beheaded chickens, you would ignore me and run off anyway?"

"You're absolutely right, Father," Beth said, impatient but not irritated. "Now let's go!"

"You won't wait until tomorrow?" he asked, persevering.

Ginny shook her head, and both Hartes could see the level of her misery in her pale skin and reddening eyes. "I don't want to stay here another minute, Judge Harte. I must go now, even if you refuse to take me."

"Humph, well, it's for the best, then. You do have a strong back lurking about for these trunks, don't you?"

"Yes, of course," Ginny said, and called for two servants, who deposited the trunks in Judge Harte's carriage and wished the two young women a pleasant trip. They asked no questions, but questions were in their eyes.

The judge pulled his daughter aside for a moment as Ginny climbed into the carriage. "You told her about Hoskins, didn't you?" he asked.

"I had to."

He grunted. "I suppose, from your view of matters."

"What's that supposed to mean?"

He waved a hand. "Later."

"Father—"

But he was saying no more. Beth followed him into the carriage, and they rode off into the sunshine. It would, Beth thought, be a warm day. Stifling in New York, no doubt, but she didn't care. She had to get away from Jared Inman. But what had her father meant? She recalled that

Jared had decided Judge Robert Lowell Harte and his daughter were a pair of incorrigible idiots. Had Jared been to see her father? Was that why he had been late?

They stopped at the Clarendon so the judge could collect his bags. He suggested they dine at the hotel, but Ginny wanted to wait and have lunch on the train. When he shrugged in resignation and went into the hotel, Beth and Ginny sank low into the carriage.

"This is ridiculous," Beth muttered.

"Why? You know I can't face Richard—"

"We're running away, Ginny. Look, if I've learned anything in my twenty-four years on this earth, it's that I can't run away from problems. I can't escape. Sneaking away to New York isn't going to solve anything." She sighed, impatient with herself, and was already climbing out of the carriage. "This town hasn't heard the last of Elizabeth Stanton Harte. Care to join me?"

"I can't, Beth," Ginny said desperately. "Oh, Beth—"

"It's all right, Ginny," Beth reassured her. "Father will drive you to the train station." She winked and grinned, her violet eyes glowing. "Wish me luck!"

She smoothed out her skirts, made sure her hat was on straight and, with her head held high, marched down Braodway to Congress Hall. Her stomach suddenly began to growl with hunger. She smiled to herself. Better to starve than to mope, she thought, and made her way through the crowds into the lobby. She walked straight to the front desk.

"Where's the railroad meeting being held?" she asked the thin man behind the counter.

"I—um—" he said, floundering. If Cornelius Vanderbilt and two dozen railroad men wanted to keep their meeting secret, or at least pretend no one knew about it, then a hotel clerk wasn't going to tell a prim young woman, obviously not a railroad executive or one's wife, about it.

He shook his head and sniffled. "I don't know what you're talking about."

"Of course not," Beth said crisply.

She wandered around the huge, opulent lobby. She tried to think of something else. Congress Hall had a mile-and-a-half of halls. She couldn't very well sneak through all of them and find the meeting room.

Five minutes later, Cornelius Vanderbilt and J. H. Devereux walked into the lobby from the maze of halls. Beth cursed to herself. The meeting was already over! She rushed back out onto the street and searched the crowd for familiar faces. She saw a railroad man and his wife walking down Broadway. Damn! Her resolve had come upon her too late. She should have been up and out of the house with the men instead of hanging around moping and packing her trunk.

"Oh, Jared, Jared," she said in frustration. "The things you do to me!"

Then she saw William walking across Broadway toward her. He looked exhausted even in his crisp, elegant suit, but he managed a smile when he saw her. "Elizabeth, I didn't expect to see you here!" he said, pleased.

"I came to town with my father," Beth explained. "William, I know about your gambling debts. I know about Richard Hoskins. What are you going to do?"

He shook his head in amazement. "You always know more than you should, Elizabeth," he said, taking her hands in his. "It's what I've always admired about you. If you must know—and I'm sure you will insist that you must—Richard and I have come to an agreement."

"You agreed to Richard's terms," she stated.

He squinted at her in the sun. "How did you find out? I should know better than to ask, I suppose. Yes, Elizabeth, I agreed to his terms. I nearly ruined myself with my own excesses and stupidity. I—I don't want to discuss it. It's over now."

"No, it's not," Beth said stoutly. "Your sister is in love with Richard."

"Yes, but she doesn't know about all this. It's just as well. Richard's methods may have been less than noble, but in the end he saved me a great deal of embarrassment."

Beth swallowed guiltily. "Ginny does know about Richard. I told her."

"Oh, no, Elizabeth," he said, grimacing. "What did she say? What is she going to do?"

"She is going to take the next train out of Saratoga back to New York. If Hoskins is such a saint all of a sudden, perhaps you should tell her—both of us—what has been going on around here."

William shook his head dismally. "Perhaps."

"Now, William."

"Will you walk with me in the park, Elizabeth?"

"I want to know what went on here this morning," Beth said tartly, wishing he wouldn't hold her hand. She extracted it from his grip, but he only took her by the upper arm. There had been a time when Beth would have wished for William's attentions, his touch, his understanding—years ago, when she had envisioned them working together for reforms and women's voting rights. Now she was impatient for information. She didn't want his caresses. "What happened at the railroad meeting? Were you there?"

William smiled indulgently. "You're so amusing, Elizabeth."

She gave a low growl of frustration, but followed him toward the sprawling Club House lawns. His hand was still lightly on her upper arm.

"Were any decisions made? Are they going to change the rates? Did the Commodore succeed in restricting counterproductive forms of competition?" Beth huffed angrily when William grinned stupidly at her. "I am not amusing!"

They were in the shade of a giant elm. William suddenly turned into Beth and pulled her close to him, his hands on her shoulders. "Elizabeth, I love you," he said abruptly. "I've been confused and stupid and cruel, but please believe that I couldn't be more in love with you. You're beautiful, you're courageous, you're tender. Elizabeth, you're everything I could want in a woman."

"William—"

"Please say you'll marry me."

"William!" Beth snapped, and pulled herself out of his embrace. Once she would have prayed for such words from him. What his money and prestige could do for her cause! But now she knew better. Not only did she not love him—at one time she even would have considered a loveless marriage if it would further her cause—but she knew William would tolerate her only if he were in control of her. "I'm flattered," she went on quietly. "I think you even believe what you're saying, but we both know we could never be happy together."

He drew her against his chest. "Elizabeth, please don't push me away now. I've changed. I—I want you so badly."

"William, please stop before we both embarrass ourselves. I can't marry you."

"No, Elizabeth—"

"I'm not the woman you think I am, William, and, besides that, I'm in love with another man."

He dropped his hands to his sides, and Beth quickly took two steps backward. "Who?" Then his teeth clenched, and anger reddened his face. "Jared Inman."

Beth said nothing.

"Then you aren't the woman I thought you were, Elizabeth," he said crisply, disapprovingly.

"I said I wasn't."

He inhaled sharply, humiliated.

Beth smiled, her eyes laughing. "Oh, William, don't be so angry with yourself! Just add your offer of marriage to your list of mistakes for the summer. Now, about Ginny and Richard—"

But William, without so much as glancing at her, walked away. Beth opened her mouth to call him back, but shut it again. The man had talked himself into being in love with her, and she had just talked him out of it. She told herself she should be a bit more understanding and let him get over it before she questioned him further.

She would give him thirty minutes, perhaps an hour, before she tracked him down again.

She tucked a stray lock of hair under her hat and marched off toward Congress Street. Now, she thought, what to do about Ginny? Beth doubted if in Ginny's shoes she would forgive Richard Hoskins easily, but then Beth had a much stricter code of conduct than Virginia Prentiss. She laughed aloud. Whom was she kidding? She was in love with a man accused of murder, corruption, robbery, and simple brutality.

Not accused of, she thought, suspected of. And not murder, killing in self-defense. Perhaps. What did it matter? Continuing any sort of affair with Jared Inman would be suicidal.

She was still preoccupied, musing, when she saw the man in question cross Congress Street and head down Broadway. He didn't see her. Beth lifted her skirts and ran up to him.

"Hello," she said casually.

He gave her a cursory glance, but didn't slacken his pace.

"Nice afternoon," she added.

He grunted.

"Where are you going?"

"None of your business, Beth."

"Friendly this afternoon, aren't we?"

"Don't pester me, Beth, I'm not in the mood."

She shrugged, unoffended, and found herself nearly trotting to keep up with him. "I thought you were always in the mood for me," she said with a mischievous smile.

The corners of his mouth twisted upward. "Beth for godsake!"

"Are you a criminal?"

"Not now, Beth!"

"Are you a railroad spy?"

"Leave me alone."

Two men, deeply engaged in conversation, walked directly in their path, and Beth had to jump aside to let them pass between her and Jared.

She ran to catch up with him. "Did you hire Jacques to shoot Louisiana?"

"I shot Jacques, remember?"

"Jared, damnit, will you stop a minute and talk to me! I can't keep up with you. I hardly slept last night."

He gave her a sideways glance, never slackening his pace. "Young ladies shouldn't curse."

They were nearly to the Clarendon, but looking ahead, Beth didn't see her father's rented carriage. "You're infuriating!" she seethed. "Do you know what kind of arrangement William and Richard made?"

"Yes."

She nearly ran into a stunningly dressed woman, but Jared didn't go on and explain as she had expected. "You're treating me like some empty-headed damsel—"

"I'm in a hurry, Beth."

"Aren't we the big, important man?"

He eyed her sourly.

Beth was nearly out of breath. "The least you can do is tell me if it was legal!"

He stopped abruptly and caught Beth by the elbows as she nearly catapulted past him. He grinned down at her. "If what was legal?" he asked, purposely obtuse. "This morning? It may not have been legal, darling Beth, but it certainly was fun. And this, Miss Harte, is where you stop. No more questions, no more badgering. Go find your father and have tea and crumpets with him."

"I don't have to obey you, Mr. Inman," she said, crossing her arms over her breasts. Her hat, she knew, was askew, but she didn't touch it.

Jared, however, did, setting it squarely back on top of her head. "If you follow me, Beth Harte, I am going to drag you back here by your hair and lock you in your father's room." His jaw set squarely, and he furrowed his thick brows at her. "I mean that, Beth. Don't follow me. You nearly got us both killed last night."

She scowled.

He resumed his hurried pace, but looked over his shoulder at her a final time. "I'll be back for you, Beth!"

"You'd damned well better be!" she shouted after him.

Several sets of eyes in the crowd around the Clarendon glared disapprovingly at her. Beth shrugged, smiled amiably, and went inside.

The desk clerk informed her that Judge Robert Lowell Harte had not checked out of his room. So, Beth thought, he'd never had any intention of accompanying her to New York! But she suspected he had agreed to bring Ginny to the train station in hopes that someone would get there to change her mind before the train left. Beth found herself cursing again, under her breath this time, and walked back out onto the street.

Richard Hoskins was dashing up Broadway toward the Clarendon. He saw Beth, nearly knocked over an elderly man with a cane, and ran up to her, jerking her by the shoulder. His face was white and glistening with perspiration. "I just saw William," he said. "Where's Ginny?"

"About to board the train for New York, I should think," Beth said.

He groaned, shoving his hair back with the palm of one hand. "Oh, God, how could I have gotten myself into such a mess!"

"By being deceitful," Beth said unsympathetically.

"I would have told her."

"Before or after the wedding?"

He beat one of the graceful columns of the hotel with his fist.

"That isn't going to solve anything," Beth said tartly. "I suggest you trot yourself over to the train station and do some fast explaining. Be dead honest with her, Richard. I've told her everything." She grinned boldly. "You can thank me later."

"How did you know?" he asked, even as he turned to go.

"Abraham Wood is a good friend of mine," she said to his back. "We're the only people we know with violet eyes." He turned and glared at her in horror. She grinned and waved. "Better hurry."

And he was gone.

CHAPTER 19

Jared Inman did not come.

Beth waited in the busy lobby of the Clarendon Hotel, but he never returned. She told herself she wasn't surprised. She expected as much from him. She was just as glad he hadn't come. But then the big lobby doors would push open, and her eyes would shoot up to see who it was. She would make a face, fold her hands on her lap, and continue to wait.

Her father found her in that position. He was alone, looking calm and not at all confused, more amused, Beth thought, than anything else. He nodded to a half-dozen people who recognized him as he made his way to his daughter's velvet chair.

"I see you've had a change of plans," he said mildly.

"I couldn't run away," Beth replied. "Where's Ginny?"

"With her Richard. He was most repentant, it seemed to me, but I retreated rather discreetly." He yawned and rubbed his chin. "Would you care to join me in a cup of tea?"

"Tea! Father, after what's happened, you can stand there and calmly invite me to a cup of tea?" she huffed in exasperation. "I don't want tea!"

"Then I suggest you return to the Prentisses and resume your vacation."

Beth groaned.

Her father put a bony hand on her shoulder. "You know William and Richard have settled their differences?"

"Yes."

"Have you wondered what Elijah Dobbs plans to do now that William has pulled out?" the judge asked quietly.

Beth's eyes shot up to his. "Find someone else to put up money for this railroad scheme of his." She bit her lip. "Father, there must be hundreds of men willing to go in with Dobbs!"

"So why did he choose William for his partner?"

Her father was speaking as though he knew the answer. Beth frowned. "Well, why did he?"

"I don't know," he replied maddeningly.

"We're assuming William was planning to go in with Dobbs," Beth said pensively. "We don't know that for certain."

"That we don't."

Beth stared up at her father. He had removed his hand from her shoulder and shoved it into a trouser pocket. She waited for him to explain himself.

"Jared Inman came to see me this morning."

Beth stiffened.

"He said something about our being incorrigible—"

"Idiots," Beth finished.

"No, no, he didn't call me an idiot."

"Lucky you."

Her father smiled. "He's an interesting man. He said he planned to stay on in Saratoga for a few more days."

Beth's eyes narrowed.

"I believe he will remain a guest at the Prentiss cottage, unless—"

When he stopped midsentence, Beth prodded him. "Unless what, Father?"

"Oh, just something he said." He seemed to shake off a distracting thought and looked down at his daughter. "I believe he and certainly Elijah Dobbs, and perhaps even William, bear further watching."

Beth rested back in her chair and gave her father a long look. "You want me to continue spying for you."

"Gathering information for the worthy cause of ending corruption in our society," the judge replied airily.

She snorted.

He withdrew his hands from his pockets and looked at his watch. "Of course," he went on, seemingly absently, "we have yet to settle the matter of Jacques LeBreque."

Suddenly, Beth paled. If Richard Hoskins had put Jacques up to terrorizing Ginny and shooting William's horse—

How could she have even considered reuniting Richard and Ginny!

"You may take my carriage," her father said. "I'll be in touch."

Beth rose slowly. Jared still hadn't come. She knew now that he wouldn't. She pursed her lips firmly, glanced at her father's retreating lanky figure, and left.

She was nearly fainting with hunger when she halted the carriage in front of the Prentiss cottage, but she saw no servants about when she climbed down. She scowled at the monstrous trunk in the back of the carriage. Tracking down a strong back, as her father would say, would only cause delay. She grabbed one handle of the trunk and could just barely reach around to grab the other.

"Here we go with the Hercules act again."

Beth whirled around to see Jared Inman, sauntering toward her from the house. He looked taller than usual. He was dressed handsomely in a double-breasted black frock coat, vest, stiff white shirt with a black string tie, and leather boots. He had a glass of scotch in one hand. Beth realized her heart was beating in her throat. She glowered at him and turned back to her trunk.

Jared leaned over and set his glass next to the trunk. Then he covered her hands, still clenching the handles, with his. She could smell the scotch on his breath. Without a word, he lifted the trunk, with her in between, crushing her fingers. He turned her and the trunk around as he dropped it on the ground, just missing her toes.

Beth tried to turn into him, but there wasn't enough room. She tripped and landed squarely on the rounded top of the trunk.

"Should I be impressed?" she asked sarcastically.

He shrugged and retrieved his scotch. "If brute strength impresses you," he said, eyeing her, still sprawled on the trunk. "Where have you been?"

"Waiting for you, fool that I am."

"You planned to go to New York."

She rose and examined her sore fingers. "I should have."

"You were going to run out on me, Beth," Jared told her as he moved closer. "If you had, I still would have come for you. You know that, don't you? You can't run away from me, Beth.''

She scoffed and started toward the house.

He grabbed her by the upper arm and spun her around. His face was close to hers, and she could see his jaw set firmly, his black eyes narrowed. "You should take my feelings for you seriously," he said in a harsh whisper.

She looked away and concentrated on a maple sapling. "And what are your feelings for me?"

"What?"

She looked back at him and saw confusion in his eyes.

He dropped her arm. "I have taken you into my bed, saved your life, traveled three thousand miles to find you, and you still dare to ask how I feel about you?"

"You've never told me, Jared," she said haughtily. "And you know I don't believe you traveled three thousand miles to find me after seven years."

Jared turned away, his boots grinding on the cobblestones. "I have to go away for a few days, Beth," he said starkly. "Perhaps longer." He paused, still not looking at her. "Will you wait for me?"

Beth felt her throat tighten and her blood run hot. This morning she had meant to leave this man. Now he was asking her to wait for him. "Where are you going?"

He gulped his scotch, and Beth knew he wasn't going to answer.

"I plan to return to New York in a few days," she said. "Then wait for me there."

"For how long, Jared? A few days, maybe longer. What does that mean? Until Christmas? Spring? Until I begin turning gray? How long, Jared?" She walked toward him and touched his hand. "Take me with you."

"No."

"Why not?"

He spun around at her. "Because I won't! You're not

going with me, Beth. You're going to stay here and wait
for me. If you don't, I'll find you. I don't care where you
go or where you hide, I'll find you." He caught a lock of
her hair between his fingers and smiled suddenly, kissing
the few strands. "I promise you that, Beth," he added
gently.

"When are you leaving?"

"Now."

She shut her eyes, but Jared lightly kissed each lid.
"You can't order me about," she said.

"You're right. I don't have any business ordering you
around. Please wait for me, Beth, and accept that you
can't go with me." He brushed her cheek with the back of
one hand. "Please."

"If you'll tell me where you're going."

"I can't."

"Because you don't trust me," she said heavily.

"Beth—"

She backed away without a word, then turned and went
inside. Jared didn't stop her. She closed the door behind
her and leaned against it. Her heart was racing, her head
dizzy with hunger and fatigue, her brow perspiring. He
was leaving! The questions still unanswered flew at her,
but Beth resolutely rose up straight and calmed herself.
She would eat, then she would make her plans.

She requested a tray be brought to her room and headed
upstairs to peel off her dusty clothes. She wondered if
Ginny would take Hoskins back. His dealings with William
were underhanded to be sure, but no worse than the tactics
of the most respected businessmen in the country. Certainly more despicable practices went on daily. Not, Beth
thought, that she approved. They were precisely the sort of
thing she and her father were trying to end.

A scrap of paper lay on her pillow. She picked it up and
scowled at the familiar scrawl: "I stole your carriage. That

should keep you put. Even if you don't wait for me, darling dear, I'll find you. Remember that. J.''
She read it again.

She could hear his taunting voice, his deep laugh, see the amused look on his face as he wrote the note. It was all a joke to him. He knew whom he was. He knew if he had hired Jacques LeBreque. He wasn't a mystery to himself.

She stomped around her room.

''The arrogance of it!'' She glanced at the slanted ''J.'' Not ''Love. Jared,'' but simply ''J.'' She scowled and made a face at the words in her hand. '' 'Darling dear.' Ha!''

But even as she stomped around, she realized she wasn't angry. Jared hadn't left without thinking again about her. He hadn't left in a huff. She was, she thought, oddly reassured.

She looked at the note in her hand once again. '' 'Even if you don't wait for me, darling dear, I'll find you.' '' She shrugged, sighed, and crumpled the paper in her hand. ''If you can find me wherever I hide, Jared Inman, I can find you.''

And with that, she ate a huge lunch and took a long, soothing, hot bath. She had the feeling if she wanted to know where to begin looking for Jared Inman, she should ask one Judge Robert Lowell Harte. Her father, she had begun to suspect, had not told her everything.

Beth did not see her father until the following morning. She was standing on a rock above the still water of Lake Saratoga, her dress, the sky, and the lake all the same shade of gray. Her hair curled loosely down her back, tied off her face with the thinnest of velvet ribbons. She was ready to leave Saratoga. Her trunk was packed, and she had arranged for transportation into the village for the afternoon train. She would ask her father to join her, but she would leave without him if necessary. Already she had begun to despair of picking up Jared Inman's trail.

Judge Harte walked up beside her with his pipe in hand. "Rain before dinner," he predicted.

"Good morning, Father," she said, and stepped down off the rock. "I wasn't expecting you."

"I've decided to return to New York today, Beth," he said without preamble.

"So have I."

"I'm not surprised," he said mildly.

"Jared's gone, LeBreque's gone, and William's leaving this evening—"

"I beg your pardon?"

Beth smiled smugly. So she knew something her father didn't for once! "He announced at dinner that he planned to return to New York this evening. I think he's too embarrassed to stay here."

Judge Harte thoughtfully chewed on the end of his pipe. "I see."

"I don't see how I can continue my mission for you with only Ginny and her parents here to observe," Beth added.

What about Hoskins?"

"Ginny's sent him back to Baltimore—and I believe he had to report to Mr. Garrett in any case," Beth explained as they started across the lawns. "She will forgive him, but I think she wants to make him suffer first. What he did to William—and her—was nearly unforgivable. I believe Ginny wants to be sure she's not making another mistake. I'm still the only one who knows that they had actually agreed to marry."

"Then she doesn't have her father's permission?"

Beth shook her head.

"Well, I'm sure a prison sentence would be no worse punishment for Hoskins," the judge mused. He pulled his pipe out of his mouth and pointed it at his daughter. "You could stay here and have that vacation you so richly deserve. Enjoy the races, the springs, the company of your friend—''

"I would rather track down Jared Inman."

A smile snuck across her father's face, but he quickly stuck his pipe back in his mouth.

"I am not trying to amuse you, Father," Beth said hotly. "I should think you would want the answers to all the remaining questions—''

"But are you dispassionate enough to help find those answers?" he asked levelly.

Beth scowled. "I am not dispassionate, and neither are you! Why should we be? For heaven's sake, I was nearly killed because of this whole affair!"

"As I understand it," the judge began wryly, "you were nearly killed because of your incorrigible idiocy."

Beth stopped abruptly in the dew-soaked grass and stared at her father. He was trying to be inscrutable. "You've seen Jared," she accused.

He waved his pipe. "He returned the carriage."

"How good of him."

"We had a nice cup of tea together."

Beth snorted and kicked a tuft of grass. "You like anyone who'll have a cup of tea with you. What did he say?"

"That he was leaving Saratoga."

"I know that much!"

"Be patient, Beth," Judge Harte admonished gently, his eyes twinkling.

Beth growled.

"He mentioned that Elijah Dobbs and his family were returning to St. Louis today."

"A regular exodus," Beth muttered.

"Indeed."

"What else did he say?" she prodded.

"He refused to tell me where he was going himself

because he knew you would drag it out of me." He glanced at his daughter. "I am an incorrigible idiot, too, you know," he said facetiously.

"Jared is an arrogant bastard."

"Your language, my dear."

She kicked another tuft of grass, but they resumed their course to the house.

"I think there is far too much secrecy between you two," the judge went on placidly. "You don't trust each other because you don't know each other."

"I don't need a lecture, Father," Beth said, not entirely exasperated with him yet. "I need directions to where to find Jared."

"Oh, he'll turn up," he replied with what Beth thought was totally unreliable confidence. He was waving his pipe at her again. "In the meantime, I would like to send you on another little mission."

Beth simply shook her head and noticed that the ends of her skirts were wet from the grass. Like Jared, Judge Harte would tell his daughter only what he chose to tell her. Beth knew this, but she also knew that, unlike Jared, it had nothing to do with her being a woman. Her father's occasional reticence about his "matters" derived from his peculiar sense of how to accomplish a task and from his own ideas of how the world should be run—not to mention his sense of adventure. Beth had more opportunity to see how the mind of Judge Robert Lowell Harte worked, but that didn't mean she understood it any better than anyone else. She merely knew how to deal with it.

She knew, in essence, when to wait.

They were nearly to the back door when her father resumed. "I would like you to travel to St. Louis."

Again Beth waited.

"I have arranged for you to speak about women's voting rights before a group of Episcopal women—at one of their luncheons, I believe." He puffed on his pipe. "I thought you might be anxious to get back to your work."

Her brow furrowed, but still she waited.

"And, of course, you would want to look in on the Dobbs family while you're there. You and Melissa became tolerable friends, did you not?"

"Tolerable," Beth admitted.

The judge opened the back door for his daughter. "Good, then it's settled. Would you like to borrow fare for your trip, or do you have enough money left after your fiasco at the casino?"

Beth shook her head even as she grinned. "Father, I think Jared Inman is right about us."

Her father laughed heartily. "So do I, daughter!"

CHAPTER 20

Two days later, Beth was in Baltimore boarding the B & O's American Central Line to St. Louis. She had traveled up and down the Eastern Seaboard, but never to America's heartland. Even alone and preoccupied with her thoughts of Jared Inman, she was looking forward to her trip. It would take less than forty-eight hours and require the services of four of John Garrett's railroads: the B & O to Wheeling, the Northwestern Railroad of Virginia to Parkersburg, the Marietta and Cincinnati to the latter, and the Ohio and Mississippi to St. Louis. As much as Beth complained about railroad corruption and inattention to safety and passenger rights, she did consider it the most efficient and comfortable way to travel.

Her two-day journey was spent aboard one of George Pullman's new ladies' sleeping cars. It was a coach by day and a sleeper by night, and its elegance rivaled that of many city houses. Beth wondered at the intricate inlaid woods, the rich red velvet drapes, the plate-glass mirrors, the finest linens. Everything was done to make the wealthy passengers feel pampered and not too far from home.

By day Beth worked on her notes for her speech and watched the American countryside pass by her window. Her father had warned her that the Beecher-Tilton scandal would no doubt prompt an even deeper hostility toward the vote for women among her audience. Henry Ward Beecher, a proponent of women's suffrage and one of the nation's most prominent and respected ministers, was accused of engaging in an adulterous relationship with Libby Tilton, a member of his congregation.

"The public wishes to believe that the good reverend and the shy Mrs. Tilton are above such a human act," Judge Harte said, "but I believe the investigation will reveal that indeed they are not."

"You mean they did have an affair?"

"Years ago," her father said with a wave of his pipe. "It would have been forgotten entirely if Victoria Woodhull had kept quiet."

Woodhull was not popular. She advocated such radical ideals as free love and open divorce, besides women's suffrage, and had even dared to run for President of the United States. Judge Harte and his daughter regarded her as a spirited and well-intentioned eccentric, but the public was less charitable. In some circles, hanging was considered too good for Victoria Woodhull.

"She announced that Libby Tilton and Henry Ward Beecher had been lovers," Beth said.

"And so Theodore Tilton, Libby's former husband, brought charges against Beecher," the judge added, "and the public, bored with stories of corruption and economic collapse, seized upon the scandal. All summer we have heard nothing but how this minister and kind lady have become the victims of flamboyant Victoria and low Theodore."

Theodore Tilton and Victoria Woodhull had surely practiced her free-love principles, but they weren't minister and lady and no charges were brought against them. So Henry Ward Beecher was spending the summer defending himself against scandal.

"I don't think it's anybody's business," Beth declared. "Henry Beecher is a good man, even if he did have a brief affair with Libby Tilton."

"Well, Beth, whatever is the outcome of the investigation, I fear the suffrage movement will suffer," her father said seriously.

Now, as Beth perused the back issues of several New York newspapers, she suspected her father was right. The Beecher-Tilton scandal would leave a bad taste in people's mouths. Elizabeth Cady Stanton and Susan B. Anthony were caught hopelessly in the middle. On the one hand was Henry Ward Beecher, president of the American Suffrage Association. On the other were Victoria Woodhull, flamboyant advocate of women's equality, and her sidekick Theodore Tilton. Who had done what, rightly or wrongly, wouldn't matter in the end. In the end, Beth guessed people would blame women and their quest for voting rights. The scandal would be used over and over against them.

She shook her head and wondered what she would tell the Episcopal women of St. Louis. She could hear their

outraged questions now. Miss Harte, wasn't it Reverend
Beecher's interest in suffrage that corrupted him? Miss
Harte, do you truly wish to give the vote to women like
Victoria Woodhull? Miss Harte, do you believe Mrs. Tilton's
husband ever would have strayed if women kept to their
proper sphere? Miss Harte, in light of what has happened,
how can you continue to advocate women's suffrage?

And, of course, the ever-present, ever-unasked question:
If women do receive voting privileges, will our husbands
turn against us?

Beth smiled. No, she wasn't afraid of any of their
questions. Ah, how she missed her work!

On the second day of her journey, Beth saw a familiar
face in the dining car. Just as she was entering the ornate
car for lunch, William Prentiss, Jr., was leaving. She was
sure he hadn't seen her. She sat down to a luncheon of
broiled quail, but hardly tasted a morsel. Was this just a
harmless coincidence?

"There are," she muttered, "no such things as coinci-
dences."

Then what was William doing on a train to St. Louis?

Elijah Dobbs. Beth was positive William was going to
see Elijah Dobbs. But why? He had no money for Dobbs's
secret railroad!

She would wire her father the moment she reached St.
Louis and tell him about this new development. Would it,
she wondered, surprise him?

Late that afternoon the train crossed the just-opened
Eads Bridge into the sprawling river city of St. Louis.
Beth had read about the bridge. It was the first to span the
Mississippi River and had employed the most advanced
engineering techniques the world had to offer. It was over
a mile long and promised to be safe, but Beth still felt her
heart beating rapidly as she stared down at the muddy
river, crowded with boats, far below. Above the railroad

tracks, a platform had been laid so wagons could cross the bridge, thus giving it a dual purpose.

St. Louis was a city of some three-hundred-thousand inhabitants, the gateway to the West, the entry port of the Mississippi, from which it was protected by an intricate system of levees. East-West and North-South trade crossed in St. Louis.

At the train station, Beth waited for a porter to bring out her trunk and watched for William. She caught her breath, quickly dodging behind a post, when she saw him being met by Elijah Dobbs. The porter followed as she raced outside. Elijah had a hooded carriage waiting. Beth quickly flagged down a cab, but as the porter and driver together hoisted her trunk aboard, she realized there was no hurry. Her father had given her Dobbs's address. When she was ready, she knew where to find him.

And William.

Now she longed only to find a hotel and shed her trim mustard traveling dress and take a sudsy, tepid bath. St. Louis was stiflingly hot and humid, particularly in comparison to Saratoga Springs.

She tipped the porter and prepared to climb into the cab.

"Well, Beth, you're as dowdy as ever," Jared's voice said behind her.

She flew around, almost into his arms. He looked down at her, his black eyes betraying the anger the rest of his face so carefully concealed.

"Funny, isn't it," he said through clenched teeth, "I'm not surprised to see you."

She straightened up haughtily, recovering from her shock. "Nor I you," she said coolly.

He was wearing his usual sack coat and trousers, both of brown twill. His hair was tousled, and sweat dripped from his temples. His boots were dusty. He did not look happy to see Beth.

Her violet eyes sparkled with determination. "If you'll excuse me, I need to find a room."

"Dammit, Beth, you just hopped off a train on a bright and sunny day in a strange city and don't even know where in hell you're going to spend the night?"

"More or less."

He groaned in exasperation. "Your father sent you, didn't he?"

She opened her mouth, but nothing came out.

"You're both outrageous! You do exactly as you please, don't you?" His eyes darkened suddenly. "You followed your precious William."

Beth lifted her shoulders airily. "I would have followed you, but you didn't tell me where you were going."

He muttered something, then pushed past her and spoke to the cab driver. "I'm on horseback. You can follow me."

Beth grabbed his elbow. "Jared Inman, how dare you make decisions for me? I'll—"

"You'll follow me," he declared.

She watched in frustration as he stalked off. The driver turned questioning eyes toward her. She sighed and pointed vaguely toward Jared. "Follow him," she said dryly.

She thought the driver grinned.

Jared led them through the streets of St. Louis, past blocks of factories and warehouses, and, finally, to the riverfront. They rode along the docks and levees, and Beth stared, fascinated, at the dozens and dozens of massive steamboats coming into dock, just pulling out, or chugging along in the great brown waters. The Eads Bridge was high enough for them to pass beneath it, but Beth knew any bridges too low for riverboats would have a difficult time crossing the Mississippi.

At last Jared stopped in front of a hotel, or at least a badly painted sign above its front door claimed that was what it was. Beth climbed out of the carriage, paid the driver, and wrinkled her nose at the unpretentious wooden building in what she guessed was not one of St. Louis's finer neighborhoods. Jared stepped past her and hauled down her trunk.

"I should be getting used to this," he muttered, and carried it into the hotel lobby, such as it was.

He didn't pause at the front desk, and Beth, confused, trotted after him up the plain oak stairs. There were no marble floors or allegorical paintings or dining rooms that could seat a thousand. No rugs, for that matter, Beth observed. Jared walked up two flights and dropped the trunk in front of an unnumbered room. He dug a key from his pants pocket, unlocked the door, and dragged the trunk inside.

Beth followed.

It was a small room with a brass double bed covered with a thin white spread, an oak bureau, a washstand, and a clothes rack. Beth swallowed. Jared's clothes hung from the rack, and his good pair of boots stood at the foot of the bed. He was breathing hard when he rose up straight from the trunk and looked at her.

"You look like a virgin ready for sacrifice," he said.

"Jared, I can't stay here with you!"

"Why not?"

She breathed in through her nose. "It's not right."

"This is St. Louis, Beth. Nobody cares. Nobody knows you or Judge Robert Lowell Harte." He raised his left leg and placed his dirty boot on her trunk. "Or would you rather stay with William?"

Beth didn't move from the doorway. "I am to speak before a group of Episcopal women. If they discover I'm staying here with you—"

"You're what?"

"I came to St. Louis to address a group of Episcopal

women on the subject of women's voting rights," she said primly.

Jared laughed.

"Father arranged it."

Jared laughed harder.

"I take my work seriously," she said icily. "I don't think it is amusing."

"You and your father," he said in mock despair, and shook his head. "Close the door, Beth."

A softness in his eyes, his hushed, pleading, insistent voice, made Beth sigh and close the door. The room was hot. All of St. Louis was hot. Perspiration dripped down her temples.

"I would like to take a bath," she said.

"There's a tub down the hall."

"A common bathroom?"

Jared laughed. "You sound like your father. It has a lock, Beth. If I'd known you were coming, I would have asked for a room with a bath. There might be one or two in this place. Then we could hop into the tub together." He grinned, then frowned. "Are you sure you didn't follow William?"

Beth made a face and stooped down to open her trunk.

Jared came around beside her and, with his hands under her arms, lifted her to her feet. His mouth came down hard on hers, and his tongue pried her lips open. Even against her hot skin, she could feel the heat of his touch, and she threw her head back so that he could better devour her mouth. His hands slowly moved across her midriff, and just the thumbs caressed her corseted breasts. She forgot her exhaustion and threw her arms around his neck, holding the hard muscles, running her fingers through his sweaty hair. Desire rose up in her, making her tingle and ache at her very core.

"I've missed you," she whispered as he pulled her tight

against him and held her. "Jared, Jared, we can't go on like this!"

He stood back and let his arms drop to his sides. "I know, darling," he said. "We do have our problems." He grinned suddenly, maddeningly. "But none of them are physical."

"What are you doing in St. Louis, Jared?"

He turned and headed toward the door.

"Jared!"

"Have a good bath."

"Where are you going?"

He grinned over his shoulder. "To water my horse." He dug into his pocket and tossed her the key. "Be here when I get back."

Beth didn't move for a long time after he'd left. She looked at the key in her hand. No, she wouldn't do it. She walked downstairs and asked the man at the front desk for a room. With a bath. He said they were all out of rooms with baths. She would take a room without a bath. He took her money and handed her a key for a room on Jared's floor. She gave it back and asked for a room on the fourth floor. He looked at her strangely and said there was no fourth floor. She took the key to the room on the third floor and went upstairs. She still had Jared's key. Well, she thought, he could figure it out for himself. She wasn't about to tack a note to his door. She dragged her trunk down the hall to her new room.

Then, sweating and exhausted, she took a bath and fell naked into bed for a long nap.

CHAPTER 21

Beth slept for five hours. When she awoke, the late afternoon sun slanted through her dusty window, and the small, plain room was stiflingly hot. She rolled out of bed, splashed cool water on her face, and dug into her trunk for something appropriate to wear. But what was appropriate in this particular part of St. Louis? She settled on a cotton lawn dress with a pale green tunic that dropped tightly over her hips and was gathered up and back over a small poushe. The underskirt was white with two-inch lace trim, the bodice high and close-fitting with lace along the neckline.

She pinned her cameo brooch over her breastbone, put on a sturdy pair of walking boots, and combed out her hair, which she promptly tied at the nape of her neck with a dark green velvet ribbon.

She glanced at Jared's key, still on her bureau. "Watering his horse, my foot," she muttered.

She left the key where it was and walked down the two flights of stairs to the lobby. Three men leered at her, but she ignored them and stepped out onto the street. There was a sidewalk, but just barely. It was narrow and dusty and not acknowledged by horses. Or mules. With distaste, Beth passed the dirtiest, stinkingest mule she had ever seen in her life. It was drinking water out of a leaking bucket.

"Well," she mumbled to herself, "at least Jared is not an elitist."

In this section of town, there were more horses than carriages, more men than women, and no children. Beth had a feeling she wasn't exactly around the corner from the home of Elijah and Beatrice Dobbs. She turned back around and went into the hotel.

The balding man at the front desk was still there, chewing something Beth assumed was a wad of tobacco. Brown juice dribbled down his chin, and he wiped it away with the back of his hand. Repulsed, Beth quickly thought of her mother nursing the wounded during the war and knew there were worse sights than tobacco juice on an unshaven chin. But why had Jared brought her here? She shuddered. Perhaps he wanted her to sample his normal way of living.

"Excuse me," she said, clearing her throat and unfolding the slip of paper with Elijah Dobbs's address. "Could you tell me where I can find this place?"

The man coughed and spat behind the desk. "Across town," he said with one glance at the paper.

"Within walking distance?"

"Nope."

"Well, do you rent carriages?"

"Nope. Horses, no carriages."

Beth supposed she could walk somewhere and find a cab, but she honestly did not want to walk any more than she had to among smelly mules and filthy streets. "All right," she said crisply, determined not to flee back to her room. "I would like to rent a horse."

He leaned over the desk, looked from her neck to her feet, and slowly shook his head. "Ain't the kind of horses a lady would want to ride."

"I only want one horse," Beth said with a confident smile. "And I assume it will be the cleanest and most gentle you have. I would appreciate it if you would have it saddled while I change."

The desk clerk shrugged. "Suit yourself."

He didn't argue when Beth paid for the horse and left an enormous tip. She didn't want a filthy, stinking mule that drank water from a leaking bucket.

What she got wasn't much better. It was a fat old quarterhorse that looked too tired to carry its tattered saddle, much less a person. It didn't stink as much as the mule. Beth wrinkled up her nose and with a resigned sigh mounted the beast. It plodded down the hot, dusty streets, and Beth, in her neat riding clothes, watched for the landmarks and street signs the desk clerk had told her would get her across town. As the hotels grew taller and more elegant shops and banks and businesses began to appear, so did carriages, women, and children. Beth began to relax, even if she did feel ridiculous on the old horse.

At last she came to a wealthy residential section of the city. The houses were mostly Greek Revival, with classic columns, hipped roofs, and attractive belvederes overlooking trim lawns. Beth was reassured that St. Louis wasn't simply a wild frontier town. It was a city with many different sides.

Elijah Dobbs's house was one of the largest on the street, glistening white with spacious lawns baking in the sun, and a carriage house at the end of a long cobblestone drive.

Beth lingered on the street. Now that she had found the place, what did she propose to do? She frowned, thinking. There was only one thing to do. She dismounted her horse, looped the reins over a spoke in the wrought-iron fence, and walked up to the front door.

A very tall black woman, dressed in black with a starched apron around her flat middle, opened the door on Beth's second knock. She didn't say a word. Beth smiled at her. "Hello," she said cheerily, "this is the Dobbs residence, isn't it?"

The woman, not over forty, nodded slightly.

"My name is Elizabeth Harte. I'm a freind of Melissa Dobbs. We met in Saratoga Springs. I'm in town unexpectedly, and I thought I would stop by and—"

"I will announce you," the woman said in a quiet, deep voice.

Beth opened her mouth to say thank you, but the woman was already gone. Beth wondered why she hadn't been invited in to wait. But then she glanced at her boots and saw that they and her riding habit were covered with dust, and she had picked up a bit of the horse's smell. Well, she thought, that explains being left out on the front steps.

The woman returned, but her only indication of disapproval was her slightly flared nostrils. She nodded, again ever so slightly, and said, "This way, please."

Beth followed her through the opulent house onto a terrace. Melissa was sitting alone on a wicker love seat amid a stunning garden of late summer flowers. She was wearing pink with a string of daisies in her hair.

"Why, Beth, what a surprise!" she said happily, not rising. "Come sit down. Would you like something to drink?"

"Water would be wonderful, thank you," Beth said, and sat in a wicker chair next to Melissa. "I apologize for dropping in on you like this, but—"

"Oh, no, no! Don't apologize! I'm delighted to see you. I've done nothing at all since that awful train ride but sleep and sit in the garden."

Beth discreetly brushed dust from her jacket. "I didn't expect you to leave Saratoga so suddenly," she said idly.

"Oh, I thought we would be staying through August," Melissa lamented. "I wanted to be there for the International Regatta, but Father had to return for business and he didn't want to leave Mother and me alone. St. Louis is so hot and miserable in the summer!"

"It's a beautiful city," Beth put in, restraining herself from asking too many questions. "So alive."

"I suppose," Melissa said doubtfully, pouting.

The black woman appeared with a glass of mineral water, which Beth took gratefully. "I'm in St. Louis on behalf of the women's suffrage movement," she said. "I'm to address a group of Episcopal women."

"Are you? You never told me."

"I thought I did," Beth said, and shrugged. "Well, sometimes I'm in such a fog I forget whom I've told what."

Melissa liked her admission of fallibility. "Yes, you intellectuals!" She giggled. "But whatever happened to you and Jared Inman?"

Beth looked at the pretty pink, innocent cheeks and realized Melissa had no idea Jared Inman was in St. Louis as well. "He's gone his way," she said vaguely, "and I've gone mine."

"Well, you'll catch someone," Melissa assured her. "You're pretty enough."

"Yes, I suppose," Beth said, restraining herself again. "Of course, I'm lot nearly as pretty as you, Melissa."

It was exactly the right thing to say. Melissa leaned forward and reached out for Beth's hand. Beth noticed her hands were still red from the unpretentious reins of her brute of a horse. She hadn't thought to bring along riding gloves. Melissa didn't seem to notice.

"Won't you have dinner with us tonight?" she asked, almost pleading. "It would be such a treat for me!"

"Why, I'd love to, Melissa," Beth exclaimed, she hoped not too eagerly. "Are you sure I won't be intruding?"

Melissa released Beth's hand and sat back. "Of course not! Heavens, it's been absolutely deadly dull here, especially after the Springs. You don't want to eat alone in some hotel! Where are you staying, by the way?"

Beth realized she had never gotten the name of her hotel and wasn't even sure it had a name. She remembered one of the more elegant hotels she had seen on her way across town and gave its name to Melissa.

"Wonderful! I'll send a carriage for you at seven." She smiled contentedly and fingered the daisies in her hair. "Isn't this such a nice surprise!"

"For me, too," Beth said, and meant it. She hadn't expected such kindness from Melissa Dobbs. "Seven o'clock, then."

On her way out, Beth felt only the slightest twinge of guilt at knowing that she had wanted Melissa to invite her to dinner only so she could continue her mission for her father. She could also feel guilty, she thought, that her primary reason for being in St. Louis was to investigate railroad corruption rather than preach on women's suffrage. Still, she was addressing a group of women, and she was happy to see Melissa.

A stable hand had watered her horse, but still the old creature didn't look anxious to resume their journey. Beth patted him and mounted him as carefully as she could. She thought it would have been very dramatic to go off at a gallop, but all the old quarterhorse could manage was his steady plod.

She returned the horse to the hotel stable herself and promised the manager at least a day's pay if he would brush down the poor horse, clean up the saddle, and give the creature a proper bucket of oats. The horse was fat with poor food, not overdeveloped muscles. Then, rather pleased with herself, she headed up to her room.

Jared's key was still on her bureau. Beth scowled at it and peeled off her dusty, sweaty riding clothes. She took a sponge bath with cool water and sat naked on the edge of her bed. Where was Jared? She huffed, disgusted. He expected her to stay locked in a dingy hotel while he went gallivanting all over St. Louis. The arrogance of it! Of course, perhaps he was off killing people in bars or planning a train robbery. What did she know?

Someone pounded on her door.

"Who is it?" she called.

"Beth!" came Jared's livid voice through the thin wood. "Open this damned door before I break it down!"

Beth was unintimidated, but she couldn't hold back a smile of relief. "Just a minute. I'm not dressed—"

"Now, dammit, or—"

He pounded the door hard, once, and Beth knew he meant what he said. She also knew the clientele and proprietors of the hotel would hardly swoop in to her rescue. There wasn't time even to dig into her trunk for a robe. She pulled her towel around her and opened the door.

"My, my," he said as he walked past her. "You did mean not dressed."

She slammed the door shut. "Well, you've got your way. I suppose you came for this." She pulled the towel around her tightly and marched over to the bureau for his key. She threw it at him, but he caught it in one hand. "Now go."

He sat down on the edge of the bed. "Where the hell have you been?"

He wasn't simply asking her, he was demanding, which only infuriated her more. She stayed close to the bureau. "None of your business," she told him hotly.

He breathed through his mouth, his teeth clenched, controlling himself. "Damn, you're beautiful," he said, but shook his head, as if shaking off the thought. "I've been worried sick about you, Beth. You have no idea what you're involved in—"

"So you threaten to beat down my door."

He shrugged without apology. "So I was mad, too. You can be trying, you know. Beth—" He sighed again and shook his head. "I can't be your nursemaid and keep my eye on you every minute—"

"I haven't asked you to."

"Beth, dammit, I asked you to stay put!"

"Told me. Commanded me." She pulled the towel even more tightly around her. "Demanded I remain here until you returned. It certainly didn't take all afternoon to water your horse, Jared. Where were you? Never mind. I don't want to question you the way you question me."

She could see his anger surge again, but he held it at bay. Only his granitelike eyes betrayed his fever. "Where did you go?"

She refused to answer.

He looked at the pile of dirty riding clothes. "You went to the Dobbses, didn't you?"

"I had a glass of water with Melissa on the terrace," she admitted.

"That's all?"

She nodded, but winced in frustration when tears sprang up in her eyes. She couldn't brush them away and hang onto her towel at the same time, so she let them spill down her cheeks. She turned away from Jared, but he was already crossing the room. He brushed away her tears with his fingertips.

"I feel like such a fool," she whispered hoarsely. "You don't want me here, Jared. You—you don't want me, do you? I should have stayed in New York. That would have been a more gentle way of letting me down. It was what you planned, wasn't it?" She cocked her head up at him, her eyes still filled with tears. "You never would have come for me. But I—I had to follow you."

His fingertips traveled from her cheeks down her throat and across the smooth white curve of her shoulders. "You are a fool, Beth," he said gently, a small smile softening his features as he placed a hand on each of her shoulders and turned her toward him. "But only because you are so very wrong about me." His hands, palms downward, traveled the length of her arms. "Darling, believe me, I would have come for you."

Their kiss was burning, longing, Beth still holding the towel as her lips tasted Jared's mouth and her tongue mingled with his. The ache of desire coursed upward through her body, quickly overshadowing the physical ache from her long ride through St. Louis and the wrenching ache of knowing so little about the strong, mysterious man who could make her feel like this. She kissed his chin and smiled as she ran her fingers down to his chest and deftly unbuttoned the top few buttons. She slipped her hand against his warm skin and felt his heartbeat.

"Beth, darling, I don't have time—"

She unbuttoned the rest of the buttons and put both hands inside his shirt, letting them feel his strength, absorb it, as her palms slowly coursed down his hard stomach. "Would you have come for me?" she asked breathlessly, as the towel, on its own for the last moments, loosened across her breasts and fell to the floor.

Jared groaned. "How can you ask that?"

She slid her arms around his back and let her cool, naked breasts press against his taut chest. She kissed him from one shoulder to the other until her face tilted upward and he claimed her mouth. His hands were on her hips now, but suddenly he clenched her at the waist and lifted her to her feet, their mouths still locked.

He laid her on the bed and quickly discarded the rest of his clothing. They were ready for each other, but Jared lay beside her and slowly kissed every inch of her body. When he grabbed her hips and pulled her on top of him, Beth couldn't speak or even think, but looked deep into his eyes with her love unabashedly written in hers. They came together with an openness that was at once terrifying and exhilarating, everything Beth had ever hoped for in a relationship with a man. She put a hand on each of his shoulders and pushed herself up so that she could look at the man beneath her. She whispered his name once before she collapsed onto him and gave herself up to the abandon of their passion.

They drifted off to sleep together, still joined, but it was only for the shortest of catnaps. Beth disentangled herself from Jared's long legs and sprang out of bed. Her body was pink and hot from their lovemaking. She squeezed the sponge in her washbasin, the water now tepid, and quickly ran it over her body. Jared stirred and rolled over onto his side. She smiled at him, marveling at the thickness of his thighs.

"What are you doing?" he asked groggily.

"I have to get ready," she replied. "Melissa invited me to dinner tonight—"

"What!"

He was out of bed, beside her. Beth felt something clog

her throat, but she refused to say it was nervousness. She wrung out the sponge in the basin. "Melissa Dobbs invited me to dinner this evening," she repeated primly. "I accepted her invitation, and she is sending a carriage for me at seven."

"You can't go."

"I am going."

Jared kicked his pants into the air and caught them in one hand. He dressed quickly, tearing his clothes on in silent fury. Beth calmly finished her sponge bath and brushed out her hair.

"They don't know I'm in town," he told her, begrudging this one fact she had already assumed. "I want it kept that way."

She pulled clean undergarments from her trunk. "Certainly."

He growled and stalked out, slamming the door when he left.

Beth was adding the finishing touches to the bustle of her violet dress when Jared burst into her room again. He raked his fingers impatiently through his thick hair. "You won't change your mind about going?"

"Of course not," she replied airily.

"All right, then I may as well put you to work." He ignored the eager flash of Beth's eyes. "I want you to talk to William—"

"That's a switch," Beth said with light sarcasm.

Jared eyed her darkly, and she decided to keep further remarks to herself. "I want you to tell him that you've learned that Elijah Dobbs sent LeBreque after Ginny and that damned horse of his. Tell him your father told you or you learned it on your own. I don't care. Just don't bring me into it. Suggest he leave St. Louis at once."

Beth stared at Jared. "You think William is in danger?" she said, not sure whether she was asking a question or making a statement. Jared said nothing. "But, Jared, what—how did you find out about Dobbs? Why can't you tell William yourself? Jared!"

He gave her a twisted smile and patted her on the cheek. "You like living a dangerous life, Beth," he said. "Have fun."

"Jared Inman!"

He ignored her completely and pulled open the door, pausing as he glanced over his shoulder. "Don't get yourself killed, Beth," he said lightly, and closed the door softly behind him.

CHAPTER 22

Beth almost talked herself out of joining the Dobbses for dinner, but she resolutely finished dressing and with Jared's help hired a carriage to take her cross-town to the hotel she had blindly named to Melissa.

"Elizabeth Stanton Harte told a lie?" Jared asked in mock horror. "Goodness, what would your father the judge think?"

"I'm not in a very good humor, Jared," she said darkly.

Unimpressed, Jared laughed. "And I thought you liked the thrill of danger, the excitement of the world beyond the ladies' boudoir—or do you prefer smoking cigars in the billiard room and disguising yourself as a man to get into a poker game to putting yourself to the test in the real world?''

''Am I supposed to laugh or defend myself?'' Beth asked coolly, but she and Jared both were spared continuing the discussion by the arrival of her carriage. She climbed into the passenger seat and gave him her haughtiest look, but there was a betraying glint in her violet eyes. ''Good evening, Mr. Inman.''

Jared said nothing until the carriage pulled away, at which point he called out loudly, ''You're one of a kind, Beth!''

She allowed herself a smile, but grew serious again when she began to rehearse her lines to William. If only he would listen to her! And, of course, there was the added difficulty of warning William against Dobbs in Dobbs's own house.

Precisely at seven Beth was met by a sparkling two-wheel open chaise in front of the elegant hotel. To her relief, William was its driver. She climbed in beside him before he had a chance to get out to help her.

''William! It's good to see you—''

''Elizabeth,'' he said coolly.

''You don't approve of my being in St. Louis,'' she guessed lightly. ''Well, neither do I, under the circumstances!''

He looked at her unsympathetically as the carriage made its way toward the Dobbses' neighborhood.

Beth decided to be serious and get to the point. ''William, I must talk to you. I believe—William, I believe you could be in danger.''

His pale features hardened as she spoke, but he didn't look at her again.

''Elijah Dobbs had Jacques LeBreque break into Ginny's

room and then try to kill Louisiana," she went on quickly. "I believe this was in retaliation for your coming to terms with Richard Hoskins. William, I don't know why you came to St. Louis, but I don't believe Elijah Dobbs is the sort of man who would take being double-crossed easily. And you did double-cross him, didn't you, by pulling out of his railroad scheme?"

The carriage stopped on a quiet, treelined street. Beth held her breath. What if she were wrong? What if Jared were wrong? Suddenly, she realized that William and Dobbs could have made another deal. Perhaps together they had double-crossed Hoskins and William was only playing the part of a victim.

And Beth was in a carriage alone with William. He knew she was in St. Louis to spy on Dobbs. She twisted her fingers together, breathing rapidly, waiting for William to speak.

"I know Elijah Dobbs is a scoundrel," he said at last, "but I don't believe I have put myself in any danger. You see, Elizabeth, I have asked Melissa to marry me."

She whirled around at him. "What!"

"She is a kind, sweet girl, Elizabeth, and she deserves better than her father. I want to get her away from him." He sighed, studying the reins in his hands. "I'm taking her back to New York."

Confusion was making Beth's head spin. "Does her father approve?"

William smiled bitterly. "Of course. He'd love to have access to the Prentiss fortune. I've pretended I don't know he had my sister attacked." He looked at the still-blue summer sky, the humidity hanging heavily in the air. "I don't expect you to approve of the match, Elizabeth, but Melissa will make a fine wife. Her father's business ethics are as low as they come, but I succumbed to them myself for a while. It is not an easy time for an honest man to be in business, Elizabeth. I think Elijah went too far, but I can't damn his daughter for what he is."

Beth took his hand and squeezed it. "You're wrong, William," she said, and smiled at his hurt but unsurprised look. "I do approve of the match. I also believe you're much more like your sister than either of you ever thought."

"We're both romantics," William said with a sudden grin. "I'm glad you approve, Elizabeth."

And then they resumed their ride to the Dobbs house. As they arrived, William had one further comment. "Speaking of scoundrels, Beth, I have good reason to believe Jared Inman has been in Elijah's employ as well as Jacques LeBreque. It's just as well you two have separated."

Beth bit her lip, remembering her afternoon in bed with Jared, and was unable to ask what William's good reason was before they were on their way into dinner.

Dinner began with a discussion of the weather and ended with a discussion of fall fashion. Beth resigned herself to a dull evening. Elijah Dobbs was curt but amiable enough, and Beth hoped he didn't put too much stock in her being in St. Louis. William, so absorbed in his own affairs, had never pressed her on her reasons for being there. Surely, she thought, at least Dobbs and William suspected that the suffrage lecture had been a hastily arranged excuse for following them across the country. Everyone was painfully polite and, when Beth bowed out of the evening, only stopped short of offering to attend her lecture.

She was grateful, even relieved, when her host offered a servant to drive her back to her hotel. She said her good-byes, promised she would visit Melissa again, and fled.

She was halfway into the carriage out front before she noticed that the driver was Jacques LeBreque. Panic gripped her insides, but she was rational enough to attempt a quick retreat. Jacques's hand shot out and grabbed her by the wrist, and in his other hand the blade of a knife glistened. Beth, seemingly calm, climbed in beside him.

"You heal quickly, Monsieur LeBreque," she said coolly.

"I was not shot, only grazed," he said, contempt burning in his eyes. "You move, *mademoiselle*, and I will kill you."

She looked at him haughtily. "Charming."

But her words belied her fear. If she didn't move, would Jacques still kill her? Was he acting on Elijah's orders or on behalf of his own warped need for revenge?

The carriage clattered into the night. Neither spoke. Beth sat very rigid, not moving. If Jacques had been unarmed, she would have been less afraid. He was not a very big man, and she was tall and athletic. Perhaps she could have defended herself long enough to escape, but with the knife she didn't know what she should dare. She thought of Jared, but tears sprang to her eyes and so she pushed him from her mind. She had to rely only on herself.

"What do you plan to do?" she asked steadily.

"You will not spend even one night in St. Louis," he replied with a hateful, smug grin. "I will see to that."

Beth's eyes focused briefly on the knife. It was in his left hand, away from her, the reins in his right hand, next to her. It wasn't such a big knife. Sharp and efficient, to be sure, but from that angle he would be hard pressed to stab her in the heart or the back, and any other wounds would surely be superficial. If only she didn't have on that damnable dress with its yards of fabric and impossible bustle! If she tried to be cautious and ease her way out of the carriage, he would hear the rustle of her skirts, know she was moving, guess what she was planning. No, if she were going to act, she had to act quickly and boldly.

Without a word or another thought, she sprang up and

leaped out of the carriage. She landed sprawled on the cobblestones, just clear of the wheels, and was sure the loud crack she heard was a bone or two, but it was only her bustle. She had scraped her arm, sprained a wrist, and tortured her knees, but the yards of fabric and underclothing had helped cushion her fall.

Then she remembered Jacques. He would be upon her with his knife any moment. She scrambled to her feet, or tried to, but the twisted cloth and broken bustle impeded her.

"Get down, Beth, dammit!"

Jared! Dazed, Beth glanced around for him, but suddenly Jacques was upon her, knocking her back onto the cobblestones. She saw the flash of his knife and was suddenly alert once more, but Jacques was quicker. He straddled her and went for her neck with his free hand. Beth hammered his chest with her fists, but the advantage was all his.

She screamed for Jared.

He was there, plucking Jacques off her even as the knife readied for its first deadly thrust. Beth screamed again, this time in horror, when the knife found its mark in Jared's arm. But Jacques didn't linger to finish the job. When Jared groaned out in pain and released his grip on the smaller man, Jacques seized his chance and raced to Jared's horse. He was gone before Jared could curse soundly.

Beth was on her feet beside Jared. She held out shaking fingers and touched the hand holding his wound. "Your arm," she said tentatively.

"It's nothing," he growled. "I never should have let him go. Damn!"

"I'm sorry."

"It's not your fault! I should have guessed Dobbs would do something like this." He shook his head in disgust. "And I should have tied you to your bed, woman."

"Jared Inman, how dare you! I am responsible for my actions, not you." Beth whirled around, furious, anger washing away the last remnants of her terror, and she wondered what they were supposed to do next. The carriage was gone. "You have no right to blame yourself, Jared."

"I knew LeBreque was in St. Louis."

"And if you had told me, I still would have been unprepared for what happened here." She turned back around to face him. "You followed me."

His face was pale against the starlit sky, and blood oozed between his fingers. "Yes."

"And you didn't think it incumbent upon you to tell me beforehand?"

"Then you wouldn't have held hands with William, knowing I was watching." he said, biting off his words.

Beth snorted in disgust and started walking down the street.

Jared quickly caught up with her. "Well?"

"Well, what?"

"Look, I just saved your life—for the second time, I might add—and you haven't even got the courtesy to tell me what went on tonight?"

She refused to look at him. "I held hands with William."

"Beth, please, for god'sake!"

She eyed him now, coldly. "And if you hadn't hollered at me, I would have kept in mind that I was alone and stayed alert. I would never have let LeBreque get so far in his attack."

Jared laughed.

Beth couldn't suppress a smile, and she took Jared's hand. The chaise was around the corner. Not entertaining any arguments from Jared, Beth took the reins. On the way back to their hotel, she told him everything that had transpired that evening, including William's comment as they went into dinner.

"I've never worked for Dobbs," Jared stated baldly.

Which still, Beth realized, left what he did do unexplained.

They spent the night together in Beth's room. She cleaned and bandaged Jared's wound, which had stopped bleeding by the time they arrived at the hotel, and agreed that they had had enough action for one day. They fell asleep holding hands, their thighs touching.

At dawn Beth rolled over at the creak of the bed and the lifting of Jared's weight off it. She opened one eye and saw him pulling on his pants, his back to her. She opened the other eye. "Where are you going?" she asked, fully awake.

He pulled on his shirt and faced her as he buttoned it. "Out."

She pulled the sheet up to her neck and frowned at him. "Out where?"

"Haven't decided yet."

"Liar."

"Whatever."

Beth threw off the sheet and sat up. "I'll come with you."

Jared tucked in his shirt. "You're not invited."

"I don't care. I'll come anyway. It'll take me five minutes to get dressed."

"I have a few things to get ready in my room," he said, and walked to the door. "You're not coming, Beth."

"I am!"

When he closed the door, she quickly washed and dressed in a plain rose-colored poplin dress, her walking boots, and just enough corset and bustle to be proper but not confined. After women received the vote, she would wage war on the bustle. She brushed out her hair, tied it up in a hasty knot, and ran to Jared's room. The entire process had taken perhaps ten minutes, a record she was certain.

Jared hadn't waited for her. She pounded on his door, but there was no answer. Finally, someone hollered about the noise from another room, and she gave up. She went downstairs. The hotel dining room was off to one side of the lobby. Beth stood in the door and eyed the seven tables with mismatched chairs, none occupied Jared Inman. She smiled feebly at the middle-aged waitress, the only woman in the room, and decided she could skip breakfast if Jared could.

She went back into the lobby.

"Miss Harte?" the desk clerk called, waving an envelope. "Message for you."

Beth raced to the front desk. The clerk still hadn't washed his chin, but for all she knew he had been at his post the whole night. She tipped him generously and took the envelope. Nothing was written on the outside. She ran out the door and tore open the envelope in the bright, warm morning sun.

She scowled. Another note from Jared. "Off again," it read in his bold, arrogant scrawl. "Wait for me in a nice hotel. Or, better yet, go back to New York. J."

"More of the same," she muttered, and tore the note to bits.

She went around to the hotel stables and discovered her fat old quarterhorse was available for the day. She didn't bother going back to change into her riding outfit, but mounted the horse in her rose dress and headed into the city. It was just coming to life, facing yet another stiflingly hot August day, but Beth was amazed at its size and newness. It was so different from New York City, crammed onto that coastal island, so much older. St. Louis sprawled out from the river with nothing but lack of people and money to stop it.

Once again the black woman answered Beth's knock on Elijah Dobbs's front door. "Good morning," Beth said, forcing a smile. "I would like to speak to William Prentiss, if I may."

She nodded. "I will see."

This time she let Beth into the foyer. Beth had already shaken the dust out of her skirt, but it still clung to her black shoes. She shrugged, fighting off her nervousness. What would she do if Elijah Dobbs met her—or Jacques LeBreque?

But seconds later, William rushed in, seizing Beth by the wrist and half-dragging her outside. "What are you doing here?" he whispered, horrified, when he got her into the front yard.

Beth wrestled her hand from his. William was dressed impeccably in striped trousers and a dark blue coat, but he looked exhausted. His cheeks were without color, his eyes puffy, his lips set firmly together, not with determination but with a self-conscious effort to seem in control.

"You heard Elijah sent LeBreque after me," she guessed.

William nodded miserably. "Thank God you're all right, Elizabeth! He was only supposed to scare you into going back to New York. Oh, Elizabeth, please leave here! I'm taking Melissa and her mother back to New York today. Won't you come with us? Elijah knows you're spying for your father—"

"My father is a retired judge who likes to have innumerable facts at his fingertips so he can influence legislation," Beth said crisply. "He is relatively harmless."

"Elizabeth, please!"

"William, last night you said you believed Jared Inman once worked for Elijah Dobbs," Beth went on, ignoring William's pleas. "Why?"

He turned away in disgust. "So LeBreque wasn't lying," he said. "Jared Inman is in St. Louis. Beth, don't you see? That's all the more reason for you to leave!"

"Why? What have you got against Jared?"

William whirled around, his fists clenched at his sides, his mouth shut tight as if to hold back a tide of words.

"William, if you don't tell me, I'll find out for myself, one way or another."

"Jared Inman intends to kill Jacques LeBreque," William said in an explosion of words. "LeBreque is a gun for hire, Elizabeth, a lowlife. He and Inman operate in the same circles. They have no loyalties, no ethics, no beliefs. As I understand it, Inman was supposed to be protecting Juan Correrro. LeBreque double-crossed him, or got past him somehow, and assassinated Correrro. There's no proof, of course, and if you're thinking Jared somehow was noble in all this, think again. If could easily have been the other way around, Inman killing Correrro and LeBreque defending him. Just a question of who hired whom."

William paused for a reaction, but Beth only stood frozen on the sunburnt grass.

"LeBreque made Jared look like a fool, Elizabeth, and now Jared intends to have his revenge."

"By murdering him," Beth whispered.

"Precisely. *Now* will you return with me to New York?"

Beth furrowed her brow, thinking. "But why did your father allow Jared to stay in Saratoga as his guest?"

"I asked myself that—and my father—a hundred times, but I never received a satisfactory answer," William admitted. "My father has his own less than noble business tactics, Elizabeth. Perhaps he intended to hire Jared for a job himself."

Beth frowned at the unsatisfactory explanation, but she suspected she would get no more from William. "Does Elijah know you're leaving?"

"Yes, but he refuses even to see his wife and daughter off," William said bitterly. "He and LeBreque left early for the docks this morning. How I ever could have made a deal with that man! Or let LeBreque trick me into hiring him to train Louisiana! Well, it's water over the dam now. Look, I'll pick you up at your hotel in an hour—"

Beth shook her head adamantly. "I have a group of Episcopal women to address, remember? The luncheon isn't until tomorrow afternoon. I'll make my plans then."

William shook his head in despair.

"Thank you for talking to me, William," Beth said quietly. "I wish you had told me what you knew about Jared sooner. You would have saved me—a lot of pain. Good luck with your marriage."

"You won't change your mind about joining us?" He smiled and touched her hand. "Good-bye, then, Elizabeth."

"Good-bye, William."

CHAPTER 23

Beth rode her fat old horse across town and told the stable manager she needed a carriage. She didn't care what kind of carriage, but she had to have one within fifteen minutes. He grunted and scratched his head. She promised him a huge tip. He raised an eyebrow at her seemingly endless supply of money, but he said he'd find her a carriage.

Back in the hotel, Beth checked with the desk clerk. It was as she thought. Jared Inman had paid his bill and left. She ran upstairs, packed her trunk, and had it brought out to the stable. There the old manager had waiting a two-wheel chaise that looked as though it had been through the War of 1812. Its one horse was trimmer but probably as old as her quarterhorse. Beth presented the man the promised tip, had the trunk hoisted aboard, and was off, if hardly at a clip.

The docks were crowded with sweaty, cursing men and riverboats and piles of cargo just unloaded and ready to be boarded. The Mississippi lay wide and brown in the noon sun. Beth leaned over and asked a man sitting on the ground in front of a crumbling, filthy tavern if he knew where she could find Elijah Dobbs.

He bit into his sandwich and jerked a thumb down toward the water. "He'll be down with the *Beatrice*," he said, talking while he chewed. He paused to swallow. "Biggest boat going out today. You'll find your way."

Beth thanked him and urged her horse on. Within a hundred yards, she saw the *Beatrice*. The name was printed in blue on the paddle boxes covering the two huge side paddle wheels. The wheels themselves were covered with half-circles ornately decorated with orange and yellow sunbursts. Beth forced her carriage as close to the dock as she could. Scores of men were loading stacks of cargo, and a crowd of passengers had gathered in front of the gangplank awaiting word to board.

She didn't see Jared Inman.

Beth climbed out of the carriage and threaded her way through people and cargo to the huge steamboat. There was little below water level on such a boat, since it was essentially a gigantic raft, but three decks and a pilothouse towered above, and all were painted a sparkling white, with blue and red trim here and there. There was intricate scrollwork everywhere, giving the famous "wedding cake" appearance, but Beth knew most of the boat was made of thin, light wood that easily caught fire. The tragedies of steamboats on the Mississippi had become legendary.

She forced her way through the crowd of oncoming passengers to a portly man with lambchop sideburns and a balding head. He was wearing trim white riverboat garb and not smiling. Exactly what she expected, Beth thought.

"Excuse me, sir," she said. "I'm looking for Elijah Dobbs. Do you know where I might find him?"

He glanced at her, just once, briefly, and returned his gaze to the crowd boarding the ship. "What do you want with him?"

"I'm a friend of the family's," she said quickly. "It's urgent that I see him—"

"Spare me," he said, still gazing at the brightly dressed men, women, and children anxious to be on their way down the Mississippi. "He's on board. You'll catch him leaving if you stand right here."

"I must see him now!"

His eyes flickered at her again. He looked back at the remaining passengers. For a moment, he said nothing and Beth thought she had been dismissed. Then, without looking at her, he said, "Check with me as you leave. If you don't, I'll be looking for you myself." He flicked his icy blue eyes at her once again. "And you won't like it if I find you."

Beth grinned broadly and raced past him, nearly knocking over a woman and two children. She asked a cabin boy where she could find Elijah Dobbs.

"Hurricane deck," he said.

"Where's that?"

He gave her a contemptuous look born of a life spent on the mighty river. "Third deck." But he couldn't leave it at that. "You're on the main deck. Next one up is the boiler deck. Mr. Dobbs'll be in the texas."

"The texas," Beth repeated dumbly.

The boy, thin and dark, didn't take pains to make Beth feel anything but uninformed. "That's a group of cabins for the officers on the hurricane deck.'' Then he reminded her with a cocky grin: "That's the third deck."

Beth thanked him and fled before he could lecture her on the operation of a steam engine. In five minutes, she was high above the river. The group of cabins—the texas, she corrected herself—was in the center of the deck, with two huge blackened smokestacks rising up on either side. Beth crept around to one of the opened doors.

"Elijah, I think you should just tell me and get it over with," Jared Inman was saying, his voice as smooth and unruffled as ever.

Elijah Dobbs didn't answer.

"I've stated my case," Jared went on. "You know what I'll do if you don't tell me."

Beth shuddered.

Someone sighed. She supposed it was Elijah Dobbs. "The Swamp," he muttered.

There was another sigh, distinctly victorious, distinctly from the lips of Jared Inman. Beth wrinkled up her face. The swamp?

"You won't find him, Inman," Elijah added. "And don't think you'll get your hands on my neck again. I'll kill you first."

Jared ignored his threat. "Then I'll be staying aboard the *Beatrice*," he said mildly.

Staying aboard! Beth decided this was a fortuitous moment to shrink away. She found the captain watching the last of the passengers board his boat.

"I would like to buy a ticket," she said.

He gave her a wry look. "I thought you might. I've only a berth on the main deck to offer. 'Tisn't suitable for a young—"

"I'll take it."

"You've trouble written right into your violet eyes, missy."

She tried to soften him with a smile, but failed. She respected him more than that. In the end, he did sell her a ticket, against his better judgement.

"By the way," she asked, turning, "where are we headed?"

He raised his eyes to the heavens. "New Orleans, and don't be getting in my way, missy."

She promised him he wouldn't even know she was aboard. He gave her a doubtful look and had a couple of strong backs fetch her trunk. She wasn't at all concerned about the carriage. The tip she had given for it was worth more than the carriage itself.

As the *Beatrice* began its journey down the Mississippi River, most of the passengers stayed outside on the promenade of the second deck—the boiler deck, Beth remembered from her lesson—and watched St. Louis fade into the distance. Beth stayed in the crowd and scanned it for Jared Inman, but she was just as glad she didn't see him. She wanted to be well down the river before he discovered she was aboard.

When the other passengers headed inside to the main cabin, Beth melted in with them and followed. This was where the riverboat travelers would gather to dine and dance. The main cabin extended through the center of the boiler deck with the emphasis on opulence. The ceiling was paneled with rosewood scrollwork and hung with huge crystal chandeliers. Thick, flowered carpets covered the floor, and on either side were numbered doors to the elegant staterooms. Certainly the *Beatrice* didn't compare to the United States Hotel or even the pristine Clarendon, but Beth thought it was a rather interesting way to travel.

She did not see Jared Inman in the main cabin or making his way to the stateroom. Was he, like she, relegated to a berth on the main deck?

Doubting her sanity in following Jared after what William had told her about him, Beth nonetheless resumed her search, in earnest now. Off the far end of the main cabin was a barroom. Beth smiled to herself and marched directly to it.

Jared Inman, looking like any riverboat gambler, was stretched out in a chair studying his poker hand. Three other men were at the card table. Two women, brightly dressed in taffeta with heavily painted faces, feathers in their hair, and lots of exposed, plump white skin, hovered over the men. All were sipping drinks. Jared's appeared to be straight whiskey.

He was the last to glance up at the prim-looking woman who had just walked in. He didn't smile, and only his black eyes registered any hint of surprise or anger. Beth felt her knees weaken. She was crazy, outrageous, impetuous.

Alone.

Jared's companions were older and more elegantly dressed then he in their black string ties and tailcoats. One had an old-fashioned ruffle down the front of his shirt. Another wore a diamond pinky-ring. It was he who smiled at Beth and drawled, "Is there anything we can do for you, Miss—er?"

"Harte," she said boldly, stepping toward the table. "Elizabeth Stanton Harte."

He smiled even more broadly and rose with a formal bow. He was perhaps in his mid-thirties, with slicked-back dark hair, a wide face with a long, straight nose and huge brown eyes, and a long, thin frame. "Pinchos T. Elliot," he said.

Beth smiled back.

Across the table, Jared tossed out three cards and growled, "Back off, Pinky. She's mine."

"Just saying hello to the lady," Pinchos T. Elliot said quickly, but his smile wasn't nearly as broad. He sat back down and dealt Jared three cards. "Two for the dealer," he said with an ingratiating smile, and dealt himself two cards.

The two women, one on each of Jared's elbows, ignored the newcomer. Beth stood very erect and watched the poker hand. It was, she thought, somewhat more complicated than faro, but just as silly. Then she remembered Betty Bowman's husband and wondered if she should revise her opinion. No, she thought, poker wasn't the cause of Mr. Bowman's untimely death. Money was. Greed.

And Jared Inman's facility with a gun.

Pinky won with a full house. Jared seemed unperturbed. The other two men groaned and swore, remembered Beth, apologized to her, and groaned again. Beth wondered why they didn't apologize to the two women in taffeta, but she had her suspicions.

Jared calmly excused himself from the game. He rose stiffly, and Beth realized he was controlling his anger with heroic effort. She knew he wasn't angry about losing the hand. She bit the corners of her mouth and, without another thought, spun on her heels, fully intending to retreat. She hadn't taken two steps before Jared was around the table with his fingers digging into her elbow. He guided her to the bar, where the hugest man Beth had ever seen was wiping glasses with a white cloth. He glanced at Jared and Beth and waddled to the other end of the bar.

"What a coincidence," Beth said, but her words were hoarse and unconvincing, she cleared her throat and leaned cockily against the bar.

Jared released her elbow, raising his chin as he inhaled. "How did you find me?" he asked, anger clipping his words.

"Accidentally," she replied airily, but when Jared's fists clenched, she added quickly, "I was looking for Dobbs, and I found you both."

His black eyes narrowed.

"I'm not lying."

"You never lie, do you, Beth?" he ground out bitterly.

She tossed her head back. "Unlike some people I know."

"Don't push me any further—"

"Or what? You'll throw me overboard?"

He kicked the base of the shiny mahogany bar. "Beth, dammit, do you think you can keep following me around the country? I can't keep worrying about you every minute!"

"I've not asked you to worry about me even one second," Beth replied, her anger beginning to match his. "I can take care of myself perfectly well without your help, Mr. Jared Inman. If you want me to let you do as you please, then I suggest you let *me* do as *I* please!"

He stared at her, his jaw squared, his black eyes narrowed, his eyebrows curved down. "You're on your own, Beth," he said at last, and turned away.

"Fine with me!"

She watched him strut back to the card table. Even his broad back looked arrogant. The gall of the man! He had snuck out on her, left her a totally unacceptable note, never bothered to explain where he was going or why. He was impossible. She was glad she had followed him, if only to make his life more difficult. She would be thoroughly delighted to have him arrested in New Orleans. She would inform the local marshal that Jared intended to murder Jacques LeBreque, and Jared would be arrested.

And who would believe her?

She flounced to the door, but turned before she went through it. "Have you warned your fellow card players that you've been known to kill over a game of poker, Mr. Inman?" she called.

He stiffened and glared at her as he lowered himself into his chair. The other three men looked at her with raised eyebrows, then at Jared. Jared muttered something and they all laughed, a distinctly ribald laugh. Even the women chuckled. Beth reddened and flounced out.

Her berth was just large enough for a narrow bunk and, if she didn't mind climbing over it to get into bed, her trunk. It had no windows. The main deck held the kitchens, cargo areas, and bunks for the *Beatrice's* less prestigious passengers. Beth doubted her father would approve of her accommodations, even given the reasons for them.

Feeling cramped and unable to breathe freely, Beth walked back up to the promenade on the boiler deck. She looked out at the wide, brown, slow-moving Mississippi. The sprawling streets and levees of St. Louis were already a memory, in their place the plush greens of the Missouri countryside and the rocky bluffs of the upper Mississippi.

Would her father approve of her reasons for following Jared Inman to New Orleans? The judge had seemed singularly unconcerned about Jared's role in this haphazard investigation. Perhaps it was this, she thought, and her own uncontrollable feelings about Jared that kept her after him. But if her father knew what she had learned about Jared Inman in St. Louis, would he still countenance her pursuit of him? Or would he expect her to calmly and wisely call in the authorities?

Beth didn't know. She only knew that she adored Jared when he was with her, loved him wholly and completely when they were together.

But was he capable of killing a man, even if that man was as despicable as Jacques LeBreque? And was he a hired gun himself, or the man behind the scenes who did the hiring? Did it make a difference which?

And when she finally did learn who and what Jared Inman was, would it make any difference in how she felt about him?

Yes—and no.

If Jared was the scoundrel everyone proclaimed him to

be, she would leave him to his deserved fate. But she would never forget him. She would always have her memories and no regrets. Far better to have loved once in vain than never to have loved at all.

"I wouldn't be so lucky as to have you be thinking about me with such longing, now would I?" a voice said beside her.

Beth looked up and saw the bushy lambchop sideburns of the captain of the *Beatrice*. She laughed. "No, I'm afraid not."

"I thought as much. And are you enjoying your trip thus far?"

"The berth you gave me is unspeakable," she told him bluntly, "but I like being able to get outside. I just spent two days on a train and—"

"Bah, trains are for cattle!"

Beth laughed. "Out here, perhaps, but back East they're the most efficient way to get from one place to another."

"You're from the East, then," he said.

"New York City."

He grunted and looked out at the river. "Then tell me, Miss Harte, what are you doing chasing after a man from San Francisco?"

Beth looked away. So the captain had already heard about the episode in the barroom. "I'm not chasing him," she said quietly.

"It's none of my business, I know, but I hate to see a young woman ruin herself over a man like that," the captain told her. He sighed in frustration when she still refused to look at him. "Our first stop is Memphis. If I were you, I'd be getting off there."

When she didn't answer, he shrugged his shoulders and resumed his walk around the promenade. Beth, holding the rail, looked up and said in a normal tone, "I'll think about it, Captain—and thank you."

She knew he had heard her by the slight hesitation in his gait and his even slighter nod. She also knew that the captain of the *Beatrice* never for a moment thought Beth would heed his advice.

They both knew she would stay aboard until the grand riverboat stopped in New Orleans.

CHAPTER 24

The trip took three days, with stops in Memphis and Natchez. The weather grew hotter and muggier as the *Beatrice* approached the Mississippi Delta, and Beth quickly ran out of light dresses. Her berth was oppressive. She slept little, and always she waited for Jared to come to her and explain. He remained true to his word. She was on her own, and she was too proud—and too fearful of what he might tell her—to approach his stateroom.

When the *Beatrice* started into the five-mile tangle of crowded docks of New Orleans, Beth put aside her pride and went to Jared's stateroom. She had learned which was his the first night aboard. He had entered it late with a bottle of whiskey, but at least not with one of the women in taffeta.

She walked in without knocking. Jared was loading not one but two large, ugly guns. He looked up at her from his double bed. The room was spacious, gigantic in comparison to Beth's berth, and was paneled in walnut. Beth took in the marble-topped bureau, the full-length mirror, and the nightstand now holding the two guns.

"Expecting trouble?" she asked with seeming lightness.

He rose and pulled on a twill sack coat over his shirt. "You look tired, Beth," he said, even the sound of his deep voice making her knees quiver. His mouth twisted in a sardonic smile. "Haven't been sleeping well?"

She fought back a blush. "You're going into some swamp to find Jacques LeBreque and kill him, aren't you?" she asked steadily.

"And who's been telling stories about me this time?" he asked just as steadily.

"William."

"Of course."

She took two long strides to him and grabbed his hard upper arm. Her eyes were glistening, her jaw thrust out. "Look at me, Jared Inman," she said fiercely. "I'm here. I didn't stay in Saratoga. I didn't stay in New York. I didn't stay in St. Louis. I'm here, Jared, and you can't simply will me away."

"So what am I supposed to do, Beth?" he asked quietly, looking down at her.

"Explain."

"I've asked you to trust me."

"But all the evidence—"

"Is against me," he finished for her, and pulled his arm

from her grasp. "I know. I wouldn't need your trust if it was all in my favor, would I?"

Beth couldn't speak, even if she knew what to say. Her throat suddenly tightened. She closed her eyes to hold back the tears, but they spilled from beneath her lashes. She opened her eyes and let the hot tears wash down her cheeks. "I'm so tired," she said weakly, and turned away.

Jared caught her by the wrist before she took a step and turned her to face him. He lightly brushed her tears away with the tips of his fingers and whispered her name. He kissed her gently.

A loud knock on the door interrupted them, but Jared held Beth's hands as the door opened. A lanky black-haired man with a scrubby black mustache walked in. He was wearing a white linen suit and carrying a shotgun. Beth went pale, certain Jared was about to be arrested. But the stranger, not a passenger on the *Beatrice*, laughed and shook his head. "Figured I'd catch you with a pretty lady, Inman."

Jared grinned. "Marshal, I'd like you to meet Elizabeth Stanton Harte. Beth, Marshal Jean Guidrion."

She wrested her hands from Jared and nodded politely. "Marshal."

"My pleasure, Miss Harte," he said nobly. "If you'll excuse us, I would like to have a word with Mr. Inman."

"I'd prefer to stay."

Guidrion looked at Jared. "The hell she would." He looked back at Beth and jerked a thumb toward the door. "Out."

Jared folded his arms on his chest and grinned. "You want to argue with him, Beth?"

Beth stalked out without a parting glance at either of them. Another man was posted at the door, so she was unable to eavesdrop. She gave him a withering look and went out onto the promenade.

The passengers were beginning to disembark. Beth leaned against the railing and looked out at the sprawling docks, peers, and levees that made those of St. Louis seem insignificant. New Orleans, carved out of the delta swamps, was the second-largest—and busiest—port in the country. Beth thought it looked it.

The *Beatrice* was nearly emptied when Marshal Guidrion finally departed. Jared wasn't with him. Beth, dazed by the heat and the waiting, sprang to life and raced to Jared's stateroom.

He was gone.

Panic seized her. She dashed back outside to chase down Marshal Guidrion, but the captain of the *Beatrice* caught her by the arm on the main deck.

"Now hold on there, missy," he said. "You're not used to this heat. You'll be fainting before long."

"I'm in a hurry—"

"I know what you're after, but he's gone," the captain said kindly, his grip softening with his words. "He asked me to tell you."

Beth stared into the older man's clear blue eyes.

"He said you were probably tired of notes by now. The man has five thousand riding on his head, missy. It's just as well he's gone."

"What?"

The captain released her arm and scratched his lambchop sideburns. "That little squirrel who does Dobbs's dirty work has been offered five thousand dollars to kill Jared Inman. One scoundrel doing in another, if you ask me. Leave them to each other, missy, and get yourself home to New York."

The blood drained from her face, and she had to fight to catch her breath. She grabbed the captain's arm to steady herself. "Did—did Jared tell you this?"

"No, no, heard it from the marshal. No. Inman said—I don't know if I should be telling you this, missy—"

"Captain, please!"

"He said for you to wait for him in New York," the captain said quietly. "He'd be back for you." Then he added gruffly, "If he lives that long, and if you ask me, you'd be better off if he didn't. Asked me to look after you and see you back to St. Louis, which I mean to do—never mind his say-so."

Beth steadied herself, still holding the captain's arm and trying to breath in the heavy air. "Captain, what's the swamp?"

"The Swamp is no business of yours, missy," he said darkly.

"Captain, please tell me."

He sighed, frustrated, and shook his head with a huff. "It's an open sewer of murderers and thieves, the worst part of New Orleans. 'Tisn't a dozen blocks, but an officer of the law hasn't stepped foot there as long as I can remember. He wouldn't come out alive. Bodies of murdered men keep floating up in the river—about a half-dozen a week, they say."

"That—" She hesitated, closing her eyes briefly. "That's where Jacques LeBreque is hiding out."

"I figured as much, but Guidrion told me so this morning."

Beth nodded and straightened up, collecting herself. "What else did Marshal Guidrion say, Captain?"

The captain didn't answer.

"I assume the marshal told you about the five-thousand-dollar reward," Beth went on, in control of herself now. "How does he know?"

"He has his spies, missy. Now—"

"Is LeBreque waiting for Jared in the Swamp? Did the marshal know this and forbid Jared to go in there? Captain, obviously I can't do anything about any of this. I just want to know what's going on."

The captain sighed, frowning. "You're a difficult woman, missy, but I won't have any peace till I've told you. LeBreque snuck out of New Orleans last night—before Guidrion could get to him. Now I don't know where he went to, because no one told me, so don't start asking me."

"But we can be sure LeBreque isn't going to pass up a five-thousand-dollar pay-off for—killing Jared," Beth mused. She glanced up sharply at the riverboat captain. "Who offered the pay-off? Dobbs?"

"That'd be my guess, but you'll not find any proof."

"But why!"

"Dobbs is as bad a scoundrel as any of them," the captain said. "As soon as I can find me another riverboat to captain, he'll be seeing me gone. But these aren't good times for the river, missy. Dobbs is fighting the future the only way he knows how, but it's not my way. Now I don't know how you got yourself into this mess, but it doesn't make any difference to me. I'm putting you on the next riverboat to St. Louis not owned by Elijah Dobbs—and if you have any sense, you'll be on the first accursed train leaving for the East."

The *Delta Princess* was even larger and more elegant than the *Beatrice*, and it left the sprawling docks of New Orleans late that hot afternoon and began churning up into the heartland of the continent. Beth was given a stateroom with a big double bed covered in satin, an ornate full-length mirror, a washstand, and a velvet-cushioned chair. She remained there or on the promenade most of the two-day journey.

When the *Delta Princess* docked in St. Louis, Beth had come to no conclusions and had no plan. She only knew that she wanted Jared to come for her. She wanted to see him again. She wanted him alive.

The captain, in deference to his comrade on the *Beatrice*, personally escorted her off the riverboat.

Judge Robert Lowell Harte was waiting, brushing dust from his conservative black suit and eyeing the men unloading cargo with distaste.

"Father!"

Beth flew into his arms and hugged him fiercely. "Oh, Father, I'm so glad to see you! What are you doing here? How—"

"Can we please go somewhere more civilized before I answer your questions?" he said, and kissed her lightly on the cheek. "You're looking fit, Beth. How was New Orleans?"

"Hot, but I never got to see the city beyond the docks," Beth said and added sourly, "Jared Inman saw to that."

"Occasionally, the man does make sense."

"Father!"

But the judge refused to say another word until they were safely in the dining room of his hotel with a pot of tea on the way.

"The Episcopal woman are quite furious with you, you know," he began. "I tried to persuade them that you were called away on the most pressing emergency, but they insist upon clinging to their belief that all who favor women's suffrage are unreliable."

Beth folded her hands on the white linen tablecloth. "I don't want to discuss St. Louis's Episcopal women at the moment, Father," she said patiently. "What are you doing in St. Louis?"

"I did intend to present evidence against Elijah Dobbs and have him arrested, but the wretch has slithered away," Judge Harte said feelingly.

"Have him arrested for what, Father?" Beth said levelly.

"Corruption, fraud, conspiracy to commit murder—the usual."

Beth kept her hands folded on the tablecloth. A white-clad waiter arrived with their tea. When he departed, Beth patiently waited for her father to add a dopple of cream and a teaspoon of sugar and stir his tea.

He took one sip and set his cup back on its saucer. "I've been investigating Elijah Dobbs for a long time. You've helped me immensely, Beth."

She knew if she betrayed any surprise, any outrage, her father would only lecture her on her lapse in perspicacity. She remained silent.

"And so has Jared, in his own peculiar way. I understand Dobbs has promised Jacques LeBreque five thousand dollars if he kills Jared." The judge chuckled, unconcerned. "I would like to be around for that fight!"

"I thought you were a pacifist," Beth jibed in place of the dozen questions she wanted to ask.

Her father waved a bony hand dismissively and sipped his tea. "If someone tries to kill a man for financial gain, he deserves what is coming to him."

Beth dumped two teaspoons of sugar into her tea. Her father was beginning to try her patience. "Then you don't think LeBreque will succeed in murdering Jared?"

"I wouldn't expect so, no."

"You seem terribly confident."

"Jared Inman inspires that particular sort of confidence." Her father paused and gave his daughter a long, studious look. "You don't agree?"

"I don't know anything about Jared Inman," she said bitterly.

Her father touched her hand warmly. "You know that you love him."

"Father, he's a killer! A hired killer! William said—"

"Oh, more rumors. I've said it before, Beth: There's far too much secrecy between you and Jared."

She looked away. "Jared's finished with me, Father. I followed him to New Orleans—"

"So he said."

She whirled around. "What do you mean? When—"

"In his telegram. He said you had followed him to New Orleans, you would be returning to St. Louis on the *Delta Princess*, and I should meet you and take you back to New York." He wiped his mouth with a linen napkin. "We're both to await him there."

"He could be killed!"

"Not likely, given his size and experience."

Beth groaned.

"I know they have guns that kill elephants and Jared is somewhat smaller than an elephant, but, truly, Beth, I believe your worry is misplaced." The judge paused, his angular face growing serious. "It's Elijah Dobbs I'm worried about. Jared has no idea he is not in custody."

"Why should he think he *is* in custody?" Beth asked impatiently.

"Because I wired him before he left for New Orleans and said I would be arriving in St. Louis to have Dobbs arrested." The judge sighed, betraying his own impatience with his daughter. "Didn't you know?"

Beth shook her head.

He threw down his napkin. "Jared didn't tell you he had received a telegram from me?"

Again Beth shook her head.

"The wretch!"

Beth had to smile.

"Has he told you nothing, then? Nothing at all?"

"Nothing."

"Why—why, this is outrageous! There is far more secrecy between you two than I even suspected!"

"He didn't want me in St. Louis—or New Orleans," Beth added.

"I can see perfectly why he didn't want you to follow him to New Orleans, but he should have seen how useful you could be here in St. Louis," the judge said, musing. An eyebrow arched at his daughter. "You didn't wire me any of this."

"There was no time."

He sighed. "Tell me everything."

And she did, from the moment she arrived in St. Louis to the moment she had flung herself in her father's arms. His only visible reaction was her description of the hotel in which Jared had insisted she stay, and that was merely a distasteful wince. In the end, they had consumed two pots of tea, and Beth was convinced her father, while not lying outright to her, was being less than frank.

"Well, daughter," he said, "do you wish to return to New York and wait patiently for this scoundrel to return to you?"

"I doubt I would wait patiently," Beth said carefully, suspecting her father had a plan of his own.

He wiped his mouth and laid his napkin next to his teacup. "There is no doubt in my mind that Jared can dispense with Jacques LeBreque independently of us," he said mildly, "but I am less certain of Elijah Dobbs, particularly since I have no way of knowing if Jared realizes Dobbs is still free."

"Father," Beth said, knowing she was interrupting his train of thought, "is Jared Inman a criminal?"

Her father snorted. "Would I hire a criminal?"

That was all Beth could wheedle out of him before he outlined his plan for the Harte family to track down one Jared Inman in his hometown of San Francisco.

CHAPTER 25

Judge Robert Lowell Harte had hired Jared Inman to investigate Elijah Dobbs. He had also cajoled his daughter into
investigating Elijah Dobbs, however informally. Inevitably
the paths of Jared Inman of San Francisco and Elizabeth
Harte of New York had crossed.

"Inevitably," Beth said with a heavy sigh as she settled
into a luxurious Pullman car of the Central Pacific Railroad at Omaha, Nebraska. Her father was busy looking out
the window and paid her no attention. He hadn't spent the
past two weeks traipsing up and down the continent, Beth

thought sourly, and huffed slightly so that he would know she was irritated.

He smiled innocently and pointed out a group of Sioux on the platform. "Fascinating," he said. "Don't deserve the abysmal treatment they've been receving."

"So why don't you have Jared Inman investigate on their behalf?" Beth inquired sarcastically.

"You're being petulant, my dear."

She snorted and refused to look at his Sioux.

Twice during the trip from St. Louis to Omaha she had told him what William Prentiss, Jr., had said about Jared Inman, but he adopted his inscrutable judge demeanor and declined comment. She suggested that very possibly he had made a mistake in hiring Jared—that indeed Jared could have outfoxed him and escaped before the judge could find out—but her father only snorted in his own fashion.

And so, when the Pullman chugged out of the Central Pacific Railroad station in Omaha on the first leg of the transcontinental journey to San Francisco, Beth knew no more than when they had left St. Louis. Indeed, she thought, more and more infuriated, since she had left New Orleans.

Had Jacques LeBreque led Jared to Elijah Dobbs, and thus, somehow, to Judge Harte? Jared had been protecting, in some capacity, Juan Correrro, who was, according to her father an honest railroad man. Jacques LeBreque had killed Correrro apparently upon someone else's orders. Jared sought out LeBreque not to avenge Correrro's murder but to avenge himself. LeBreque had made him look a fool. But by the time Jared caught up with LeBreque, the Frenchman was already working for Dobbs.

"And Dobbs had Jacques hire on as William's horse trainer so he could keep an eye on him on Dobbs's behalf," she mumbled to herself for the thousandth time.

"It's seventeen hundred miles to San Francisco," her father pointed out mildly. "I should think you would want to rest your brain."

"A Harte's brain never rests," Beth countered, "and I quote."

He scoffed. "I never said such a thing!"

"That's why you sent me on that stupid mission when I was supposed to be on vacation," Beth said.

"Nonsense," he replied smoothly. "You wouldn't have gone otherwise."

"That would have been far smarter than traipsing after thieves and murderers the entire summer!"

Her father yawned deeply. "You wouldn't have gotten far with women's suffrage this summer, Beth, not with the Beecher-Tilton scandal. You know that."

He was trying to divert her from the subject, but she wouldn't take the bait. "Think of the scandal if pristine Judge Harte has had working for him one of the most despicable scoundrels of the Wild West," she said. "I can hear the cries from the society people now!"

"You still don't trust him?" her father asked, one eyebrow raised.

Beth lifted her chin and folded her hands in the lap of her mustard traveling dress. That, of course, was the crux of the matter. Did she or did she not trust Jared Inman?

Clearly, her actions of the past week demonstrated that she did not. She had badgered him with questions, heeded the gossip about the unscrupulous man from San Francisco, followed him wherever he went. She had only trusted him with herself.

And now, if he were honorable and if he survived the promised attempts on his life, he would have nothing further to do with her. He would cast her aside like a dirty mop.

She moaned and shut her eyes against the onslaught of tears.

But why should she have trusted Jared Inman! Did he give her any reasons for his conduct? Did he give her any reasons for the rumors?

Indeed, did he do anything besides treat her like an incorrigible idiot and a silly, weak-minded woman!

While Beth stewed and fretted, her father showed his determination to enjoy his trip. He apparently had studied for a transcontinental journey and had come prepared. At Cheyenne, Wyoming, he pointed out to his daughter that the now-bustling town was but one house eight years ago. At Shuman he insisted they go out on the car's platform and look south, where, one-hundred-sixty-five miles in the distance, Pike's Peak rose up into the hot summer sky. As the train rolled through the vast, uninviting miles of the Great American Desert, where the sun beat down, boiling hot, Judge Harte rambled on about such points as Laramie City, Creston, Point of Rocks, Bryan, Carter's Station, Wasatch, and Echo City.

Beth thought only of Jared.

They rested in Ogden, where the Mormons were carving life out of the desert with the most spectacular results. Beth, exhausted from worry, self-pity, and anger, roused herself and admitted she was impressed. By the time they boarded the Union Pacific Railroad at Promontory, Utah, her optimism was nearly fully restored. Jared wouldn't be killed, he wouldn't turn out to be a scoundrel, and she, Beth Harte, would tell him she loved him.

Together she and her father remained by the windows of the railroad car and looked out, transfixed, at the spectacular scenery of the Rocky Mountains and the Sierras. The train seemed so small and insignificant. As they passed through the High Sierras above the canyon of the American River, Beth found herself unable to breathe and her hands white, clinging to the thick velvet drapes. Her father quietly provided names for all they saw: Donner Lake, the snowsheds above Cisco, Emigrant Gold Run, the heart-stopping abyss below Cape Horn, Blue Canyon.

And then they were over Summit Mountain and cruising down through the American River Canyon into Sacramento.

California. Jared's country. The thrill of the journey faded, and Beth sat rigidly in her seat, her heart beating rapidly, her hands white, her mouth dry, not at the magnificence of the view but at the prospect of finding out at last who and what Jared Inman was . . . and what she meant to him.

"Do you think he's dead?" she asked her father.

He glanced at her with distaste. "Don't be morbid, Beth."

They left the Union Pacific Railroad and took the steam boat ferry across the bay to San Francisco. It was much larger than Beth had expected, and not at all the dirty dusty frontier town of her imagination. Its waterfront was still one of the most dangerous in the world, but beyond it built into the hills of northern California, was a city with its own peculiar mix of grace, respectability, and stubbornness.

"I should think basing your operations on behalf of women's suffrage here in San Francisco would be quite interesting, Beth," Judge Harte mused. "Quite."

"Father, please!"

He shrugged his thin shoulders, but his face suddenly lit up as they started off the steamboat. "Ah, how fortuitous!"

Beth paused to glare at him, but he was already trotting nimbly out to the dock. When she looked up, a scowl on her face, she saw him shaking hands with a tall, dark figure.

Jared.

She hung back and quickly straightened her dress and tucked a few strands of hair back into their pins before she joined the two men.

"I thought we would surprise you," the judge was saying.

"Nothing either of you two does surprises me anymore," Jared replied. "In fact, I've been expecting you to turn up sooner or later, so I—" He noticed Beth and stopped, his black eyes locking with hers. He nodded slightly. "Hello, Beth."

"Hello, Jared," she said stiffly. "I—I see you're not dead."

A slow grin crossed his face, lighting up his eyes.

"Dobbs?" her father inquired sternly.

Jared tore his eyes from Beth. "In custody."

"LeBreque?"

"Likewise." He glanced down at Beth. "He's not dead either."

She raised her chin. "Why weren't you arrested?"

"I did the arresting, you little idiot!"

Beth stared.

Jared turned in confusion to her father. "Didn't you tell her?"

"Not my place, my boy," the judge replied lightly as he withdrew his pipe from an inner coat pocket.

Jared groaned loudly. "All right, into my carriage, both of you."

"Jared—"

"Beth," her father cut in mildly, "don't argue with the man now, for heaven's sake."

She shut her mouth and didn't say another word. Her thoughts raced on, and when they were all in Jared's carriage, she opened her mouth to speak. With a dark look followed by a wide grin, Jared shut her up. The judge lit his pipe and commented on the scenery. He was delighted with the cable cars and noted that they had been installed only last year. Beth folded her arms on her breasts and fumed.

By the time they reached a trim brownstone in the heart of San Francisco, Beth didn't know whether to be more angry or worried. Jared Inman apparently was wholly trustworthy, but how was she to have known? She was supposed to have trusted him. He had been romantic and wonderful with her, and she was supposed to have believed that that was the true Jared Inman. Now she was certain he would have nothing further to do with her, and yet she couldn't possibly have trusted him under the circumstances.

They stepped out onto the sidewalk, and the judge scrutinized the brownstone. "Marvelous," he said in appreciation, "just marvelous."

Jared informed him he could wander around outside and promptly escorted Beth into a first-floor office. It was lined with shelves of law books and contained a massive walnut desk and two leather chairs. An open door led to yet another office. Both looked unused. Jared leaned against the desk and nodded to one of the leather chairs. Beth walked nobly across the room, aware of his eyes on her, and sat on the very edge of the chair.

"I suppose you want an explanation?" he asked gruffly.

She gave him her most withering look.

He grinned. "As I thought." But his face grew serious, his firm jaw tightened, and he rose and faced the window, his broad back to Beth. "Nearly three months ago, my uncle and closest friend was murdered," he began baldly. "Juan Correrro."

Beth pulled in her upper lip to prevent herself from speaking. Juan Correrro was Jared's uncle?

"Juan had been launching plans for a new railway to run west and south of St. Louis. It would be in direct competition with the north-south trade route on the Mississippi. When Juan died, so did his plans for the railroad."

Beth twisted her fingers together and studied her nails while Jared paused, not looking from the window.

"I did some investigating and learned that a man by the name of Jacques LeBreque had actually killed Juan, but LeBreque was only a hired gun. I wanted the man who had paid him to murder my uncle."

He paused again. His words were short, bitter, tortured, and Beth found an urge to put her arms around his broad shoulders. She didn't speak.

"So I contacted the only man I know who has the national contacts and the courage to investigate something like this. Everyone urged me to let it drop. I couldn't bring Juan back to life, and I would only cause more trouble and even get myself killed if I tried to avenge his death. But I didn't just want to avenge Juan, I wanted to do something to help put a stop to this sort of thing. People have to know they can't get away with murdering their competitors." He paused again and turned slightly, so that his eyes locked with Beth's. "So I contacted Judge Robert Lowell Harte."

Her mouth dropped open. "My father?" she said hoarsely, numbly.

Jared's face twisted into a small grin. "The absent-minded do-gooding former judge, who also happens to be the organizer of a small, secret committee, loosely approved by and associated with our federal government, that monitors railroad corruption." He glanced at Beth for reaction, but got none beyond her dumbfounded expression. "I became part of that committee when it was first formed seven years ago. Judge Harte had asked me to meet him at a ball in Saratoga Springs, and I did."

Beth fell back into the chair and kicked her legs out straight. She scowled at Jared's grin. "Go on."

"I had been too busy to be more than nominally involved with the committee, but seven years later when

Juan was killed, I knew the judge would be the one person who could help me.'' Jared turned back to the window and shoved his hands deep into his trouser pockets. ''Together we learned that Elijah Dobbs, a confirmed riverboat man, was planning his own railroad to run west out of St. Louis and had also vowed never to relinquish control of the north-south route to any railroad. He was also way out on a limb financially after last year's panic. What we didn't know and certainly couldn't prove if we did was whether or not Dobbs had hired LeBreque to murder Juan.''

''So you joined Dobbs on his trip to Saratoga Springs,'' Beth put in, recovering.

''To Dobbs, it was just a chance meeting on a train,'' Jared said, still facing the window. ''He had no idea I was investigating him or that I was Juan Correrro's nephew.''

Beth licked her lips, wishing she could see Jared's face. Did he hate her for having to explain all this to her? ''And in Saratoga you found Jaques LeBreque working as a horse trainer for William Prentiss.''

''I looked for a connection between Jacques and Dobbs and William and Dobbs, and, of course, I found it.'' Jared walked back to the desk and hoisted himself onto the edge. He crossed his arms and narrowed his black eyes at Beth. ''I also found out that dear, unearthly Judge Harte had sent his beautiful violet-eyed daughter to help me.''

Beth cleared her throat and absently smoothed her skirt, a hopeless case. ''You were against my involvement from the beginning.''

''Vehemently. Your father said I was underestimating you and assured me you were quite sensible, but neither of you has had much experience with men like Dobbs and LeBreque.''

She tossed her head back airily. ''I didn't get myself killed, did I?''

''Thanks to me.''

"You made up that story about traveling three thousand miles to see me to scare me off, didn't you?" she asked sharply.

He grinned unabashed. "More or less, although if I'd known you were still as beautiful and wild as when I caught you skinny-dipping in Lake Saratoga at age seventeen, I would have traveled three thousand miles to see you. I was in love with you, Beth, the moment I saw you trying to drag that trunk upstairs."

She stiffened and looked away. *Was.* He wasn't *still* in love with her. "So you discovered William planned to pull out of the B and O and invest in the St. Louis Western with Dobbs," she said quietly.

"Yes," Jared replied, his voice suddenly sharp. "I told his father what I suspected, and he reluctantly agreed to have me as a guest if I would help William. I didn't take any pains to make my interest in his affairs seem honorable."

"You didn't take any pains to make yourself seem honorable to anyone!" Beth snapped, but she quickly calmed herself and added, "In any event, Hoskins put the screws to William and he backed out on Dobbs."

"And Dobbs retaliated by sending LeBreque after Ginny and William's horse," Jared went on. "Then Dobbs quickly took leave of Saratoga and went back to St. Louis."

"Then William showed up. My God, he could have been killed!"

'You *both* could have been killed," Jared said emphatically.

"Nonsense," Beth said, mimicking her father. "Besides, would you have intervened on William's behalf? You were trying to nail the coffin lid down on your case against Dobbs and LeBreque, weren't you? You weren't interested in saving William. I did that—or I would have if he hadn't already figured things out for himself."

Jared groaned in disbelief.

"You and my father have been communicating regularly?"

"More or less."

"He wired you we were coming to San Francisco?"

"Not until you were in Sacramento, but I was hardly surprised."

She sat up straight. "All right, Jared Inman, who are you? What about all those rumors? What about Betty Bowman's husband?"

"Betty Bowman's husband pulled a gun on a federal law officer with every intention of killing him, and so killed him."

"How noble of you," Beth said ironically. "Did the federal law officer thank you?"

"I was the federal law officer, Beth."

She raised one eyebrow. "You?"

Jared couldn't suppress a grin. "Me. Betty knew it, but she saw her chance to pay me back by trying to scare you off. I went to her and suggested she keep my background to herself. The rumors I cultivated myself—with your father's help. I thought they might prompt you to return to New York, but, of course, they worked in reverse and kept you clinging to me like a damned shadow. You're a tenacious woman, Beth Harte."

Beth laughed, but she was nonetheless nervous when she walked to him and took his big, callused hands in her. "Jared, I haven't known what to think, what to believe. I wanted to trust you—"

He touched her lips with his fingers. "But I didn't trust you," he said quietly. "Beth, darling—"

"I love you, Jared."

He grabbed her around the waist and brought her mouth up to his. They kissed again and again, only their lips touching, until Jared moaned and opened his mouth against hers. She responded immediately, wrapping her arms around his neck and pulling him to her, holding him, tasting his

"Beth, darling, I love you so much," he whispered hoarsely, and kissed her again. He drew back, still holding her. "I was so sure I would lose you when I left you in New Orleans—"

"But you wanted to take care of LeBreque—and Dobbs, as it turned out—without my or my father's help," Beth finished for him, not angrily. "The big lawman of the Wild West."

He grinned. "Not anymore."

"Oh?"

"I resigned. I'm going into private law practice."

"Oh?" Beth said again, dumbly.

"Yes, and if you'd been more interested in finding out the facts about me instead of chasing down rumors, you would have discovered that I attended Yale and am the son of Sarah and David Inman of New Haven."

"Sarah Inman? Why, Jared, she's a suffragette!"

He smiled. "I thought you'd like that. I came West after Yale to help out Juan—he was my mother's brother—and ended up as a lawman."

Beth ran her hands up his strong arms. "Now you're going to be a lawyer."

"Do you think you could live in San Francisco? I could live, Beth, but—"

"I think it would be thrilling."

He grinned and kissed her on the forehead, his fingers grazing her hair, promising so much. "Your father will be pleased," he said. "He and I—well, we—he hasn't told you, has he?"

"As you have seen, he has told me very little," Beth said dryly.

Jared picked her up firmly by the waist and set her down on the desk. Then he went into the other office and came back with a large wooden sign. He cleared his throat, rather nervously, Beth thought, and turned the sign so she could read it.

Her eyes opened wide. "Inman and Harte, Attorneys-At-Law—Jared!"

"During all this mess, I mentioned to your father that I was in love with you, and he decided he needed a new adventure. So we worked out the law partnership. I don' think he wanted to be in New York with you out here, and I certainly didn't want to break you two up—not tha living with you will be peaceful—" He stopped suddenly and set the sign on one of the leather chairs. "Beth—"

"You don't have to ask, Jared," she said, grinning. He eyes glistened. "Of course I'll marry you."

He looked at her, surprised, then threw his head bac and laughed heartily. "Shall we break the news to you father?"

They found him outside smoking his pipe on the fro stoop. "I shouldn't talk about too much secrecy betwee Jared and me if I were you, Father," Beth said crisp when he rose to greet them. "You haven't exactly bee open with me about your secret committee—"

"Then it wouldn't have been a secret, and, of cours you know the federal government and its attitude towa women—"

"Or about your plans to take up the practice of law San Francisco."

The judge arched a brow at Jared. "You did tell everything, didn't you?"

Jared grinned.

"Yes," Beth went on, "and I've asked Jared to ma me—"

"And I've agreed," Jared said.

Judge Harte shrugged. "Whatever works."

Jared and Beth laughed.

"Now if you two don't object, I would like to ind

myself in a proper bath and a proper cup of tea. You do have a dwelling somewhere nearby, do you not, Jared?''

"Of course," Jared said, a glint in his black eyes. "Juan left me his villa on Nob Hill. It's not too ostentaious—"

"His word is gaudy," Beth put in.

The judge wrinkled his face in distaste and waved his pipe at his daughter and future son-in-law. "That's all right, I suppose, Jared. Beth will marry you anyway.''

ENJOY ALL OF THESE TITLES
FROM PARADISE PRESS